Praise for th

# A NASCAR *Holiday*

"Humor, witty dialogue, a good setup and a great hero and heroine make [Raye's] book sparkle."
—*Romantic Times BOOKreviews* on *Texas Fire*

"St. Claire will likely be one of the most talked about authors in the genre. This is an author who's on the fast track to making her name a household one."
—*Publishers Weekly*

"Webb moves effortlessly between two very diverse romances and masterfully keeps the reader on the edge until the last page."
—*Romantic Times BOOKreviews* on *Striking Distance*

# Kimberly Raye
# Roxanne St. Claire
# Debra Webb

# A
# NASCAR
# *Holiday*

HQN™

ISBN-13: 978-0-373-77156-1
ISBN-10:    0-373-77156-8

A NASCAR HOLIDAY

Copyright © 2006 by Harlequin Books S.A.

NASCAR® is a registered trademark of the NATIONAL ASSOCIATION FOR STOCK CAR AND AUTO RACING.

The publisher acknowledges the copyright holders of the individual works as follows:

LADIES, START YOUR ENGINES…
Copyright © 2006 by Kimberly Groff

'TIS THE SILLY SEASON
Copyright © 2006 by Roxanne St. Claire

UNBREAKABLE
Copyright © 2006 by Debra Webb

Printed in U.S.A.

# CONTENTS

# LADIES, START YOUR ENGINES...

## Kimberly Raye

This story is dedicated to NASCAR fans everywhere (*especially* the ladies). Here's to the greatest sport in the world!

# CHAPTER ONE

THERE WERE MEN. AND THEN there were *men*.

Savannah Calloway stared across the gigantic garage at the man who leaned under the hood of the blue and black Chevy race car. He wore faded brown cowboy boots and a snug pair of worn jeans. The denim cupped his tight tush and molded to his muscular legs. A frayed rip near the middle of one thigh played peekaboo with her as he leaned down, giving her a mouthwatering glimpse of tanned, hair-dusted skin. A white T-shirt outlined his broad shoulders. The sleeves clung to his sinewy biceps as he worked the wrench with his strong hands.

While she couldn't see his face because he leaned under the car's hood, she didn't have to. She knew the view would only get better because Mackenzie Briggs had killer blue eyes and a drop-dead gorgeous smile to go with his hunky body.

Yep, she knew that firsthand.

Which was why she made it a point to keep her

distance from said hunky body and that drop-dead gorgeous smile and, in particular, those killer blue eyes.

Her stomach hollowed out and panic rushed through her. She became acutely aware of the dimly lit garage and the fact that it was half-past midnight on a Saturday night in December. In other words, it was off-season—the last race had been in November, and there was no one—*no one*—inside the massive building that housed the cars for Jamison Racing.

Just Mac.

She swallowed her rising panic.

While she'd always avoided him in the past, things were different now. Savannah no longer worked for Calloway Motor Sports. Not only the largest racing team in the Fort Worth area, but one of the biggest on the NASCAR NEXTEL Cup circuit. Much bigger than Jamison Racing—a small, one-car operation whose headquarters sat just north of downtown Fort Worth, only a few miles from the track. Two of the top three drivers in the NASCAR NEXTEL series—her twin brothers Trey and Travis—raced for her father's team.

*Her* team.

Or at least it had been.

Up until Will Calloway had given her the old heave-ho.

*"I know this is upsetting, honey, but it's for your*

*own good. I know you're busy here, so it only makes sense that you should take some time off for yourself. You're not getting any younger. Why, your mother had already had the four of you by the time she'd turned twenty-eight. Of course, she hadn't looked a day over twenty-one, God bless her. Even after four kids, she was every bit as pretty as the day I first married her."*

Pretty and smart and perfect. That had been the late Eileen Calloway. The woman had given birth to four kids, loved and cared for them, supported her husband's dream of being a car designer and owner, and looked picture-perfect while doing all of it. Savannah was ten when her mother died of an unexpected heart attack, and she could still remember the attractive blonde flitting about the kitchen in a pink dress and high heels, a twin in each arm and dinner simmering on the stove. She'd always had a smile for everyone and never a cross word, no matter how overworked she'd been or how stressed. She'd been perfect, all right.

Savannah had spent the past twenty-eight years following in her mother's perfect footsteps. Right down to the pink high heels.

She glanced down at the pair of three-inch stilettos she wore. Her toes whimpered in protest, and she wished she'd thought to swing by her condo to change. But she'd been so devastated when she'd left

Calloway, pink slip in hand to match her outfit, that her only thought had been *"What am I going to do now?"*

She was officially unemployed. Jobless. *Desperate.*

Not hormone-deprived, mind you (the kind that had sent her straight into Mac's arms six years ago for a night of unforgettable pleasure). This time it was pure survival instinct that had driven her to Jamison Racing at a quarter past midnight in search of Mac.

*And if he says no?*

He wouldn't. Because he needed her as much as she needed him. He just didn't realize it yet.

THE SOFT FOOTSTEPS ECHOED IN Mac's head and it took everything he had not to toss the wrench down and turn toward her.

*Her.*

He still couldn't believe it, but there was no mistaking the scent that pushed past the sharp aroma of motor oil and car exhaust to tease his nostrils. Vanilla mixed with light, fluffy whipped cream. Sweet. She smelled so damned sweet. She always had.

Of course, he hadn't had an up-close whiff of Savannah Calloway in nearly six years, but he still hadn't forgotten.

He caught the occasional glimpse of her sitting in the owner's box at the track. But since she was

Calloway's marketing manager and, more importantly, since her father had always been so adamant
about keeping her out of the garage, she spent more
time in the business office than she did in the trenches.

Thus nixing any encounters of the close kind.

Lucky for him.

But his luck seemed to have finally run out
because she was here. Now. *Here.*

He stiffened as she came to a halt next to him, but
he didn't turn toward her. Instead, he concentrated
on unscrewing the massive bolt that held part of the
carburetor in place.

"Mac? Can I talk to you for a second?"

"The answer is no." He twirled the wrench a few
more twists until the nut rolled off the bolt and into
his palm.

"No, I can't talk to you?"

"No, I'm not driving for your father again. I like
driving for Jamison. It's a small team, but we're
family and the owner is committed for the long haul."

"That's nice, but I'm not here about your driving
skills. Even though you did make an impressive
showing this past year."

"So why are you here?"

"Because I need you."

He looked at her then. He couldn't help himself.
Her words rang in his ears and his head swiveled.

Her soft brown hair streaked with blond hung

past her shoulders in soft waves that made his fingers itch to reach out. She had hazel eyes as rich as hot caramel and just as addictive. She wore a pink blouse, fitted pink skirt and a pair of high heels that made her legs seem endless. The small spot of grease near her collar was the only indication that Savannah Calloway liked to get down and dirty in the pit when no one, especially her father, was looking.

He knew then that she hadn't changed much from the twenty-something who'd come down to the garage every day to spend her lunch hour changing spark plugs or tightening pins. Before her father walked in and chased her back to the office, that is.

"What I mean is—" she licked her full, pink lips "—you need me. We need each other."

He set the wrench aside, leaned one hip against the car and folded his arms. "How do you figure that?"

"Let's face it. You're good, but you're not better than my brothers." Trey and Travis were the only twin brothers racing the circuit and they'd all but locked down the first and second positions since they'd hit their stride two years ago. "But you could be."

"Meaning?"

"You let me make a few adjustments to your car in time for the New Year's Eve charity race. I've been watching you. You're close, Mac. You just need a little something to push you up to the next level. I'm that something. You want a championship? I can set you up to win one. The New Year's exhibition race will be next season's predictor. Whoever wins will set the pace for next year. It could be you."

"And what do you get out of it?"

"A chance to prove to my father that I belong on his team. Specifically, in the garage." She stiffened. "I should have stood up to him years ago, but he's always been so adamant about keeping me out of the garage and I've always been so busy with everything else…" She swallowed, and sadness flashed in her eyes. "Too busy to argue. But all that's changed now. He let me go."

"He really *fired* you?"

She nodded. "He wants me to get a life. Settle down. Find Mr. Right." She shook her head. "But that's not what *I* want."

"You have something against living happily ever after?"

"Not at all. But who says happily ever after involves a man?" When he arched an eyebrow, she shook her head. "I like men, but that doesn't mean I need one. Besides, men don't like women who can change a tire faster than they can."

"Maybe you're going out with the wrong men."

"That's the problem. They're all wrong and I'm

tired of wasting my time. Better to focus on something I can actually fix, like my career. Or lack thereof." She motioned around. "I want to be here. In a garage. Doing what I love. He won't take me seriously unless I do something serious. Something drastic."

"Like help the competition."

"Exactly. He can't dismiss it as tinkering if you win the race and then tell everyone that you couldn't have won without my expertise. He'll realize that I'm a valuable member of the team and he'll give up this crazy idea about me getting married and having babies. Not that I don't want to get married someday. But not today. Or any time soon. I know I'm not getting any younger, but I'm only twenty-eight. That's not old."

"Hell, no. And neither is thirty-two."

"Well, I wouldn't go that far." She grinned and his heart skipped a sudden beat. "So, can we do this?"

*This and anything else you have in mind.* That's what his body said. But Mac had been pushing himself far too long to give in to his ungentlemanly urges. Even when it came to Savannah Calloway.

Especially when it came to her.

He eyed her. "How do I know this isn't just a setup? A way for you to get the inside scoop on me?"

"I wouldn't do that."

She wouldn't. He could see the sincerity in her gaze. The determination. The desperation.

Even so, he wasn't about to let just anyone touch his car. "I finished fourth this past year. Calloway has four drivers. I'm sure your father's itching to dominate the top positions."

"My brothers are already sitting at number one and two. While Linc Adams has been consistent every year and did manage to finish third this past year, I seriously doubt he holds the spot once my father introduces his new engine at the New Year's Invitational." Linc raced for the MacAllister Magic, a reputable team owned by legendary driver Clint MacAllister. "It's that fast. And that good."

"Which means it'll eat my lunch, too."

"Not necessarily. My dad knows his stuff, but I know mine, as well. You've got a reliable car. You just need a few tweaks if you want to win."

*If?*

There was no *if* about it. He'd been racing the NASCAR NEXTEL Cup Series for ten years. *Ten.* And he'd yet to place in the top three, much less win a championship. He'd come close. He was close right now. So close that his Granny Briggs was convinced this next year would be the Big One.

She knew it, but Mac wasn't as convinced. Ten years was a long time to stay fixated and focused and hungry.

*Too long.*

He pushed the thought out of his head the minute it struck. Or, at least, he tried to shove it away. But it stalled in the back of his mind. A reminder that he wasn't as young as he used to be. And maybe, just maybe, he didn't want it nearly as much.

"Everyone who's anyone will be racing New Year's Eve," she went on. "All the biggies. Trey and Travis included." Her youngest brother, Jack, raced for the NASCAR Busch Series. "If you win, it'll set a precedent for next season. You'll show everyone what you're made of and what your car is capable of doing."

"And what you're capable of?"

She nodded. "I can help you." Her gaze met and locked with his. "You know I can."

He knew, all right. He'd seen her work her magic under the hood. And he'd also seen her sitting *on* the hood, her hair gleaming in the moonlight...

Mac narrowed his gaze and studied her. She wasn't the most beautiful woman he'd ever been with. But for some insane reason, she was the one he couldn't seem to forget.

"We'll have to keep things quiet," he told her. "Even if I buy the story about you getting fired, I can promise you that hardly anyone else will. My crew will be suspicious. Since it's the holidays and a charity event on top of that, there's no round-the-clock prep going on. But everyone will be here during the day, so we'll have to do our thing at night after everyone leaves. Every night."

"That works for me." She smiled then, and if he hadn't already agreed to her proposition, he would have done so at the first tilt of her luscious mouth. Her lips parted and her eyes twinkled and his chest hitched.

No, she wasn't the most beautiful woman he'd ever been with. But she did have one hell of a smile.

Hands off, he told himself. He'd seen for himself how much one night of hot, wild passion could mess with a guy's head. He'd lost the next five races after the episode with Savannah, so many that her father had given him his walking papers at the end of the season, and all because he hadn't been able to get her off his mind.

She spelled bad luck with a capital *B*, and Mac wasn't about to jinx himself again. He was steering clear of Savannah and her warm smile and keeping his priorities straight.

*Winning*.

"Tomorrow night," he told her. "Meet me here around eight and we'll get busy. On the car," he added when a graphic image pushed into his head. "We'll get busy working on the car."

The car and nothing but the car…no matter how sweet she smelled.

# CHAPTER TWO

"*Tomorrow night.*"

Mac's words echoed in Savannah's head as she pulled into the parking lot of her condominium complex a half hour later. Her heart revved that much faster.

He'd agreed. He'd really agreed.

Excitement made her hands tremble as she killed the engine and slid from behind the wheel of her classic Mustang convertible. She could still see her father's face when she'd driven the piece of junk home after she'd graduated from college.

"You bought a muscle car?"

"It's a classic."

"It's a pile of junk."

"Now. But give me six months."

Thanks to her father, who'd promptly handed over Calloway's PR schedule, the restoration had taken nearly six years. She'd been busy with work, as well as family commitments—as the only female in the bunch, she'd become responsible for holidays, birthdays and even Sunday dinners. Which meant she'd had very little time to pursue her own interests.

While the last thing she'd wanted was to get fired, her father had been right about one thing. She did need to start thinking about herself. But not in terms of marriage and babies. That was his dream for her.

This... She ran her hand down the smooth, cherry-red finish of the car and a thrill of excitement zigzagged up her arm.

*This* was her dream. It always had been. She'd just been too busy to pursue it—and too afraid to let anyone down. Her father had wanted a daughter as picture-perfect as his wife. And her brothers had needed a mother in their lives. Savannah had been both.

No more.

She walked up the winding concrete path that led to her condo. The main selling point when she'd first looked at the place had been its location just north of Fort Worth. She was less than five minutes from Calloway Motor Sports and the racetrack. Over the past eight years, however, Savannah had come to appreciate the community itself.

It was a nice, friendly place where the folks knew each other and always waved hello. People walked their dogs every evening and kids played in the large, well-manicured yards that connected the buildings. Large, potted poinsettias sat here and there amid the cluster of two-story white brick buildings. Red Christmas lights lined the cement walkways. The doors sported matching frosty-white wreaths dotted with tiny, red velvet bows.

Every door except for one.

As usual, Savannah had been working late, scheduling appearances for her twin brothers, when her neighborhood association had had its monthly meeting. Last month's topic? Holiday yard decorations. She'd contributed to the decorating fund thanks to old man Peterson, who lived in the condo that adjoined hers. He'd been waiting for her and her donation—coffee can in hand—when she'd gotten home that night. But while she'd helped fund the decorative lights and flowers, she hadn't had the time to run by the building office and put her name down on the order form for the wreaths.

"It just ain't right, I tell you."

The old, crackly voice slid into her ears and she turned to see a shadow sitting on the adjacent porch. A single flame pushed back the darkness as Jacob Montgomery Peterson—Skeeter to everyone at the local VFW hall—lit his pipe and took a long, deep puff. He was a small, wiry man with snow-white hair, a thick mustache, piercing blue eyes and a bad case of insomnia.

"Hi there, Mr. Peterson. Can't sleep tonight?"

He ignored her question and motioned toward

her door. "It's like a bad apple in the orchard, that's what it is." He motioned toward her door. "A cryin' shame, I tell you. A real cryin' shame."

"I'm sorry I forgot to sign up. I've been really busy."

"Baloney. You young-uns are always rushing here and there, thinking you're all so important 'cause you got them fancy cell phones glued to your ear. I've got one word for you—brain cancer."

"That's two words."

"Don't you go gettin' all smart on me. I got grand-kids for that."

She smiled. "How are the girls doing?"

"Fine and dandy. Their ma said thanks for those autographed NASCAR caps you gave 'em last week. Girls loved 'em." Skeeter had triplet granddaughters who descended on him every Saturday afternoon.

Actually, they descended on Savannah because Skeeter took an afternoon nap and the triplets couldn't help but get bored. There is only so much *Reader's Digest* a girl can handle before she goes searching for some real reading material. They'd come knocking on Savannah's door, desperate for an issue of *Seventeen* or *Glamour*. Savannah had been more than happy to oblige. She'd also fed them a few issues of *Popular Mechanics*. Needless to say, all three fifteen-year-olds could now change a flat tire, check an oil gauge and follow a NASCAR race without help from the commentators, all while wearing the latest eye shadow and lip gloss.

"It was no trouble."

"I'd say not on account of you probably have piles of that stuff lying around at your work. 'Course, you're too busy to remember to bring one to your favorite neighbor."

"Mr. Sinclair wants a hat?" She stared across the yard to the condo opposite hers.

Skeeter frowned. "Ebenezer Sinclair wouldn't know the difference between a race car and a Pinto."

"But you would."

"'Course I would. I'm a red-blooded American, ain't I? I watch NASCAR like everyone else down at the Senior Center. And I got my favorites, too. No offense, but those brothers of yours—whatstheirnames? Trent and Troy? Tim and Terry?"

"Trey and Travis."

"They ain't got a chance in Hades of winning the New Year's Eve race."

A girl could only hope.

"My money's riding on Linc Adams. 'Course, Mackenzie Briggs is a pretty good fella. Seems nice and not nearly as self-centered as Tom and Toby."

"Trey and Travis," she told him.

"Whatever. 'Course, if you just happened to bring me a couple of Tom and Toby's caps, I'd be obliged to wear 'em on account of it's the neighborly thing to do and I'm a good neighbor." He pinned her with a stare. "You won't catch me rushing off to work every day and ignoring my responsibilities."

"You're retired."

"That's beside the point. Folks can count on me, which is more than I can say for present company."

"I didn't mean to miss the meeting. It slipped my mind. Things were really crazy at work."

"*Humph.*" He snorted. "You don't know the meaning of the word *crazy* 'til you play ten bingo cards during one sitting." He waved the pipe in her direction. "Now there's a challenge fer ya."

"You play *ten* bingo cards?"

"Every Tuesday night. Wednesday, too, when *Lost* is running reruns."

"That's impressive."

"Did twelve once, but it doubled my blood pressure and I damn near had another heart attack. It's been ten ever since. And I can eat a foot-long chili-cheese dog and a plate of hot wings while I'm doin' it."

"Shouldn't you be watching your cholesterol?"

"Ain't that the cat calling the kettle black?"

"I don't have high cholesterol."

"'Course you don't. I'm talkin' 'bout tendin' to your personal business. Which you ain't. On account of your door, there, is as bare as a toy store shelf the day after Christmas." He took a long drag on his pipe. "You best be gettin' inside. All this yappin' is giving me heartburn."

Savannah suspected the culprit was the now-empty bag of fried pork rinds sitting on his lap, but she kept her thoughts to herself. There was no winning with Skeeter Peterson. The best a person could hope for was escaping before he started talking about his World War II scars. Talking always led to showing and, frankly, she'd already endured enough pain and suffering that day.

"Sleep tight, Skeeter." She slipped inside her apartment and closed the door behind her. Sliding off her shoes, she collapsed on the sofa and leaned her head back. She was just about to close her eyes when the phone rang and the answering machine kicked in.

"This is Savannah. You know the drill." *Beep*.

"I know it's late, but I just heard." Jaycee Anderson's familiar voice filled the room.

Jaycee was Savannah's best friend and the only female driver currently racing in the NASCAR NEXTEL Cup Series. Jaycee was the daughter of the late Ace Anderson, a legendary car designer and team owner who was still making headlines six months after a fatal heart attack because he'd left ownership of his race team to Jaycee's half sister, Riley Vaughn. Riley owned Sunny Side Up, a string of tanning salons, and knew absolutely zip about stock car racing. She'd waltzed in and taken charge, however, as if she'd been born in a race car, and so Jaycee—who could take apart said car and put it back together with her eyes closed—was this close to strangling her most of the time.

"Dads," Jaycee went on. "They can really screw things up. Do you know that Riley wants the team to wear *pink* hats? Hell will freeze over before I put a pink hat on my head, I'll tell you that much. Even if it is the signature color of our new sponsor. She can just find another sponsor, or better yet, another driver. We've already lost half the crew, including our crew chief. Sam quit today. Said he wasn't going to work for a woman who didn't know the difference between a Chevy and a Kia. But I know you don't want to hear about my troubles. You've got your own. I'm here if you need to bitch and moan. Call me." *Click.*

Silence filled the room all of ten seconds before the phone rang again.

*Beep.* "And don't do anything stupid," Jaycee's voice floated over the line again. "Like eat an entire pizza or a whole bag of Doritos. Not that I have anything against the two, but don't do them together. In their entirety. With a thirty-two-ounce chocolate shake. Trust me, she's not worth it. I mean *he*," Jaycee blurted after what sounded suspiciously like a muffled burp. "Your dad's not worth it." *Click.*

The phone rang again and Savannah picked it up.

"I feel sick," Jaycee told her.

"I know. I still can't believe it."

"No, I really feel sick." A bag crumpled in the background. "I ate too much."

"So you're bingeing in honor of Sam's departure?"

"Not about Sam. With every other member of the crew walking, it was only a matter of time before he followed. I'm talking about the hat."

"You're making too big a deal out it."

"Would you wear a pink hat? Don't answer that." Jaycee rushed on. "You're the poster girl for pink."

"I am not." Pink had been her mother's signature color. "Not anymore." She collapsed on her couch. "But I bet you would look terrific in the color. Especially if it's a hot, vibrant shade."

"I don't care about looking terrific. This isn't a fashion show. It's a race team. And for the record, we're talking Pepto-Bismol pink."

"Oh."

"Exactly."

"So explain to Riley how you feel."

"I already did."

"And?"

"And I also told her where she could go and how fast to get there. She's not speaking to me right now. Which is the only good thing to come out of this day." Her voice softened. "So he really *fired* you?"

"He prefers the term 'laid-off.'"

"Are you sure he's getting enough oxygen to his brain? Before my dad had his heart attack, he started acting kind of crazy. In fact, I'm totally convinced that's when he drafted his will and left Riley in charge."

"Dad's not lacking in oxygen, he's lacking in grandchildren. At least, he thinks he is, thanks to Uncle Pete." Uncle Pete was Will's younger brother by ten years. "My cousin Sally just had a baby." Savannah toed the announcement sitting on her coffee table and sent it sailing over the edge.

"Uh-oh."

"Exactly." Will Calloway wasn't a NASCAR icon for nothing. He took competition very seriously. Both on and off the track.

He wanted grandchildren and he wanted them now, and Savannah was the obvious means to an end.

While she didn't agree with his way of thinking, she understood it. The team owner in him refused to sacrifice his sons because he needed them to keep Calloway thriving. They were drivers, after all. Vital to the success of a race team. Which meant Savannah got to be the sacrificial lamb. She was the eldest, the only female and, even more, merely the company's marketing manager. She wasn't an important member of his team.

But that was all about to change.

"I've got an idea." She gave Jaycee the details of her plan to help Mac crack the top three.

"What sort of tweaking are you going to do?"

"I'm going to give the car a once-over first, then I'll start with the obvious. Spark plugs. Points. Fuel lines—" *Beep.* Her other line clicked in and she checked the caller ID. "It's Trey. I have to go."

"Call me when you get home tomorrow night."

"Will you still be up?"

"Actually, I won't even be home. I've got my own car to worry over until I can get someone to replace Sam. Why don't I call you?"

"Sounds good. Bye." Savannah punched the button and switched to her second line. "Hey, Trey."

"Vannah? Thank God you're home. I've been going nuts since I heard the news."

Tears sprang to the back of her eyes and she blinked frantically. "Can you believe he actually fired me?"

"What? Who?"

"Dad. I figured you already knew."

"Dad fired you? Oh, yeah. You mean the layoff. Sorry about that. Listen, can you believe he's going to let Travis run the new engine on New Year's Eve? I busted my ass this year to win the cup. If anyone should run it, it's me."

"The engine? That's why you're calling me?"

"You have to talk to him. Tell him I should drive it."

"He fired me, Trey. That means I no longer work for Calloway and my opinion no longer counts."

"That's crazy. He'll listen to you. Come on, sis. I need you here," he pleaded and for the next few seconds, Savannah was eleven years old, standing in the grocery store with her father's list, the five-year-old twins clinging to her legs and her baby brother Jack in the carrier in the front of the basket.

*"Please, sissy." Trey tugged on the bottom of her sundress. "Can we have some bubble gum? Please, please, please."*

She'd given in then, just as she gave in now. "Okay." She swallowed past the lump in her throat. "I won't talk to Dad, but I'll talk to Travis. Maybe I can persuade him to step down and hand over the new engine to you."

"You're the best."

"Sure. That explains why Dad fired me." Her voice softened. "I can't believe he actually—"

"I hate to cut you short, but can we do this later? I'm doing laps first thing in the morning and then I've got a commercial for one of the new sponsors. I've got to get to bed."

"Sure. Good—" *Click.* So much for crying on her brother's shoulder.

She contemplated calling Travis, but he would probably be in bed by now, too. His schedule was just as busy as Trey's. And he was just as sympathetic.

Not that she blamed them. She'd practically raised both of them after their mother had died, and so it only made sense that they looked to her to solve their problems. And that they refused to see that she had any of her own.

Yes, it made sense. But the knowledge did little to ease the tightness in her chest.

She pushed to her feet and walked into the kitchen. A few minutes later, she settled on the couch with a pint of fat-free yogurt. It wasn't Ben & Jerry's, but it would do.

It always had.

Savannah had learned that a long time ago. While her friends had been scarfing French fries and sucking up malts at the local diner, she'd been dishing out healthy snacks to her brothers while herding them around the racetrack. She came from a long line of athletes, after all, and she was the eldest. It had been her responsibility to look after the younger Calloways and promote good eating habits while her father worked on his latest engine.

She'd done her job well. Thankfully. While she'd inherited her mother's looks, she'd gotten the slowpoke metabolism of her Grandma Bess who'd been as plump and soft as a teddy bear. Which meant everything Savannah ate went straight to her hips.

Of course, that might change. Working with the

pit crew would mean being on her feet constantly, rushing here and there, burning calories the way her father's prized car burned up a track during a race.

If, that is, she managed to tweak Mac into first place and prove to Will Calloway that she deserved a position on his pit crew.

*If?* More like *when.*

In two weeks, she vowed to herself. On New Year's Eve. Then it was bye-bye strawberry granola and hello fudge brownie madness.

Until then, however, she wasn't taking any chances.

## CHAPTER THREE

"IF I'VE SAID IT ONCE, I've said it a thousand times. Never play strip poker with a man who wears dentures, bifocals, a hearing aid *and* a prosthetic foot."

The familiar female voice carried through the screen door, along with the faint sound of the Top 40 station playing on the radio, just as Mac stepped up onto his granny's back porch.

It was late afternoon after a full day spent working with his crew chief and his head hurt like a sonofagun. Thanks entirely to a sleepless night spent tossing and turning and replaying Savannah's proposition.

He was meeting her tonight. *Tonight.* In just a few hours.

The knowledge made his heart pound that much faster. All the blood rushed to his brain and excitement zipped up and down his spine. He'd tried to keep working once everyone had left the garage, but without the noise and voices to distract him, he'd found himself thinking about her and anticipating the night ahead.

And so he'd come here. To eat some of his granny's home cooking, clear his head and get his priorities straight.

He *was* excited about tonight.

But in a purely professional sense.

"You'll die of old age before he ever gets down to his skivvies," his granny went on. A popular pop song beat a steady rhythm in the background.

"But Morty Stanbauer is as cute as a button," another crackling voice said.

"With all of the above firmly attached," Granny Briggs said. "Without it? He's old."

"Aren't we all?" the comment came from yet another voice.

Laughter drifted from the kitchen, along with the warm, sugary scent of fresh-baked cookies. Mac was about to walk in on his granny's baking group— the Baking Bunnies—and one of their meetings.

Mac frowned. While he had nothing against baking, he wasn't too thrilled with the way his granny's group now operated.

Since her heart attack, Margaret Briggs had been on a quest to recapture her youth. She'd traded her house dresses for neon warm-up suits and sparkly flip-flops, and the Baking Bunnies were following in her footsteps. They'd said adios to their hot tea in favor of frozen margaritas (low-carb mix for the dia-betics in the bunch) and they were now tapping their toes to the Pussycat Dolls.

Mac took a deep breath, gathered his courage and pushed open the door.

"I heard this strange creaking noise when I was tying my shoes the other day." Mabel Carlyle was a petite woman with snow-white hair and a bright orange sundress. She stood at one of the counters, her walker beside her, and rolled out a blob of dough. "I was this close to calling Ghostbusters when I realized it was me. My joints just aren't what they used to be."

"There are no such people as Ghostbusters. That was just a movie." The comment came from Kate Rogers, who stood next to her sifting flour into a mixing bowl. "And a damned good one."

"I heard there are people like that." Margaret Briggs rimmed a glass with salt. She wore a bright yellow T-shirt with matching running shorts and a pair of white Nike tennis shoes. She looked as if she'd just come off the track.

She'd been doing aerobics again. He knew it even before she paused to do a couple of stretches before reaching for another glass and resuming her role as bartender.

"I was watching the Effects channel the other day," Mabel went on, "and they have this new reality show about a ghost chaser who goes to these haunted houses and contacts the ghosts who supposedly live there. She actually went over to England and supposedly talked to the ghost of Attila the Hun."

"Attila who?" Mavis Shriner was the fourth member of the group. She hoisted a platter of cookies from the oven and set them on a nearby counter before taking the drink that Granny Briggs poured for her.

"Not Attila who. Attila the Hun." Edna poured a glass for herself and sipped. "It's his name. He was this really bad fellow who chopped off people's heads and shishka-bobbed them just because he felt like it. I think he had issues. And it's *FX*—the letters—not *Effects*."

"He was a fella, you say?" Kate asked.

"Yep."

"You're sure? Because my second to youngest daughter, Sarah, went through the 'change' last year, and she came this close to yanking my son-in-law's head off with her bare hands. If your Attila person was a woman, that would explain a lot."

"Sure enough."

"Amen."

"So what color undies was he wearing?" Mabel asked.

"I don't know." Margaret shrugged. "I don't even think they had underwear back then."

"Not Attila the Hun." Mabel turned toward Kate. "Morty."

"I don't know. I was catching my death when he was just peeling off his shirt. We had to call it quits."

"That's a shame. He looks like a brief man to me."

"I say boxers."

"I say long johns."

"Morty?" Margaret shook her head. "I say neither."

At that Mac cleared his throat before things got worse.

"Dear? Is that you?" Margaret turned.

"In the flesh." Unfortunately. While Mac loved his granny dearly, he had no desire to hear her views on men and underwear. Or the lack of.

Especially the lack of.

"It's Mac!" Kate declared.

"My, my, but that television don't do him justice," Mabel chimed in. "He's such a looker."

"Amen."

"So young and virile."

"Do you wear underwear, dear?"

"Ladies." He planted a kiss on his grandmother's cheek. "I didn't just hear that."

"Don't be such a fuddy-duddy." She patted his arm. "It's just a question. You get asked them all the time."

"If it doesn't have anything to do with my car, my

driving or my sponsor, I plead the fifth. There are certain things a man doesn't discuss with his grandma, and underwear is one of them."

"Sex is the other," Margaret informed her friends before turning on her grandson. "And just how do you think you came into being, young man? Immaculate conception?"

"Honestly, Gran, it's not something I sit around thinking about." He kissed her cheek. "I'd say go back to what you were discussing, but if you could give me a head start out the door, I'd really appreciate it." He grabbed a couple of cookies from the tray. "I didn't mean to bother you ladies." He kissed his grandmother's cheeks again. "Cut down on the margaritas, okay?" Mac asked. "You've been lucky, Gran. Don't push it."

"Nonsense. Luck isn't something that happens. People make their own luck. I've always been healthy and my reward was surviving a heart attack. And I don't intend to waste one minute of the time I have left."

"Still, you don't want to overdo it," Mac told her. "Speaking of which, cut down on the aerobics, too."

"I'm working on my abs."

"You're eighty-six. You don't have abs. Ladies—" he winked and nodded at the rest of the group before turning "—take care."

"Wait." Margaret pulled a long, white box from

beneath the cabinet. It was an old shoebox with faded red Christmas bell cutouts glued to the outside.

He'd made it for her back in the sixth grade when he'd come to live with her after losing both his parents in a car accident. Every year since, she'd filled it with Christmas treats for him.

"Here are some sugar cookies. We're doing gingerbread and appletinis tomorrow."

He grimaced.

"We're drinking the appletinis while making the gingerbread."

"Whatever happened to good, old-fashioned lemonade?"

"The old part," Margaret told him as she handed him the box. "Now get back to work and let us be."

Mac took his cookies and walked back out to his car. The mouthwatering scent of sugar and vanilla drifted from the warm box and his nostrils flared.

Oddly enough, it wasn't the cookies he pictured as he pulled out of his granny's drive and headed back to the garage. It was Savannah. And her soft, pink lips.

His heart kicked up a few beats and his nerves buzzed in anticipation.

So much for getting his priorities straight.

# CHAPTER FOUR

"OKAY, CHIEF. SHOW ME what you got."

The deep, husky voice slid into Savannah's ears and a dozen possibilities raced through her mind. All courtesy of last night's triple-decker fantasy starring one very hot, very hunky and very off-limits Mackenzie Briggs.

Off-limits, she reminded herself. As in *no. Not now. Not ever again.*

She slammed her mind shut and concentrated on retrieving the notes she'd made. She circled the car until she and Mac stood on opposite sides. Even though she could still see him—he wore tight jeans, a plain, gray T-shirt imprinted with his sponsor's logo and a sexy grin—she could at least breathe without drinking him in.

Sort of.

His scent still lingered in the air, teasing her senses. Her nerves went on full alert and her tummy tingled.

*Get real*, a voice whispered. *You haven't had a decent date in ages, your hormones are seriously deprived, and Mac looks entirely too good in a pair of jeans. This isn't going to work.*

But it had to.

Mac was not only her one chance to stay in the game, he was her opportunity to actually make a move, to finally do what she wanted, rather than what her family expected. She concentrated on the familiar aroma of oil and exhaust that lingered in the air and shifted her attention to the sleek car in front of her. The metal felt cool on her fingertips.

"Overall, this baby is in excellent shape. Definitely a contender. It's the little things that are holding her back."

He stared at her over the hood and arched a dark eyebrow. "Such as?"

"She's a little shaky in her turns."

He nodded. "Dane thinks it's the strut." Dane Travers was Mac's crew chief and one of the best mechanics in the business.

He was also wrong. At least in Savannah's opinion.

"Shaky engines usually point to the strut. But the engine's not shaky all the time, right? Just on the turns?" He nodded and she shrugged. "It's your air flow. When you make a turn, the engine stops breathing for whatever reason and it causes you to tremble. Not much, mind you. Just enough to slow you down and jar your control. When you come out of the turn, it takes you a few extra seconds to get the car back in line and up to speed. I'm thinking it's a combination of your shocks and your brake cylinders. Maybe even your fuel pump, too." When he started to protest, she added, "I know a constricted fuel pump makes the engine stutter, not shake, but what if the constriction just occurs in the turns? The stutter combined with the angle of the wheel and the pressure on the shocks might create a subtle shake rather than the usual stutter."

"That's a big *might*."

"True, but I'd like to check everything, make a few adjustments and see what happens."

"Dane's already checked the shocks. And the cylinders. And the fuel pump. *And* the line."

"I'm sure he has. He checks one thing and it looks fine, so he moves on to the next. But they work together in the turns, more so than when you're eating up straight pavement."

"Meaning it's not the part itself. It's what it does when I turn the wheel."

"Exactly. Dane's looking for one big, obvious problem. A bad part. An ineffective one. An obsolete something. But I don't think that's what's holding you back. It's all the little things. So small that no one on the crew really notices, and, if they do, they blame it on the driving."

"I'm not losing control on my turns."

"You know that, but they don't. They're not in the

car with you. And when someone does a test drive, the change is so subtle that they probably attribute it to their own inexperience behind the wheel. You know better. And I know better."

"What makes you think it's not the driving?"

"Because I've watched you drive. When you raced for my father's team, you never shook on your turns. Because you didn't have a problem, and neither did the car. You take the driver's seat for Jamison, and bam, your turns are shaky. It's the car. We all know that one quirky shock isn't going to keep you from winning a championship. But what if there are ten other parts each with their own quirks? If they act up at the same time, it's just enough to keep you here—" she held her hand waist high before lifting it overhead "—when you want to be here." She shrugged. "At least that's my theory."

Mac wasn't sure that he agreed with her. But with only two weeks until the race, he was willing to try anything. The car looked in the same tip-top shape that it always did. Good. But not quite good enough.

Not yet.

"I've got a list of ten adjustments that I think will make the car much more capable all the way around." She smoothed her palm over her list, softly stroking the paper, and his memory stirred. He felt her touch on his back, sweeping up the length of his spine, her fingers digging into his shoulder blades.

"So what do we do first?" he managed, despite his suddenly dry throat.

"*We* don't." Her gaze met his. "I was raised in a garage. I know my way around. I'm perfectly capable of making the adjustments on my own."

"There's no doubt about that." He folded his arms across his chest and leaned against the front bumper. "But if you think I'm leaving you alone with my car, think again."

She planted one hand on her hip. "What's that supposed to mean?"

"You work for the competition. *My* competition." He shrugged. "What do you think it means?"

"I *used* to work for your competition. I was terminated, remember?"

He shrugged. "You're still a Calloway."

"This isn't about my family. It's about me. This is my chance to do something I love. To do something, period. I've spent my whole life dreaming about working in the garage, and now it's right there. So cut it with the suspicion crap. Either you trust me or you don't." Her gaze met his. "So which is it?"

"I trust you." Even so, he didn't budge. He couldn't. She smelled too good. Like the fluffy, frosted cupcakes his granny made every year on his birthday. The warm, sugary aroma made him want to lean forward, trail his tongue along her plump bottom lip and see if she tasted even half as sweet.

She would. He remembered all too well, and the memory urged him to peel off her clothes and fall into bed with her all over again.

Crazy. That's what he was. One hundred percent certifiable. He was surrounded by beautiful women all the time. Women with bigger breasts and longer legs. Not a one of them stirred his lust the way Savannah Calloway did.

Even more, she didn't prance around in short-shorts, flirting and teasing and gushing every time a man looked at her. She'd always been much too dedicated to her father's race team for that. And damned if that quality didn't make her all the more appealing.

It always had.

Which was why he'd forgotten all about his point standing that night so long ago when they'd driven out to the beach after the Napa race. He'd meant to take her home, but they'd ended up sitting on the hood of his car, watching the surf roll in. She'd congratulated him on a phenomenal win and then she'd kissed him. It hadn't been an invitation to fall into bed. But it had been enough to let him know she was interested.

She'd wanted him.

He'd gladly obliged her and taken charge of the situation. He'd kissed her long and slow and deep, and then he'd swept her up into his arms.

They'd gone to the moon that night right there on

the beach, with the stars twinkling overhead and the surf rolling onto the sand.

The trouble was, while Savannah had managed to come down to earth the morning after and get back to business as if nothing had ever happened between them, Mac hadn't. Not until it was too late. He'd made six of the poorest finishes of his entire career after their heated encounter and irreparably damaged his reputation with his sponsor.

He'd been as mad as hell when her father had terminated his contract. At the same time, he'd been relieved.

She'd wanted only a one-night stand and he'd wanted her. Again. And again. Being so close to her week after week, seeing her around the track and in the garage, wanting her so badly and not being able to have her, had damn near killed him *and* his career.

Not this time.

He'd managed to pick himself up and get back in the game driving for Jamison Racing. His sponsor, Skull Creek Auto Parts, trusted him. He'd worked hard over the past six years to get past that night with Savannah. He wasn't about to let history repeat itself.

This time he was keeping his head on straight and, most important, his hands off. It was all about the racing.

His gaze roved over her. She'd shed the skirt and blouse in favor of an oversized Astros baseball jersey and jeans. In his mind's eye, he could see all the delicate curves hidden beneath. Her pert breasts, the curve of her hips, the smooth line of her pale thighs.

Hey, there was no law that said a man couldn't look.

As if she could read the thoughts racing through his head, she frowned. "Well don't just stand there." She folded her notes and shoved them into her pocket. Pushing up her sleeves, she pointed to the tools spread out on a massive table. "Hand me a wrench and let's get to work."

SHE WAS THIS CLOSE TO PASSING out by the time she crawled into bed just before midnight. Not only did her arms ache from all the adjustments she'd made, but her nerves were shot from being on constant alert. She needed to close her eyes. To sleep.

Her eyelids drifted shut and just like that, Mac's image appeared. His twinkling blue eyes and slow, easy grin and—

Her eyes snapped open and she sat up. So much for sleeping. She crawled out of bed and had just collapsed on the sofa when the phone rang.

"Where the hell have you been and why didn't you answer your cell phone?"

*None of your business and none of your business.*
That's what she thought, but she heard herself

say, "I've been out and the cell phone is a company phone. Since I no longer work for the company, Travis, I no longer carry the phone."

"Oh, yeah? Okay, so did you send off the press releases for the New Year's race?"

"Hello? Did you not just hear what I said? I don't work for Calloway."

"No wonder that reporter from the Speed Channel didn't know that I'm running the new engine. Trey's telling everybody and their dog that he's trying out Dad's new design, and everybody believes him because they haven't got the official announcement that it's me."

"Maybe you should let him drive."

"I won the Cup last year. I earned the chance to preview the new engine. You have to get those announcements out."

"I can't."

"Please, Vannah. I can't deal with all these people calling me, trying to verify facts. I've got to concentrate. It's making me crazy."

"I suppose I could send out an e-mail." She wouldn't actually have to go into the office, and it really wasn't much trouble, considering she'd already drafted the press release and all that it required now was a press of the button to send it to her media list.

"Great. I knew you'd come through. You always come through."

"Good old me," she murmured as she slid the phone into place. She powered up her laptop. She'd barely hit the send button when her youngest brother, Jack, called.

"Why aren't you answering your cell?"

"I've been kidnapped by aliens and they won't let me."

"That's great. Listen, I've got trouble and you have to help me out. I'd just gotten a haircut before I went for my headshot for the latest publicity photos and the hairdresser spiked me a little too high."

"What?"

"He put mousse in my hair and spiked it. Anyway, it looks like I've got a horn on the left side of my head. They scheduled a new shot, but in the meantime, this is all I've got to work with and press packs have to go out the day after Christmas..."

By the time Jack had finished, Savannah had agreed to help him fix the pictures being included in the press kit.

They still saw her as their employee, and that obviously wasn't going to change until she proved that she was more than media contacts and a sympathetic ear. Then they would stop treating her like the hired help and give her the respect and consideration she deserved.

*And the love.*

She ignored that last thought, closed up her

computer and considered the yogurt sitting in her freezer. Unless it morphed into a pint of fudge brownie madness, she wasn't likely to sate the hunger gnawing inside of her. Since that obviously wasn't happening, she headed for the bedroom. She didn't climb between the sheets this time, however. Instead, she walked into the bathroom and straight into a cold shower.

## CHAPTER FIVE

MAC HAD ALWAYS CONSIDERED himself a leg man when it came to women. He'd been eight years old the first time he'd seen Daisy Duke prance around on television in her blue jean cutoffs, and he'd been hooked from then on. As far as he was concerned, nothing got him hot and bothered quicker than a pair of long, shapely, tanned legs.

Except maybe a cute belly button.

He stared at Savannah, who lay stretched out on her back on the padded creeper, her upper body partially hidden underneath the car. She wore jeans and sneakers and a white Calloway Motor Sports T-shirt. The soft cotton had crept up past the waistband of her jeans, giving him a tantalizing view of her bare midriff.

Mac stared at the smooth expanse of skin and barely resisted the urge to reach out to see if it felt as soft as it looked.

As soft as he remembered.

"...me another socket wrench? This one keeps slipping and I can't get the spring off."

"Uh, sure." He forced his gaze away and turned toward the tool cart. He hunkered down next to her. "Here you go."

"Thanks."

Her silky fingers grazed his as she took the wrench. Electricity sizzled from the point of contact and raced through his body faster than a rookie headed for his first victory lane. As if she shared his reaction, her hand trembled and stalled.

"My pleasure," he murmured when she finally managed to pull away.

*Liar.* He hadn't gone nearly far enough for pleasure. And he *wasn't* about to. They had less than two weeks to get his car into winning shape.

Winning, a voice prodded. It was all about staying focused and primed and *winning*. That's all he'd ever wanted. All he still wanted.

It's just that with all that warm, silky-looking skin only a few inches away, he wasn't so sure anymore.

His gaze lingered on her belly button for several heart-pounding moments before he managed to find his control and force himself to his feet.

"I think the back right spring will give a more optimum spring rate on the left front tire," she went on as he rounded the car. "Your suspension's a little loose."

"My crew thinks it's me," he called out.

"They obviously didn't follow your career back when you were racing for my father."

"And?" He pulled a creeper from where it hung on the wall and sat it on the floor.

"And you weren't loose in your turns then. That car had great suspension. Optimum spring rates on every tire. If you were the problem, then you would have been a problem back then. I think you just need to switch a few springs around. The difference won't be drastic. Just barely noticeable. But that small margin will make the difference when you're revving close to 8,900 rpm."

"Maybe." But there was no maybe about it. He'd thought the same thing himself, but since he was the expert when it came to driving, he did his job and let his crew do theirs.

"This is going to work," she said. "It has to."

The last sentence echoed soft and desperate in his ears, and a rush of admiration went through him. She had guts, he had to give her that. She was going up against her father, of all people. The man was a genius with race cars—he'd been building his own for over twenty years and every one had made it to first place at one time or another. Once Mac left, Trey Calloway had slid into the driver's seat and won a NASCAR NEXTEL Cup Series championship.

The championship that would have been Mac's if he hadn't let Savannah get under his skin and into his head.

And his heart.

Before he could think too hard on that last thought, he plopped down on the creeper and slid under the car from the opposite side.

Savannah glanced toward him as he shimmied over to her. Her eyes widened and her grip on the wrench faltered. "I can do this myself."

"So can I. With our time limited, I figure two sets of hands are better than one. You just tell me what you have in mind and I'll see what I can do."

Better to be under the car helping her work than standing idly by watching her. Wanting her.

Nope. He wouldn't watch. The wanting he couldn't help, but at least he could distract himself.

He drew in a deep breath. The scent of oil and metal filled his nostrils. Unfortunately, a whiff of sweet, teasing vanilla followed, stirring his nerves even more.

Maybe being cooped up underneath the car wasn't the best idea. If they hadn't been doing this on the sly, he would have wheeled the car over to the main Jamison garage and put it up on the block for easier access. But their resources, like their time, were limited.

Cramped working conditions aside, at least he was *doing* something.

Something that didn't involve kissing her senseless.

"So you want to switch out the front right spring with the back left spring?" he asked.

"That's the plan." She turned her attention back to the spring and started cranking the wrench. "After that I want to take a look at the spark plugs. I've been researching some manufacturers online. One company's come up with a pretty reliable plug that runs colder. I don't know if it will work, but it's worth a try. If it does work, I don't think we'll have any trouble getting it through inspection."

"You're the boss."

No way was she going to kiss him.

Savannah made that promise to herself several hours later. They'd finished adjusting the front and rear suspensions and had decided to take a quick break. She took a long sip of the water bottle she held and tried to ignore the drop-dead gorgeous man standing a few feet away near one of the work-benches.

*Absolutely no way was she going to kiss him.*

No matter how much she'd dreamed about him, or how her mind had replayed the memory of their one night. This wasn't about the past, or her ridiculous fantasies. This was about her future. Her professional future.

Which meant no kissing. Nada. Zip. Zero.

Even if his eyes twinkled when they met hers. And his lips crooked into that sexy grin. And he looked even more yummy than the fat sugar cookie snowman decorated with white frosting and red sprinkles that he pulled from a white cardboard box.

She watched as he took a big bite. A speck of frosting dotted his upper lip as he chewed, and her stomach grumbled with need.

He glanced up, a knowing light in his eyes, and his mouth slid into a grin. "Want some?"

The *some* stirred all sorts of images that Savannah did her best to ignore. "I…" She swallowed. "I really don't do sugar."

"Oh. You're one of those."

"What's that supposed to mean?"

"A health nut."

"I'm not a health nut. I just like to be able to fit through the door."

"And one cookie will kill your chances? Haven't you ever heard of moderation?"

If only. But one would only make her want another and another. Her gaze lingered on his lips, and a memory rushed at her.

"Come on." He motioned to the box. "They're homemade."

"And here I thought you spent your days behind the wheel or under the hood." She set her water bottle aside, took a wrench and turned back to the car. Mac was off-limits and definitely not on the list of possibilities. Therefore, no looking. No wanting. Nothing.

"The Baking Bunnies made these." He came

up behind her and the smell of fresh cookies tempted her.

"The mystery unfolds."

"The Bunnies are my Granny Margaret's friends. They've been baking holiday goodies together for as long as I can remember. They start two weeks before Christmas and bake something different every day. Today they did sugar cookie cutouts. Tomorrow it's banana nut bread. Of course, the baking sessions aren't exactly what they used to be. But the end result is the same."

"What do you mean?"

"I mean now they drink margaritas and appletinis and dance around the kitchen like they were in their twenties. Which they're not. They're all well into their eighties."

"Eighty-year-olds can't dance?"

"Not eighty-year-olds with heart conditions." When she flashed him a questioning glance, he added, "My granny had a heart attack last year. Up until then, she was like any other grandmother. She played bingo and wore orthopedic shoes and watched "Wheel of Fortune." All that's changed now. It's as if she's trying to prove something to herself, but all she's really doing is pushing fate. She needs to take it easy."

"Have you told her that?"

He shrugged. "She never listens to me." A grin

teased the corner of his mouth. "That's the only thing about her that hasn't changed." His expression grew serious. "I just worry about her."

She tried to ignore the warmth that swelled in her chest. "That's my specialty. All I do is worry over everyone else."

"So do they worry over you?" His bright blue gaze zeroed in on her, and she had the fleeting thought that maybe he actually cared about the answer.

"Yes." He kept staring at her as if he didn't quite believe her and she shrugged. "In their own way. They're all really focused on their careers. Since I don't have a transmission and tires, they don't give me too much thought."

"But you're their sister."

"Their older sister. They see me more like a mom. Meaning, they only pay attention when they want something."

"But that's going to change, right? When you tweak my car, they're going to see you as an equal."

"Something like that."

"Maybe you shouldn't hold your breath."

"What's that supposed to mean?"

"It seems to me that your brothers are grown men and, therefore, responsible for the way they behave. They should treat you with more respect because they love you, not because you can keep their car purring like a kitten."

She'd thought the same thing herself, but she'd dismissed it. Because that would mean that they didn't love her the way she loved them. The way she wanted to be loved.

"It's not their fault," she told him. The way she'd been telling herself for years. "So your granny bakes? In addition to the drinking and dancing, I mean?"

"Yes." He finished off his cookie and reached for another. "So what's your favorite kind?"

"Of what?"

"Cookies."

"Oreos."

"I'm talking a real cookie."

"So am I."

"Oreos are not real. They're store-bought. What's your favorite homemade cookie?"

She shrugged. "I don't really have one."

"Get out of here." Realization seemed to strike. "You've never baked cookies, have you?"

"Actually, I'm the queen of baking. I don't have a favorite because I like them all. Which is why I refrain from turning on my oven unless required for a holiday or birthday."

"I'm talking real baking. Not rolling out a tube of cookie dough."

"Sugar. Flour. Eggs. The whole nine yards."

"Impressive." He winked and reached for another sweet. "You sure you don't want one?"

She took one look at the speck of frosting on the corner of his mouth and pictured herself leaning forward, flicking the small bit of fluff with her tongue. Her stomach growled.

He grinned. "Or two?"

*Just you*, she added silently. A thought she quickly ignored. She didn't need a relationship now any more than she had six years ago. She was too busy. Which was why she'd walked away after their night together and refused to look back. That, and the fact that her father would have seen it as a form of treason. While Mac had been racing for Calloway, he'd still been competing against her brothers for driver points. She couldn't very well have had an ongoing relationship with the enemy.

Not that he'd asked for one. He'd treated their night together as a one-night stand, just as she had. He'd never called. Never made any attempt to contact her and initiate anything further. Nothing.

Because back then he hadn't wanted a relationship any more than she had.

And now?

He wanted to win. And even if he had wanted more, she couldn't afford to get sidetracked. She wouldn't. This was her chance and she wasn't going to blow it.

He held out a cookie. "Come on. You know you want it."

The *cookie,* she reminded herself.

It wasn't the forbidden apple, for heaven's sake. Biting it didn't mean selling her soul for a few moments of indescribable pleasure.

Been there. Done that. Not happening.

It was just a cookie. One measly little goodie to sate the hunger turning her inside out. Then her stomach would stop growling and she could stop staring at that speck of frosting on his strong, sensuous mouth. Problem solved.

*One*, she promised herself.

She reached out.


SHE'D EATEN AN entire dozen.

The knowledge followed her all the way home after she left the garage and Mac and the now empty box that had held his granny's cookies.

A full *dozen.*

They churned in her stomach as she set aside her purse and collapsed on the sofa. What had she been thinking?

Nothing, that's what. She hadn't had one single thought. She'd simply *wanted*. No, make that *craved.*

Mac had felt too warm and smelled too potent and stood entirely too close. Every time she'd turned around, he'd been there. Her stomach had growled and she hadn't been able to stop herself. She'd reached for something—anything—to keep from reaching for him. Sure, she'd tried to slow down. To nibble rather than swallow big mouthfuls. But still, she'd consumed a full twelve.

Okay, so it had been more like thirteen. A baker's dozen. *Ugh.*

The phone rang and Savannah snatched up the receiver, eager for a distraction.

"I've been trying you all evening," her father's voice came over the line. "Where have you been?"

"Eating."

"For four hours?"

"Unfortunately. Probably all the stress from being unemployed."

"Make sure you call the *Fort Worth Star* and invite them for preparty cocktails," her father said, ignoring her comment.

"Preparty what?"

"Preparty cocktails. Before the Christmas Eve Party? The annual Calloway Christmas Eve Party. And make sure you get there at least thirty minutes before cocktail hour to greet them."

"Dad, I'm not going to the party."

"Why not?"

"Dad, you fired me. I no longer work for Calloway. Therefore, it's not likely that I'll attend the Christmas party."

"Nonsense. The party isn't just for Calloway employees. You know that. All the other race teams are invited, and the drivers. That's why I had to book the grand ballroom of the Dallas Hilton this year. To fit everyone. Not to mention, all of the shareholders will be there, and you're still a shareholder."

"An unemployed shareholder."

"It's for your own good. Don't you want a family? Don't you want to be happy? Your mother and I were so happy, Vannah. I just want the same for you. Speaking of which, make sure you wear something pretty. Wear that frilly red number you wore last year. You looked great in that. He'll love it."

"Who?"

"My allergist. I invited him. He's really anxious to meet you."

"You didn't."

"If you won't get out and meet anyone on your own, I have no choice but to bring someone to you. You're really going to like him. He's perfect for you."

"He likes racing?"

"Actually, no."

"What about cars? Is he a car enthusiast?"

"He drives a Jetta."

"So how could he be perfect for me?"

"He's anxious to settle down himself. And he's good-looking. You'll make a wonderful couple."

"Dad, I'm capable of more than squeezing out grandchildren."

"Of course you are, dear. Now don't forget about the cocktail hour. A half hour early. And be sure to wear red."

"Okay," she heard herself say. But the last thing Savannah intended to do was wear red, or any other color that played up her skin tone and her highlights and made her look as perfect as her late mother.

She wasn't her mother. Even more, she wasn't soft and feminine and half as girly as her father believed her to be. She was a serious professional. Smart. Competent. Capable of far more than arranging schedules and hosting parties and wearing frilly red dresses. She knew her stuff. And it was high time her father started taking her seriously. Professionally *and* personally.

# CHAPTER SIX

"HOW DO I LOOK?" Savannah asked the next night as she stood in the grand ballroom of the Dallas Hilton.

"I would have worn the overalls."

"You did wear the overalls."

"Exactly." Jaycee glanced down. "This says I'm serious. Goal-oriented. And I don't take crap."

"This says you forgot to shave your legs and get a decent pedicure."

"That, too. So you really think this get-up will get your dad to take you seriously?"

"Probably not. But at least he'll see me in a different light. I do look different, don't I?"

A wistful light touched Jaycee's eyes. "You look great. That is, if you like that sort of thing." She motioned to the sensible but tasteful pumps. "Those are still much too high for me. And pointed."

"They're actually pretty comfortable."

"I'll take your word for it."

"Come on, Jaycee. You can't tell me you've never tried on a pair of heels? Even low ones?" The young woman shook her head. "You've never even pulled one off the display and slipped it on when no one was looking?"

"I'd rather have my head stuffed into a muffler."

Savannah's gaze went to the well-dressed young woman who stood near the punch fountain and stared daggers at Jaycee. "That's a definite possibility."

"She told me to lose the hat." Jaycee adjusted her ball cap. "And I told her to lose the bossy attitude."

"But she is your boss."

Jaycee frowned. "For now."

"Meaning?"

"Meaning Miss Fake and Bake isn't cut out to be a team owner, and it's just a matter of time until she realizes it. Hey, I lost my crew chief on account of her. I'm entitled to a little revenge." Jaycee glanced toward the buffet. "Boy, I'm starved. I was doing laps all afternoon and I haven't eaten a thing. What about you? Want to check out the buffet?"

"I'm too nervous to eat."

"You're just afraid to add any junk to that skinny-ass trunk of yours."

"For your information, my trunk has plenty of junk."

Jaycee shrugged. "Suit yourself. That just leaves more for me." She stepped forward and Savannah caught her arm.

"You're not leaving me, are you?"

"Since when are you so jumpy?"

"Since I just spotted my father." She stared at the man who stood across the room, his gaze now riveted on her. "He looks mad, doesn't he?"

"Not exactly."

"Irritated? Mildly agitated? Miffed?"

"I was thinking *pissed*. Royally. See ya."

"Great," Savannah muttered as Jaycee took off for the buffet and her father started making his way toward her. "Run away when I need you most."

"What's this?" he asked when he reached her.

"What do you mean?"

"The way you're dressed. You're wearing *pants*. At my Christmas party. What happened to the red dress?"

"They're called slacks, Dad." She ignored the urge to turn and run, and forced a smile. "Women have been wearing them for years, and the dress just didn't work tonight. This is much better."

"This looks like you're headed to the boardroom on 'The Apprentice.'" His gaze swept over her again. "And that hair? What happened?"

"I decided to kill the highlights and go with my natural color. Brown."

"Natural? I don't think I've ever seen you with hair this dark before."

"Maybe you've never really seen *me* before."

"Will!" The man's deep voice put a stop to the discussion—thankfully—and Savannah turned toward the man who approached them. He wore a red polo sweater, tan slacks and a wide smile.

"Chip," her father said as the man reached them. "Glad you could make it."

"I wouldn't have missed it for the world." The young man glanced around. "Is she here?"

"She is," Savannah said, drawing his attention. His smile faltered and she gave herself a mental high five.

"Savannah?"

"The one and only."

"Chip," he blurted after a startled moment. "Chip Corrigan."

"Nice to meet you. Are you okay? You look a little out of sorts."

"You, um, just look a little different than what I expected."

Ready. Aim.

"Your father said you had blond hair."

Fire. "With a good bottle job. I'm a natural brunette."

"No big deal." He grinned. "I've never really gone for blondes."

So much for hitting a bull's-eye.

"Chip here heads the ear, nose and throat unit over at that new private hospital in Dallas."

"Community Park," the man chimed in, his gaze roving Savannah from her hair, which she'd pulled back into a no-nonsense bun, to the tips of her tasteful, low-heeled pumps.

"Calloway Motor Sports is funding the children's recreation unit," Chip said. "We're all very grateful for the support."

"It's our pleasure, son. Vannah here handles all of our charity projects."

"I used to handle the charity projects. My father fired me just last week."

"She works too hard."

"There's no law against hard work."

"I work a lot of hours myself."

"You must be much too busy to date," she told him.

"Well, it *is* difficult. But I'm trying to find the time. You know the saying, man doesn't live by bread alone."

"Neither should a woman," her father chimed in.

"I don't know about that. Jaycee seems to be doing a pretty fair job." She glanced at her friend, who'd just piled a fourth fresh-baked goodie on top of her plate.

Savannah ignored her father's frown and gave Chip her biggest smile. "So, you're an allergist?"

He shrugged. "It's not the most glamorous job, but it pays the bills. So, your father tells me you're an accountant?"

"That's just temporary. I'm currently pursuing a position in the challenging world of auto racing."

"Marketing. Your father told me."

"Actually, that's not exactly right."

"Oh? Are you leaning more toward management?"

"The pit. I want to be a mechanic."

"Oh."

"Do you know much about cars, Chip?" she slid her arm into his and turned away from her father who stared at her as if she'd pulled on a jumpsuit for his biggest competitor and climbed behind the wheel.

"I'm a member of Triple A."

Big surprise. "Well, I not only know them, I eat and sleep them. I always have. I can change a tire in ten seconds flat and fix a faulty transmission with nothing but a wrench and a prayer."

"That's, um, really impressive. Boy, I could really go for a drink. What about you? You thirsty?"

"Most definitely."

"What's your poison? Cosmopolitan? Apple martini?"

"Jack Daniel's. Straight up." Okay, so she was exaggerating a tiny bit. She wanted to show him the real woman, and the real Savannah had never done a shot of whiskey in her entire life. But she was trying to prove a point. Namely, that she didn't fit the girlie stereotype portrayed by her usual ultra-femme clothes and sky-high heels. The sooner he realized that, the sooner he would call it a night and the sooner her father would finally admit that she wasn't his picture-perfect daughter. "Oh, and could you bring me a beer chaser?"

"Uh, yeah. Sure." He hightailed it toward the bar, and Savannah barely managed to fight back her smile of triumph. The night wasn't over yet.

SHE WAS HERE.

Worse, she was here with a date.

Mac took a swig of his beer, fought down the crazy urge to punch something, and did his damndest to concentrate on the words coming out of the reporter's mouth.

"Word has it this is going to be one of the most exciting and grueling races of the season."

"It's a charity event. It's all about having fun."

"Are you kidding me? Anyone who's anyone is driving in this thing. The Calloways are previewing their newest and fastest car. The competition's going to be fierce and everyone is going to be watching you. It's time you cracked the top three, man."

Mac knew that better than anyone, which was the only reason he'd agreed to Savannah's plan. But he'd never been one to talk. Talk was cheap. He liked doing. Rather than tell the man what he and the beautiful blonde—no, brunette, he saw now—had in mind for his car, he intended to show him.

If Savannah was half as good as she claimed.

And if she wasn't?

He was no worse off. She would go her own way, off to find a new job, and he would get back to killing himself to crack the top three.

"Tell me," the reporter held up his microphone, obviously eager for a quote. "What is Mackenzie Briggs doing to get ready for the race of the year?"

"The usual." Yeah, right. There was nothing usual about his behavior right now. Sure, he worked out every day and practiced with racing video games. He met with his pit crew and fulfilled his sponsor commitments.

But he spent his evenings with a beautiful woman who had no desire to tweak anything except his car.

Said woman smiled at the man who returned with her drink, and a knife twisted in Mac's gut.

No, there was nothing usual about his behavior. More like crazy. He couldn't stop thinking about Savannah Calloway. Or fantasizing about her. Or wanting her.

He knew it was seeing her every day that was doing him in, despite the fact that he went out of his way to keep as much distance as possible. They were still in the same garage, breathing the same air. Close. Too close.

Until New Year's Eve.

In the meantime, if keeping his distance wasn't helping matters, he might as well get a little closer.

"Come on," the reporter persisted. "This will be

the season predictor. What are you going to do, man, to make something happen?"

Mac grinned and winked. "I'm going to have a good time."

SAVANNAH NURSED HER whiskey and did her best not to make a face in front of Chip.

"So you want to dance?" he finally asked her after she'd given him a verbal breakdown of her father's latest masterpiece engine about to be unveiled on New Year's Eve.

She shook her head. "Sorry. I don't dance. I do like to lift weights, though. It's great exercise." Okay, so now she was just flat-out trying to shock him. But she was on a roll. "I can bench-press one hundred and twenty pounds."

"Very impressive." The deep voice came from behind her and Savannah whirled to see Mac standing there.

"I...what are you doing here?"

"Everybody in NASCAR is here. Speaking of which, there's a reporter here who really wants to talk to you. You don't mind, do you, Chip?"

"Uh, no. You go ahead. I'll just get something to eat."

"What are you doing?" she asked as he took her elbow and urged her forward.

"Walking toward the dance floor."

"No, I mean the reporter. You weren't supposed to tell anyone."

"I didn't."

"But you just said…" Realization hit. "You lied."

He shrugged and led her through a maze of couples moving to the lively country song pouring from the speakers. "I prefer to call it fibbing. And for a good cause, I might add."

"What cause?"

"I saved you from Chip."

"I didn't need saving. What are you doing?" she blurted again when he jerked her to a halt and hauled her into his arms.

"Can't a man dance with his crew chief if he feels like it?"

"First off," she said as he dipped her to the left and she clutched his arm to keep from losing her footing. She did a mental search through her dance file and came up with the steps she'd memorized back in college. "I'm not your crew chief. I'm tweaking your car."

"Which my crew chief usually does. Which means you're performing in the same capacity." He winked. "Right, *chief*? So why didn't you want to dance with Dr. Chip?"

"I don't dance."

"For someone who doesn't know how to dance, you're pretty good on your feet."

"I never said I didn't know how. You name it—
polka, waltz, two-step, electric slide—I can do it. I
just don't like it."

"Why?"

"Too much work." She spent far too much time
counting—one, two, three, one, two, three—to really
enjoy herself.

"Not if you do it right. You're supposed to relax,"
he told her as if he could hear the mental steps
echoing in her ears. "You can't relax if you're wound
so tight. Just take a deep breath and loosen up." His
hold on her waist tightened and his hand slid down
to rest in the small of her back, and an aching emp-
tiness swelled inside her. "There. Now close your
eyes and just listen to the music." He guided her, his
palm strong and sure as he urged her closer. Her
breath caught and her body trembled.

*Excuse me?* She wasn't supposed to respond to
him. She'd promised herself not to, along with not
getting too close.

She stiffened and tried to pull away, but his arm
fit around her too snugly. Too perfectly. And his
body felt too good.

"The big surprise here is you," she blurted, eager
to kill the sudden silence and remember the pain
she'd felt the morning after when he'd walked away
and never looked back. "You aren't really much of
a socializer."

"I like to socialize as much as the next guy."

"I'm talking the kind of social that involves clothes."

He winked. "I can take them off if it bothers you."

"I'm being serious. You're pretty good at this."

Too good. And much too close.

She drew a deep breath and the intoxicating aroma of warm male and fresh soap filled her head. Her heart pounded, drumming a wild, crazy beat that made her want to reach up and touch his lips with her own. Again.

No.

But even as the denial screamed in her head, her hormones shouted much louder. *Just one kiss.* One little, tiny kiss to sate the desire churning inside her. If she gave in for just a second, she could stop wondering if he still tasted as good.

No more thinking. Or wanting. Or fantasizing.

She would know. Problem solved.

She pushed up on her tiptoes and she kissed him.

## CHAPTER SEVEN

SHE WAS KISSING HIM.

Mac meant to let her take the lead. She'd finally realized that she couldn't ignore the heat between them—thankfully—and he meant to see just how hot things could get. Maybe stoke the fire a little bit, but he wasn't going to push. *She'd* walked away from *him* way back when, and so he intended to kick back and let her make the next move. And the one after that.

That's what he meant to do.

Her lips were so soft, so warm, so friggin' sweet. Just like that, his control fled and he forgot everything except kissing her back.

One arm tightened around her waist and pulled her that much closer, while the other stroked up her back to cup the back of her head, tilting her just enough to give him better access.

As eager as she was, she had yet to part her luscious lips—a problem he was more than ready to remedy. He swept his tongue against the seam of her closed mouth, asking, coaxing, until she relaxed against him.

The taste of her kiss was even sweeter than her lips. Warm sugar flavored with a hint of innocence.

*Innocence?*

The thought rooted in his mind, spurred by the way her tongue hesitated against his, the way her hands rested against his chest rather than sliding around his neck. The way her body trembled. It was their first kiss all over again, and he knew then that while she'd kept her distance for the past six years, she hadn't been keeping company with any men.

The notion sent a spurt of joy through him that made him want to hoist her over his shoulder and haul butt to the nearest bathroom or storage closet. He wanted her here. Now. *Forever.*

The truth hit him as he stood in the middle of the crowded dance floor kissing Savannah Calloway. He'd never been territorial when it came to women. Hell, he'd never cared enough about anyone in particular. Sure, he'd been attracted to each woman he'd ever been with. Likewise, they'd been attracted to him. And the time spent together had always been pleasurable. But then it had ended. No lingering thoughts. No regrets. No wanting more.

Every time, with every woman, except one.

This one.

"*People make their own luck.*" Granny's voice sang in his head.

Good or bad.

He'd blamed Savannah for distracting him. But the thing was, he'd let her distract him. He'd *let* her when he'd never let any other woman because she was *the* woman. The complete package. While she looked great in a frilly dress and a pair of high heels, she was just as sexy in a T-shirt and jeans. Cocky and self-assured under the hood of his car, and all trembling vulnerability snuggled deep in his arms. Smart enough to stir his competitive edge, yet naive enough to make him want to hold her tightly and never let go. Experienced, yet innocent. And he liked it all. He liked her. A deep down, feel-it-in-your bones *like* that he'd never felt with anyone else.

And she liked him.

She just wouldn't admit it.

Yet.

"We're not moving fast enough," he murmured against her lips when they both finally came up for air.

"Amen," she said with a deep breath.

He grinned. "The song, chief. It's a fast two-step. We need to pick up the pace."

She blinked as if to clear away the cobwebs, and her disoriented gaze met his. "The song?" Realization seemed to spark. "Oh." She stiffened, her bright gray eyes going wide as if the enormity of what she'd just done hit her. "Oh, no."

"No harm done." He grinned and winked. "But if we don't start moving, we're liable to get stampeded."

"I can't…I mean, I didn't…" She shook her head. "I shouldn't have done that." Heat spread up her neck and face as her gaze met his again. "I *really* shouldn't have done that. I—I have to get out of here." She pulled away and left him standing in the middle of the crowded dance floor.

Mac had the overwhelming urge to go after her, but he wouldn't. While he'd come to terms with his feelings, she hadn't. And if he pushed her, she would only push back. Better to give her some time to think, and plenty to think about.

Starting right now.

SHE'D KISSED HIM.

The truth followed Savannah through the ballroom and down the hallway of the upscale Dallas hotel.

*She'd* kissed *him*.

Her heart pounded that much faster, and she picked up her pace. There had to be a way out of here somewhere. An exit. At the very least, a restroom. She pushed through the first door she spotted and found herself in a massive kitchen.

Ovens lined the far wall. Pots dangled overhead. A maze of preparation tables had white-clad servers moving this way and that. A man in a chef's hat sliced roast beef. Another squeezed dollops of whipped cream onto squares of Bananas Foster. Still another piped chocolate rosettes onto a rich fudge cake. The place buzzed with activity, and no one so much as glanced at her.

Thankfully.

She scooted to the side and collapsed against the wall. Drawing in a deep breath, she tried to come to terms with what she'd just done.

She'd forgotten every promise she'd ever made to herself, risked her future and *kissed* him.

*Again.*

At least this time she'd had the good sense to make a run for it.

She drew a shaky breath and closed her eyes as her mind relived the delicious, heart-pounding moment. Dread ballooned in her stomach.

He'd been the one to pull away first. She'd still been in la-la land, eager for more, and he'd been the one to come to his senses.

Panic rushed through her just as the doors to her right swung open and a waiter rushed in.

"We're out of chocolate," the man declared as he rushed over to a nearby table, where a woman wearing a white chef's hat loaded slabs of dark, rich-looking cake onto crystal plates. "I swear I thought this lady was going to gnaw off my arm when

I told her. You've got to help me before someone starts a riot."

"Just hold your horses." The female chef fed the last few pieces onto waiting plates. "I'm almost done."

Savannah watched as the woman grabbed a white decorator's bag filled with rich, frothy cream and drizzled the slices of cake. Her stomach grumbled its excitement and suddenly everything made sense.

She'd caved, all right, and it was no wonder. She'd been in severe deprivation for most of her life, always so careful to watch her figure. To be the spitting image of her svelte, attractive mother.

Since she'd inherited her grandmother's metabolism that had meant no cookies. No cakes. No ice cream. And most of all, no chocolate.

Nothing even remotely satisfying.

She remembered the first night at the garage when Mac had waltzed in with the homemade sugar cookies. She'd been as turned on by the smell of warm, sweet sugar as she'd been by the sight of him. Almost.

She ignored the last thought and latched onto the explanation like a drowning woman clutching a life preserver.

No wonder she'd jumped Mac like a starving woman. She *was* starved.

But she was no longer playing the perfect daughter. She wasn't her mother and she didn't have to stuff herself into tight skirts or clingy dresses to impress anyone. She could indulge every now and then. Live a little. *Eat.*

Then she wouldn't be so desperate around Mac. She wouldn't crave the taste of his lips. Or the feel of his mouth on hers. Or the warmth of his hands sliding up and down her back. Bottom line, she wouldn't feel so deprived when she was around him. Rather, she would feel nice and full and satisfied.

"There." The woman set her decorator's bag to the side and pushed the tray toward the impatient waiter. "Go feed the hungry masses."

"Can I have one of those?" Savannah blurted when the waiter started past her. Without waiting for a reply, she took a slice of cake and snatched some silverware from a nearby table. Forking a huge bite, she slid the sweet into her mouth and let it melt on her tongue.

Mmm...

Okay, so it wasn't half as sweet as Mac. But it would do.

At least that's what Savannah told herself.

"Merry Christmas."

"Happy holidays."

"Ho, ho, ho!"

The greetings echoed in Savannah's ears when she opened her front door to her three brothers early the next morning.

Merry Christmas?

Happy holidays?

Ho, ho… *Oh, no.*

She blinked away the exhaustion that glazed her eyes and tried to calm the furious pounding in her temples.

She couldn't have forgotten *the* most important day of the year—besides the season opener at Daytona, that is. She was having a dream, that's all. A crazy hallucination caused—like her headache from hell—by the massive amount of chocolate she'd consumed the night before.

The cold Texas wind gusted through the open doorway and snuck beneath the hem of her pajamas. She shivered and pushed the door closed before turning to follow her brothers into the living room.

Okay, so she was having a very vivid dream, complete with sights and sounds—the cold tile seeped into the soles of her bare feet, the clock ticked away in the far corner of the room and the latest Tim McGraw video blazed on the television screen. But still just a dream.

Her gaze zeroed in on Tim, who wore a Santa Claus hat and belted out a twangy version of "Jingle Bells," followed by a "Merry Christmas, y'all."

Uh-oh.

"Why isn't the tree plugged in?" Trey stared at the lifeless spruce that took up half her living room.

"Why aren't the stockings filled?" Travis eyed the red socks with the glitter trim that lined the mantel.

"Why are you still in your pajamas?" Jack stared at her as if she'd grown an eye in the middle of her forehead.

The questions pounded away at her overworked brain and her stomach churned. The past night rushed through her mind. Mac. The kiss. The chocolate.

Oh, *no*.

"Forget the stockings," Trey said as he set a shopping bag full of presents near the tree. "I don't smell any food." He headed into the kitchen.

"No food?" Travis followed on his heels. "There has to be food."

"There had better be food." Jack pushed after his brothers. "I'm so hungry I could eat the whole bird by myself."

"Listen, guys," Savannah started after them. "I know I usually have everything ready, but I had a really rough night and—"

"There's no turkey." Trey stared into her cold and lifeless oven before turning on her. "Where's the turkey?"

"That's what I'm trying to tell you. There is no—"

"No turkey?" Travis came up behind him and

peered over his shoulder. "Holy hell, there's really no turkey."

"That's because—"

"There's always a turkey." Jack took a look for himself. "Where's the turkey?"

"And the dressing?" Travis added before she could breathe, much less explain.

"And the baked apples with the cinnamon sprinkles?" Trey asked.

"I'm really sorry, guys, but—"

"Where's the turkey?" The question came from her father.

Savannah turned to see him framed in the kitchen doorway, a stack of presents in his arms.

"Vannah didn't make turkey," Travis announced.

"I meant to. I bought all the stuff. But the past two weeks have been so stressful, and I didn't get much sleep last night and—"

"It's Christmas," her father cut in, obviously not the least bit interested in her chocolate hangover. "We can't have Christmas without turkey." He shook his head. "This is totally unacceptable."

No, *"What happened, dear? Aren't you feeling well?"* or *"You look terrible. Let us help with something."*

Just a disapproving frown and the short, clipped "This is totally unacceptable." As if he were talking to his car chief about a new spark plug. As if he didn't care one way or another about his own daughter and her feelings.

He didn't, she realized in a crystalline instant as she stood in her kitchen facing the four men she'd taken care of for most of her life. Her father didn't care about her any more than the other three. He was too busy to care. Too busy trying to marry her off to the first man who would have her so she could produce the grandchildren he felt he needed.

Just as her brothers were too busy worrying about engines and who drove what car and whether or not they had enough autographed pictures to satisfy their fans.

She realized then that they would never see her as a serious asset to the company, because they didn't *see* her, period. They were too focused on themselves. *Their* wants. *Their* needs. *Their* Christmas.

"I want turkey," Jack stated. "I need it. You can't do this to me."

"You really want turkey?" She speared Jack with a stare before she whirled on her heel and stormed to the refrigerator. "I'll give you turkey." She hoisted the twenty-pound butterball from the freezer and tossed it to him. "There's your turkey."

"Wait a sec—*humph!*" He caught the bird right in the stomach.

"And your dressing," she declared as she grabbed a bag of cornmeal from the counter and pitched it at

Trey. It slapped his shoulder and exploded in a cloud of yellow dust. "And your baked apples." She grabbed a large red piece of fruit and threw it at Travis who scrambled backward as she nailed him in the side of the head.

"What the hell—ouch!"

"Get out!" she told them as she hurled another apple and caught him in the shoulder. "You're all a bunch of selfish jerks. Just get out."

"But, sis—*ugh*!" The third apple smacked into his thigh.

"I'm glad Dad fired me from Calloway Motor Sports. I don't want to work with any of you. Even more, I don't want to be a part of this family."

"Listen, here—"

"Eggnog," she blurted. "We forgot the eggnog." She reached for a carton of eggs while her father and brothers pushed past one another to get out of the kitchen before she let the first one fly.

She nailed Jack squarely in the rear end. The shell cracked and the egg dripped all over the seat of her brother's Levi's before he disappeared.

Boots slid across her hardwood floor, and the front door slammed and Savannah found herself standing in the middle of her kitchen listening to the frantic beat of her own heart.

Her hands trembled as she sank down at her kitchen table. Oddly enough, she didn't feel the usual guilt she'd felt the few times she'd let her father down or failed one of her brothers.

For the first time in her life, she felt a sense of justice.

The feeling lasted all of fifteen minutes while she cleaned up the mess. With that done, she found herself facing her first Christmas alone. A full day all to herself. To think. And reflect. And regret.

Not about what she'd said to her father and brothers—they'd had it coming for a very long time—but about what she'd done the night before. What she desperately wanted to do again.

"Can I borrow some Oreos?" she blurted when Mr. Peterson finally answered his door much later that afternoon.

"Excuse me?"

"Or some Chips Ahoy. Nutter Butter Bites. Anything. I just need sugar." She'd exhausted her own piddly supply over an hour ago.

"I got some tapioca. Brought it home from my Christmas dinner with my daughter. She always lets me bring home the leftover tapioca on account of I'm the only one who eats it in the first place. You're welcome to some."

"Tapioca, huh?" She'd eaten what was left of a bag of Oreos and two chocolate snack puddings, and she still couldn't stop thinking about Mac. Since it was Christmas, most everything was closed and so going to the grocery store was out. Which left borrowing from a neighbor. Since Mr. Peterson was the only one home—practically everyone had Christmas elsewhere—her choices were limited.

"I've never had tapioca," she went on. "There wouldn't be chocolate in that, would there?"

"Nope. But there's plenty of prunes."

*Lovely.*

"Maybe the gas station on the corner is open."

"Wouldn't count on it. I passed by there on the way home and it's locked up as tight as my granddaddy's fist on payday." She all but groaned at the news and his gaze narrowed. "Hey, how come you're over here? Where's your daddy and brothers?"

"They had other plans."

He gave her another beady-eyed stare. "You finally tell 'em where to go and how fast to get there?"

"Something like that."

His frown eased and he grinned. "I was wondering when you were going to stop letting everyone push you around and start standing up for yourself."

"I don't let people push me around."

"I got enough money out of you to fund Easter decorations for the whole block."

"What can I say? I'm a nice person."

"You're a pushover." He eyed her. "A nice pushover, but still a pushover. So you want that tapioca or not?"

"Actually, the thought of it sounds pretty awful.

I know you like it, but prunes?" She made a face and
he grinned.

"I suppose I might have a piece of chocolate pie
in my refrigerator."

"Really?"

"Maybe even a slice or two of cake."

"I think I love you."

"Now don't go getting all sweet on me. I already
told Bernice Langley that I'd go to the New Year's
Eve dance with her, and I'm a man of my word."

"I'll try to keep my hands to myself."

He stepped back and motioned her in. "Well,
don't just stand there, then. We got ourselves some
chocolate cake to eat."

"JUST HAND OVER the box," Savannah told Mac when
he walked into the garage Monday night, the white
goodie box under his arm.

He wore jeans, a black T-shirt and a sexy-as-hell
smile.

Heat zipped up and down her spine and her
stomach grumbled, mindless of the gigantic slices of
chocolate cake she'd consumed at Mr. Peterson's
the night before. She reached out. "Now."

His gaze lit with surprise as he eyed her. "Don't
you want to know what's in it?"

"Is it edible?" He nodded as she took the box.
"Good enough."

She spent the rest of the evening scarfing choco-late-cherry cookies and *not* looking at Mackenzie Briggs.

At least she tried not to look. But every time she turned around, he was standing right there. Behind her. Next to her. Leaning in front of her. His arm brushed hers, and his hand cupped her elbow and his fingers played across her neck when she leaned her head to the side to stretch.

"Does that feel good?" he asked as he kneaded the base of her neck, and she all but melted into a puddle on the floor.

"Not really. I don't really like massages."

"Is that so?"

"I don't really like to be touched." Liar. She liked it, all right. She loved it. She craved it. "It's a phobia," she blurted, scooting away before she forgot everything—the car, the race, her future—and threw herself into his arms. "I would really ap-preciate it if you would respect my space. I'd hate to end up back in therapy."

"Is that right?"

"Most definitely. I was a big mess."

"You don't say?"

"Huge. Just huge." She scooted to her side of the car, grabbed a cookie and did her best to ignore his gaze. "What?" she finally asked in between mouthfuls.

He shrugged. "Nothing."

"You're looking at me."

"So? You have a phobia against being looked at?"

"As a matter of fact..." By the time the evening came to a close, she'd replaced his spark plugs with a lighter version she'd ordered from a new and innovative company and eaten an entire box of goodies. And she'd developed enough hang-ups to make Dr. Phil one happy camper.

Not that any of it was true. But it was survival of the fittest at this point. All she had to do was resist him for the next three days and she'd be home free.

Three days...

## CHAPTER EIGHT

HE KNEW EXACTLY WHAT she was up to.

It took him a few days and a lot of his best moves—tempting smiles, suggestive looks, teasing touches—but he finally realized Savannah Calloway was sating her desire for him with his Granny's goodies.

He watched her as she opened the box he'd just handed her.

She frowned and he smiled.

"It's empty."

"I guess I got a little hungry on the way over."

"It's *empty*."

"I guess I got *really* hungry on the way over." He winked at her. "I'll make it up to you tomorrow night."

"What am I supposed to do tonight?"

"It's only a few hours. Surely you're not *that* hungry?"

He watched as she drew a deep breath. Her chest lifted and pushed against the soft cotton T-shirt she wore and his pulse quickened.

"I'll be okay."

"Good." He took the box. His fingers grazed hers in a slow, seductive glide of skin against skin that made her visibly swallow. "Let's get to work then."

WORK? YEAH, RIGHT.

Mac did everything for the next two hours but work. Instead, he smiled at her. And winked. And handed her tools. And leaned over her shoulder. And helped her lift a particularly heavy part. And stirred her hormones until she was nothing more than a quivering mass of desperation.

"Let me help," he leaned forward and his hand closed over hers, and Savannah turned on him.

"Look. Just forget it."

"What are you talking about?"

"I know what you're trying to do."

"And what is that?"

"You're trying to make me fall into bed with you again, and I can tell you right now that it's not going to happen."

"I'm not trying to make you fall into bed with me."

"It can't happen," she rushed on, "because it shouldn't have happened in the first place. We had one crazy night, but it's over and done with. No need to revisit the past, especially when you're no more interested in a relationship than I am."

"You're scared."

"It's okay. I understand. I don't have time for a relationship, either—what did you just say?"

"I said that you're scared."

"I'm not scared of you."

"Not me. You're scared of yourself. Scared of being hurt. You've been pretending to be something you're not your entire life."

"A lot you know. I've been following in my mother's footsteps to keep from hurting my father. He went through enough when he lost my mother. I didn't want him to think he'd lost her a second time. And my brothers…they never really had a chance to know her. They deserved a mother figure, and so I was that figure."

"Because you were afraid if you stood up for yourself they might not like you. You're afraid of rejection."

"I am not." Even as the denial flew from her mouth, dread churned in her stomach. "You don't know me."

"I know you're great with cars, and you like sweets and you have a knack for getting oil on your nose no matter what you're doing under the hood." He stepped closer. "It was bad timing between us the first time. You weren't ready to stand up for yourself and I wasn't ready to let go of my desire to win."

"But you're ready now?"

"Now I realize it's not a competition. It isn't you or winning. I can have both. I want both." He stepped closer. "I'm not trying to make you fall into bed with me again, chief. I want you to fall in love with me."

Because...he felt the same for her?

The possibility sent a burst of pure happiness through her, followed by a rush of panic because the last thing, the very last thing Savannah Calloway needed was to fall in love. She'd spent her entire life hiding who she really was in the name of the emotion. And now, just when she was starting to break free of the bonds she'd created for herself, Mac wanted to lasso and hog-tie her with the wealth of feeling glimmering in his eyes.

Love?

She shook away the possibility. She couldn't listen to that now. She needed to keep her head on straight. To stay focused. To live for herself for the first time in her life.

Even more, she needed to get out of that garage before she forgot all about living and gave in to the warmth that spread through her body and urged her closer to him.

"That should do it," she declared after she'd made the last adjustment to the shocks. "New Year's Eve, here we come."

"We've still got one more day until the race."

"The car's good enough." Her gaze met his. "We're finished." And then she turned and walked away as fast her sneakers could carry her, because she meant it. They truly were finished. No way was Savannah going to let herself fall in love with Mac Briggs.

SHE'D LET HERSELF FALL in love.

Savannah came to that realization as she watched Mac zoom across the finish line in an impressive second place finish.

While her father's new engine had taken first— with Travis in the driver's seat—Mac was the real news. For the first time in his ten-year career, he'd finished in the top three.

Satisfaction rushed through her. But it was nothing compared to the pure joy she'd felt for those few moments when she'd entertained the possibility that maybe, just maybe she truly *did* love him. And he loved her.

*Maybe not.* The doubt echoed through her head, but suddenly it didn't seem half as frightening as the thought that she might never talk to him again. Laugh with him. Love him.

She'd felt happier and more special in the past two weeks than she'd felt in her entire life.

And all because she'd taken a chance. Professionally, that is. She'd fought down every fear and insecurity she'd ever faced in her career. But, personally, she was still holding back. Still afraid to put her feelings on the line for fear that he didn't return them.

No more.

She had no clue whatsoever if he felt the same way, but she was determined to find out.

"...THINK TONIGHT'S FINISH puts you in the contender seat for next season's cup title?" The reporter's question rang out above the frantic *click-click* of the cameras.

"I think it says I've got the determination to go the distance, along with a car that can definitely take me there."

"The car really outperformed everyone's expectations tonight. Faster. Smoother. What's the secret?"

"Lots of cookies." The familiar voice slid into his ears, and his head jerked up to see the attractive brunette standing just beyond the cluster of reporters that surrounded him.

"More like hard work," he said as his gaze met hers. "A lot of hard work." He blinked to make sure she was real this time and not another fantasy. Heaven knew he'd had more than his fair share over the past few days.

Hell, he'd been fantasizing about her for the past six years. She'd gotten under his skin and no matter how much he tried to push her back out, he couldn't. She was in his head. His heart.

And she was standing right in front of him.

His heart pounded and his muscles bunched and it was all he could do to keep from pushing his way through the crowd, hauling her into his arms and kissing her for all he was worth.

But he'd done that already, and she'd run the other way. He wouldn't make the same mistake again. The next move was hers.

"Savannah Calloway is the one responsible for my car's improved performance," he told the press. The announcement sparked a flurry of questions as the crowd turned to face her.

"Savannah Calloway of Calloway Motor Sports?"

"Weren't you in marketing?"

"Didn't you handle accounting?"

The questions pushed past the frantic bam-bam of Savannah's heart and she nodded. "Yes."

"To which one, Miss Calloway?"

"All of the above."

"She's a mechanic," Mac said, drawing everyone's attention. "One of the best in the business." Sincerity fired his eyes a vibrant blue and her heart skipped its next beat. "She's been working on my car for the past two weeks. The changes she made were instrumental in tonight's finish."

"You can say that again."

The familiar female voice warmed Savannah's heart and she glanced behind her to see Jaycee. Standing in the garage entrance. She wore her driving suit, her helmet cradled in her arms. "I took your suggestions for Mac's car—" she said as she came up beside Savannah "—and made a few changes to my own. *Third* place." She grinned. "Can you believe it?"

"Do you think you have a real chance this year, Jaycee?"

"What's it like being the only female racing the NEXTEL Cup circuit right now?"

"How do you like having your sister as your boss?"

The questions rang out as the reporters closed in on Jaycee. Savannah and Mac were all but forgotten.

"You were right about me." She took a step toward him. And then another. "I *am* afraid of rejection. That's why I've lived my entire life pretending to be something I'm not. Because I've been afraid to be me. To go after my dream job. And my dream man." She reached him and stared deep into his eyes. Desire gleamed back at her, feeding her courage and her determination. "You're that man, Mac. *You.*"

Before she could take another breath, he pulled her into his arms and hugged her close. "Does this mean what I think it means?" he murmured against the curve of her neck.

"Yes." She slid her arms around his neck and held on for all she was worth. "I'll marry you and live happily ever after," she said with a laugh.

He pulled back enough to stare down at her.

"Actually, I was thinking more along the lines of free mechanical advice and a lifetime supply of oil changes."

"Why would she want to give you free anything when I'm more than willing to pay her?" Jaycee's voice sounded out over the crowd of reporters. "I could really use you on my team, Savannah."

"So could I."

Savannah pulled away from Mac's embrace and turned just as her father walked into the garage. "You…" He shook his head. "I…"

"We're sorry," Travis said as he came up behind his father. Trey and Jack followed. "We're all sorry."

"For?"

"For taking you for granted. You do—*did* a lot for us, and we didn't really appreciate it the way we should have. We need you, sis. We miss you."

"That's right, Vannah," her father said when he reached her. He cleared his throat as if searching for the right words. "I knew you liked piddling around in the garage, but I didn't think you were serious."

"You never asked. None of you. You never asked me anything. You just assumed. It's partly my fault because I didn't speak up for myself." She shook her head. "But those days are over. From here on out, I'm going after what I want."

"You don't have to go after anything. You've got a place on our team."

"Actually…" Her gaze shifted to Jaycee who stood amid the reporters who were eagerly soaking up the scene unfolding in front of them. "I think I'd rather have a place on Jaycee's team. No offense, Dad." Her attention shifted back to her father. "Jaycee needs me a lot more than Calloway Motor Sports. You already have a winning crew chief."

"What about me?" Mac's voice drew her attention and she stared up at him to see all the love she felt mirrored in his gaze.

"You already have a crew chief, too."

"I don't have a wife."

"So you *do* want to marry me and live happily ever after?"

He grinned. "Actually, tonight I'd rather take you back to my place. Tomorrow I'll marry you and we can live happily ever after."

She smiled. "Sounds like a plan to me." And then she touched her lips to his and kissed him.

\* \* \* \* \*

# 'TIS THE SILLY SEASON
## Roxanne St. Claire

For Rich, who gave up Indy to meet my parents.
Now, *that's* true love.

## Acknowledgments

Special thanks to Mark DeCotis, racing reporter for
*Florida Today,* who once again shared his insight on the
infield, and revealed the real secrets of silly season.

# CHAPTER ONE

"THAT CARD HAS BEEN denied."

Lisa Mahoney closed her eyes and pressed the pay-phone receiver closer to her ear. The lunch rush was noisy, and maybe she'd misunderstood.

"I paid the minimum balance," she said, turning toward the wall and away from the watchful eyes of customers and coworkers. "I sent it a few days ago."

Did yesterday count as a few?

"I'm sorry, but I can't process your order. Do you have another credit card?"

Yes, and it was even *more* overdue.

"How many do you have left?" Lisa asked.

"They're going fast, ma'am. We expect to be out of stock by midnight tonight."

Lisa's heart dropped like Santa on a chimney free fall. There'd be no Mighty Motor Remote Control Stingray under her Christmas tree. No Mighty Flight Remote Control Viper under there, either. She choked back a dry cough. Who was she kidding? She'd be lucky if there was a *tree*.

Which normally would have been just fine. But this year, this black-and-blue and bruised year, was supposed to be different.

"Thank you for shopping with Kincaid Toys," the woman added cheerfully, as though Lisa had actually *shopped*.

She hung up the phone and peered around the corner to the dining room. A couple settled into her two-top and table six had their menus closed and those four ladies from Raleigh looked low on coffee.

Behind her, a pointed throat clearing yanked her around as effectively as if her boss had put his hand on her shoulder and spun.

"Done shopping, Lisa?" Ben Censky's cold gray eyes hardened to silver beads as he held out the order pad she must have dropped in the kitchen. "Think you might be able to wait on a customer or two now? I mean, if it's not too inconvenient."

She snagged the pad from Ben's hand. "They haven't even looked at their menus. I'm watching them."

He pointed to the dining room. "Then go sell them alcohol while they chat. Tipsy people order more."

She opened her mouth, then snapped it shut. It just wasn't worth it to argue with the man who controlled her hours. Not this close to Christmas. She needed every dime to keep her promise to the boys. Maybe she could find the toys on eBay and pay cash.

If she *had* any cash.

Glancing at the newly seated couple to gauge tip potential, she saw the woman inch closer to her companion, and something in the intensity of her coppery gaze froze Lisa's step. From her vantage point, Lisa couldn't see the man's face, but she knew women well enough to read a "listen to me I'm only going to say this once" expression. Whatever it was, Lisa wasn't doing her bottom line any favors by barging over now to get their order.

Ben gave her shoulder a shove. "Move it," he insisted. "Tables don't turn if you let them camp."

Sliding a vile look at him, she flipped the pad and headed to the table, trying to catch the woman's eye before she started talking and Lisa had to interrupt.

Just as she got into hearing range, the woman propped her elbows on the table with a thud.

"I want you, Clay Slater," she said. "I want you bad."

Oh, boy. Definitely *not* the time to announce the soup of the day.

"But not until you settle down," the woman added, clearly unaware that Lisa was headed straight into their conversation. "Sure, you're good. You're great. You're phenomenal. You thrill me every time you cross the finish line…"

The finish line? That was a new one.

"But, sorry, no deal." The woman sat back and

folded her arms, her eyes still burning across the table. All Lisa could see of the man was a few locks of thick, dark hair curling over the collar of his shirt and some seriously well developed shoulders. "I need to see some changes, Clay. I need to see permanence. Being good isn't enough. You have to be committed, accountable, responsible and decent enough for what I need. Otherwise, no. Not this year. Maybe not ever."

"Yes!" Lisa hissed out the response before a single brain cell could engage and stop her. "You tell him, girl."

The woman jerked her head up to look at Lisa, her expression only slightly more surprised than the one Lisa must have been wearing. When would she learn not to blurt out her thoughts?

But this was important. If only she'd had the nerve to say that to her ex-husband.

"Good for you," Lisa continued as she sidled up to the table. "You know, the world needs more women like you."

Next to her, the man blew out a soft breath. "Yeah, 'cause barracudas are an endangered species." At Lisa's glance of disdain, he added, "Look, it's not like it sounds. You don't get it."

One look at him and Lisa most definitely got it. Of course he had to be smokin' hot. His kind always was some version of mouthwatering. This one happened to be the too-cool-for-a-haircut, too-hip-for-a-shave, too-sexy-for-his-own-good version.

"Oh, I get it, all right," she assured him, forcing herself to look away from his smoky gaze to face the woman. "Be careful what you wish for," she said with raised eyebrow. "I'm living proof that sometimes you get it."

The woman's eyes sparked with mirth and she brushed back a long strand of auburn hair. "Unanswered prayers, huh?"

They nodded at each other with the silent connection women can make, but Lisa couldn't resist one more glimpse at the boyfriend.

He leaned back on two legs of the chair, a mix of amusement and appreciation crinkling his bedroom-brown eyes. "When you two are done male bashing, I'll take a glass of chocolate milk."

*Chocolate milk?* So he had maturity issues as well as commitment problems. "And you?" she asked the woman.

"Just coffee, please." She closed her menu. "I can't stay."

A wave from one of the Raleigh ladies pulled Lisa from the table, but when she returned with coffee and the big boy's glass of chocolate milk, it was clear the conversation had gone south. And Lisa couldn't resist lingering a moment as she set out the cream and sugar.

"I can't change who and what I am, Shelby," Bedroom Eyes said without looking up at Lisa. "At least not by next Friday."

"Then you're all wrong for Kincaid Toys."

The creamer slipped out of her fingers with a clunk.

*Kincaid Toys?*

He seized the creamer without even looking at it, righting the tiny pitcher before a teaspoon spilled. Lisa looked from one to the other, taking in their intense expressions. Did one of them work for Kincaid Toys?

"Give me a chance, Shelby," he said quietly. "If I can talk to David Kincaid, we can seal this deal."

David Kincaid? The *owner* of Kincaid Toys? She bet *he* could get his hands on a Mighty Motor and a Mighty Flight before Christmas.

"I'm sorry," the woman said, glancing at her watch. "I just can't take any more time on this, Clay. Even in the off-season, we're crazy over there." She stood and placed her napkin on the table.

"You're making a mistake," he said calmly. "All I need is one chance. One chance and I can prove you wrong."

"I only have one chance to give, Clay, and I just can't risk it on you. Thanks for coming out today. That was fun." She pulled her handbag on her shoulder and scooped up the leather jacket she'd hung on the chair with one last look at him. "It's a shame because you really can do amazing things in a Monte Carlo."

Lisa had to keep her jaw from dropping as she watched the redheaded beauty saunter out of The Lodge. After a minute, she turned back to Bedroom Eyes, and shook her head with a *tsk*. "You're crazy to let that one go."

He picked up the chocolate milk in a mock toast. "I've been called worse, doll."

"I bet you have."

"You're an opinionated little thing, aren't you?" He took a sip and held her gaze over the thick rim of the glass.

"I've been called worse, doll."

He choked so hard he almost spit chocolate milk on her. Taking a napkin to wipe his mouth, his eyes danced with a trapped laugh. "Touché…uh…" His focus dropped to her chest as though he might be looking for a name card, but she wasn't wearing one. His attention lingered anyway. *Naturally.*

"Lisa," she said. "My name is Lisa and I was going to be your server. Still can be, if you want lunch."

"I'm Clay." He raked a hand through his hair, taking the locks from uncombed to unkempt. "And what I want is a ride, but I guess I'll settle for a burger."

She nodded, writing on her pad. "And just where do you need to go?"

"Victory Lane." He crossed his arms and leaned back again, sweeping her with open appraisal. "But it appears I need a wife and two-point-five kids before I can get there."

· Huh? Add *certifiable* to the list of his problems. If Lisa had a brain, she'd drop the check and run. Fast. But she had one more question for the cute and crazy commitment-phobe. Giving the kitchen a quick peek, she crouched down to whisper. "Do you really know David Kincaid?"

He frowned, a look that made his already great-looking features just a little more…great-looking. "I'd like to."

"Oh." She couldn't keep the disappointment from her tone. "That's too bad."

"Don't tell me you want to drive for him, too?"

"What I want is two of the most elusive toys in America, a Mighty Motor Remote Control Stingray and a Mighty Flight Remote Control Viper. Can you get them for me? I'll pay you," she offered quickly.

The quick flash in his eyes sent a ripple of awareness through her. As though he wondered exactly what she'd use for currency and a number of ideas occurred to him—none of them cash.

"I can give you a check by the end of this week," she added pointedly.

"Sorry. To be honest, I don't know diddlysh…squat about Kincaid Toys. I just want to drive the car they're going to sponsor."

Lisa rocked on her heels, a glimmer of understanding dawning. "You're a race-car driver?"

"Guilty."

"And that woman…" She indicated the door with her head. "She wasn't your girlfriend?"

"Shelby Jackson?" He sounded as if she'd suggested he sleep with his sister. "She's the co-owner of Thunder Racing. She's looking for a driver, but, as you heard, I don't measure up."

Lisa raised an eyebrow. "Amazing? Phenomenal? And…what was it—a thrill every time you cross the finish line? Sounded like you measure up just fine."

Now he grinned, a slow, lazy affair that changed his gorgeous features from dangerous to downright deadly. "I also heard the words *irresponsible, undependable, indecent* and a whole boatload of other things that make being single sound like a mortal sin."

"What does being single have to do with driving a race car?"

"Good question." He jutted his chin toward the empty chair. "You busy?"

She shouldn't. For more reasons than she could think of, she shouldn't. She glanced around for an excuse, but her other table had already paid and she'd just seen Ben sneak out back for a smoke. Not to mention that the invitation was issued from a man who should come with a safety warning to all female consumers. She just shouldn't.

"Talk to me," he said in a voice so low and inviting that her toes curled in her sneakers.

Who could possibly say no to that? Other than Shelby, the smart redhead who had just walked away.

And there was that potential connection to Kincaid Toys.

She rested her backside on the edge of the chair across from him. "I know racing is like a national pastime around here," she said, "but I just moved to North Carolina this fall, so I don't know much about it."

"You will," he promised. "It's an addiction in these parts. Even this time of year, the tail end of Silly Season."

"Silly Season? What's that?"

"When all the teams and owners regroup before the next racing season and drivers get rides." He gave her a grim smile. "Or not."

"So you race stock cars? Like NASCAR?"

He nodded. "I'm in the Busch Series. Think of it like the step before NEXTEL Cup. She's—" he pointed his thumb to the door "—looking for a second car and driver for her NEXTEL Cup team. The big time."

"Oh. This was a job interview."

"Sort of."

She put her fingers up to her lips and let her eyes twinkle with an unspoken apology. "Whoops. Guess I didn't understand."

"It's all right." He winked. "I liked your spitfire."

An avalanche of goose bumps rolled down her arms. "I assumed she was talking about marriage."

"She was," he said, sliding strong, lean fingers up and down the condensation on the side of his milk glass. "The sponsor, your friend David Kincaid, will only put money behind a car and driver who meets his exceedingly high standards of—" he held up his fingers in air quotes "—family values. Shelby thinks he wants someone whose lifestyle is home and hearth and not..." He paused, searching for a description.

"Fun and games?"

"Yeah, that's one way of putting it."

"Well, that's just stupid," she replied, settling further in the chair and crossing her elbows on the table. "I mean, they are a *toy* company, for crying out loud. They promote fun and games."

He laughed and reached across the table, playfully tapping her chin with his fingertip. "You're right, Miss Lisa the Opinionated Waitress." His touch was so light she might have imagined it. But something sent a very real lightning bolt straight through her. "Wish I could help you get your Mighty Mouth or whatever you want. But I can't even make the short list to meet the great and powerful King Kincaid, so I'm afraid I'm not your man."

For the third time in a few minutes, Lisa swallowed disappointment. Was that because he couldn't get the toys—or because he wasn't "her man?" Not that she'd want this particular handful of heartache, but he sure was easy on the eyes.

"Maybe you'd like *me* to take *your* order."

Lisa jumped at the accusatory voice behind her, scraping her chair away from the table.

"Ben, this is—"

"A customer," he interrupted. "And this is a restaurant. And you are a waitress. So, may I inquire what you are doing sitting down and getting cozy instead of standing up and getting busy?"

Very slowly, Clay slid his chair back and stood, instantly towering over both of them. "She was taking the time to get my order straight. I would think you'd value that in an employee."

Lisa cringed and turned to Ben just in time to see the red spot right at the baldest part of his head deepen to a nice ripe raspberry color. Then—oh God—it started to pulse.

She opened her mouth to speak, but Ben had his sinister glare set on the customer and Lisa braced for trouble.

"What I value in an employee, mister, is productivity and service. As long as she's sitting on her skinny butt flirting with long-haired hippies, she isn't doing what I hired her to do."

"Ben." She held up her hand. "Don't. I'll go check on my orders." Please, not this week. Not before she had a chance to give her boys the Christmas they'd never had. She knew her days were numbered, but she had to get some money before he let her go. "Just...relax."

Ben burned her with a look. "Unlike you, I don't *relax* when I work. While you were busy exchanging phone numbers with Romeo, I gave table six their lunches. And the women on nine paid their bill. I didn't see a tip on the table, but then they may have gotten tired of waiting for you."

"Ben, I—"

Clay stepped around the table. "I asked the lady to join me. She was accommodating my request because she wants to keep her customers happy. Unlike the management."

The red spot throbbed on Ben's head. *Please say this wasn't happening.* "Oh, I bet she's very accommodating."

Lisa's throat closed up. She knew this was going to happen. The minute she'd pried Ben's disgusting fingers off her 'skinny butt' three weeks ago with a mouthy warning that she'd kill him if he touched her again, she knew that all he needed was an excuse.

Clay took another threatening step toward Ben, looking a good six inches down his nose. "I don't like your implication," he said, a deep Southern drawl she hadn't noticed earlier giving his voice an even more menacing tone. "And I think you owe this lady an apology."

"I don't owe her crap and I'd like you to leave."

The bedroom eyes turned...menacing. "I'm not going anywhere."

"Please," Lisa finally stepped in, hating the silence that had fallen over the restaurant, the attention the scene was attracting. "Please." She gave Clay an imploring glance. "I need this job."

She saw those eyes soften ever so slightly, but his jaw was still clenched as tight as the fists at his side. His attention moved from her to Ben then back again to her. "Nobody needs a job that bad."

She closed her eyes. "I do," she whispered.

For a long moment, he just stared at her. Then he reached into his back pocket, pulled out his wallet and removed a bill, never taking his eyes from her. He slapped the money on the table, and left.

In a second, the buzz of conversation resumed and customers turned back to their lunches.

Lisa watched the door close behind that gorgeous, dangerous, enigmatic stranger and felt a chill right into her heart. He'd actually tried to rescue her. To fight for her.

She'd never see him again. And that, she knew, was good for her already damaged heart, even though it might be bad for her very lonely soul.

## CHAPTER TWO

BEFORE LISA TURNED from the door, Ben snatched the money from the table. He was quick, but not fast enough to hide the three digits in the corner of the bill.

A hundred dollars! She sucked in a breath and stared at Ben. "What do you think you're doing?"

"This'll cover my time for having to handle your customer relations problems."

He slithered to the back, ignoring a waved hand from a customer. Lisa marched after him but just couldn't walk by that customer, and several more.

Four hours later, Lisa leaned against the time clock with fury rolling through her veins, watching Ben's office door, which had remained conveniently closed and locked all afternoon.

Looking at her watch and knowing her babysitter was even more impatient than she was, Lisa banged on the door. "Ben! I need to talk to you."

The door jerked open. Ben peered at her, his anger now simmered down to something else, something more threatening.

"You want that money, Lisa?" His suggestive leer dribbled over her body like slime. "How bad?"

"Stop it, Ben. Give me my tip and let me out of here."

He glanced behind her. "Everyone gone?"

Her gut clenched. "Give me my money."

He took one step closer. "What are you willing to do for it? That long-haired freak must have expected something for his generous tip. So do I."

"You son of a…" She never got the curse out because her palm thwacked across his jaw, channeling all her hate and disgust into one swift power-crack delivered so fast he didn't have time to duck.

He stumbled back, rage sparking in his eyes. "Get out of here. And don't come back," he said. "Ever."

"Don't worry. I won't." She pivoted on one rubber sole, yanked her down jacket from the employee rack and marched through the empty kitchen to the back door.

A gust of icy wind blew in her face, and a flurry of snow nearly blinded her. She blinked into the cold, the midwinter day so short that the lights had already come on in the parking lot, glistening over the drifts that had formed during the afternoon.

She almost slid on a patch of ice when she looked up and saw someone next to her minivan. Catching herself by grabbing a nearby car, she squinted into the dark to watch the tall, shadowy figure brush snow from her windshield.

As she took a few more careful steps, another car drove through the lot, headlights illuminating her van and the person next to it.

She inhaled a breath of freezing air and simply stared, her jaw slack. It was *him*. Clay. All afternoon she'd thought of his name, his cinnamon-brown eyes, his endearing attempt at chivalry.

As she got closer, he looked up and flashed a movie-star smile, made all the more beautiful by snowflakes on his hair.

"You worked late," he said, finishing up the corner of the windshield. God, he didn't even have gloves on. He wore a down vest, not nearly enough in this cold, but it was a splendid showcase for his muscular shoulders and narrow hips tucked into a pair of tight-fitting jeans.

"I had a meeting with my boss." She finally reached him, a smile tugging at her mouth. She'd just been fired. Why was she smiling?

Because a chocolate-milk-drinking, sweet-talking, dangerous-looking race-car driver was standing in the snow, waiting for her. How could she not smile?

"A meeting with Mr. Personality. I bet that was fun," he said drily.

"I quit. Or maybe I got fired. Either way, I'm out of a job."

He swore under his breath, lightly kicking one booted foot against the frozen asphalt. His arms lifted as though he were going to reach for her, but then he stuffed them into the front pockets of his jeans. "Sorry to hear that."

"It wasn't your fault," she assured him. "I clocked him."

His eyes popped open and he released a grin of pure admiration. "You hit him?"

She nodded proudly, holding out her hand, palm up, to show him her weapon. "I'm impulsive like that."

"Impulsive is good," he said quickly. "I like impulsive. But I hope I didn't incite the boxing match."

She shrugged. "It's been a long time coming. And, you know, I really didn't need to lose my job at Christmastime, but maybe it's a blessing in disguise."

"How's that?"

"This might be the kick start I need to finally do my own thing. But I could have used the income through Christmas." She almost laughed at the understatement of that. Used the income? She was stone-cold broke.

He nodded sympathetically, as though a man who littered restaurants with hundred dollar bills could possibly understand how stone-cold broke felt.

"What are you going to do?" he asked. "What's your business?"

She tilted her head and beamed at him. "It's called Rent A Wife."

"Excuse me?"

"Well, I've been noticing that there are so many working women who just can't get stuff done—you know, bake cookies for the Cub Scouts, cook a real dinner, even find the time to take an exercise class or do their grocery shopping." She dug her hands deeper into her jacket pockets and squeezed her fists. Did this sound stupid? "So, I was planning to set up a little business as a private personal assistant. You know, kind of like a wife to wives. As a joke, I'll call it Rent A Wife."

His eyes brightened. "I bet you'll do great."

"Thanks. It's just something I can do while my boys are in school and I won't have to work nights unless I want to." She laughed humorlessly. "I've never had a really good job, but I was pretty good at being a wife."

A flicker of interest passed over his face. "Was?"

"I'm divorced," she said quietly. At the beat of silence, she asked, "You haven't waited out here all this time, have you?"

"Nope. I went shopping." He searched her face for a moment, his close scrutiny short-circuiting her brain. "I got a present for you."

Surprise and delight poured over her. "Me? Why would you do that?"

He cocked his head toward the next parking spot. "C'mere, my truck's warm."

The engine of a massive white pickup truck rumbled one spot over. In two steps, he reached the passenger door and opened it, letting the inviting, heated air roll toward her.

"Come on," he said. "Climb in."

She gave him a wary look as he reached his hand toward her. She put one foot up on the wide running board.

"I'm perfectly safe, I promise," he assured her.

He wasn't safe. He was a scary, wild thrill ride and the embodiment of bad boy and, Lord, hadn't she learned her lesson?

The smell of new leather and warm air almost pulled her inside, but she hesitated. "Why don't you just show me?"

He chuckled. "You don't trust me."

"Not entirely."

"All right, I'll stand out here and you sit right there." He eased her into the passenger seat. "Now turn around and reach into the back."

She sat gingerly on the edge of the seat.

"Come on," he urged her. "I want to see the look on your face."

Her face? What could he possibly have that—oh! She whipped around and stabbed her hand into the back cab, her fingers closing over cardboard and cellophane. "No!" she said, a giddy bubble of laughter rising up in her chest. "You didn't!"

"I did. The last two in North Carolina, as I understand it, but I got 'em for you."

She stared at the purple and yellow boxes, the grin of the beloved Kincaid clown logo seemingly wider than ever.

"I thought it was the least I could do after shooting my mouth off to your boss."

"Oh…" Lisa swallowed the lump that suddenly took up residence in her throat. "I can't believe you…" She looked up, and he was so close she could practically count his mile-long eyelashes. "I can't believe you went out and…" Unable to finish, she threw her arms around his neck and pulled him into a hug, an incredible, woodsy scent and a few locks of long hair tickling her nose. "Thank you," she whispered into his ear.

"I can't have you thinking I'm that much of a hero," he chuckled. "They had some promotional stuff from Kincaid at Thunder Racing. So I used the excuse to bother Shelby again."

She pulled back, but he remained perilously close. Kissably close. "Still, it was thoughtful."

"I got you fired."

"No." She shook her head. "And I can't let you believe that. Ben has wanted to let me go for weeks. I've just been holding on…for Christmas. I needed to…"

She purposely let her sentence trail. She couldn't

explain that she'd never had a Christmas before. Most people just looked at her like she was nuts. Even when she told them why and how. Especially after her little boys were born...

He didn't need to know all that.

She touched the shrink-wrapped packages lovingly, imagining the looks on Nick and Keith's faces. It was just too much.

"How can I repay you, Clay?"

Another one of those smoky looks darkened his eyes and, for one crazy second, she thought he was going to kiss her.

"Not necessary," he said, his attention slipping to her mouth, then back to her eyes.

Blood pumped in her head so loud she couldn't think of anything. Her whole body tensed and she gave into the urge to let her own gaze drop to his mouth. The beautiful shape of it. Those perfect teeth. Never had a millimeter of beard growth looked so inviting.

Her eyes nearly closed with the ache of wanting to kiss him. But somewhere, somehow, she found the power to pull back.

"I better get going," she said softly, shifting away.

She expected a smile, but he looked...serious. Then he gave her his hand and helped her step down. "All right. You be careful driving home."

"I will." She clutched the two boxes to her chest. "I won't let anything happen to these."

When she opened her van door and climbed in, he crouched down to her level. "You sure you're going to be okay? I mean, we had a decent amount of snow today. How far do you have to go?"

"Just a few miles. What about you?" *Where do you live? Will I ever see you again?*

"Lake Norman."

"Lake Norman?" She cursed the obvious disappointment in her voice. "That's two hours from here."

"My truck can make it and, trust me, I'm a good driver."

"Of course you are." A race-car driver. Who lives on Lake Norman. With a fun-and-games lifestyle. *Run, Lisa, run.*

"Not good enough for Kincaid, though," he said, as though he just remembered his own problems.

"I'm sorry I can't wave my magic wand and get you what you wanted today." She tapped the toys. "Like you got me these."

"I'm afraid you can't…" His voice trailed off.

"Bye, Clay."

His expression had turned expectant and odd. Slowly, he stood, still studying her face. "Bye, Miss Lisa, the Opinionated Waitress."

Somehow, she liked "doll" better.

She tugged at the door, and he let go. Reluctantly. She shot him one more smile, threw the van in reverse and hit the accelerator just a little too hard.

There. She'd done it. She'd escaped temptation. Sexy, sweet temptation. The last thing she needed was some hotshot racer running all over her emotions, no matter how sweet and kissable and seductive he was. No, she needed a job. She needed money. She needed to figure out a way to have the Christmas she promised her kids.

With a steadying breath, she stopped at the light on Route Four and closed her eyes for one second. She'd forget him in no time—until Christmas morning when her boys opened their presents. Then she'd remember the angel who'd dropped into the parking lot to deliver a little Christmas magic.

Now, all she had to do was figure out some way to pay for a tree, decorations—real ornaments, not homemade—and a turkey for dinner and—

The tap on her back bumper popped her eyes open and she let out a little "Oh!" of surprise.

All she could see in the rearview mirror was a great big silver grill and a mountain of white truck. The driver's door opened and her heart did about fifteen handstands before it landed in her stomach. Clay knocked on the window.

"You hit me," she accused, lowering the window.

"Bumper tap. Don't worry. I'm an expert." Snow danced around his face as he leaned closer, almost in the open window. "I have a question for you."

Resolve and common sense melted as fast as the

fat flakes that landed on his long lashes. Whatever he was about to ask her…for a date, for a kiss, for a phone number…whatever it was, she knew she'd have to say yes. No force of nature could stop her. She'd have to say yes. "What is it?"

"Would you marry me?"

## CHAPTER THREE

"WHAT'S A PERSONAL assis...assist...thing, Mommy?"

Lisa glanced into the rearview mirror to meet the questioning face of her younger son. "Assistant, Nicky. A personal assistant is like..." A *wife*, a little voice called out in her head. Or, in this case, a temporary actress who'd agreed to participate in a week of insanity. "A private helper who can do stuff you don't have time to do."

"What kind of stuff?"

Wasn't that the million-dollar question? Or, according to her new employer, the five-thousand-dollar question. "Well, in this job, I'm going to decorate Mr. Slater's house for Christmas and—"

"You don't know how to do that!" Keith suddenly accused.

She glanced over her shoulder at the eight-year-old, his expression so much harder and more distrustful than his younger brother's.

"I can figure it out," she said gently. "With your help. And, boys, remember. Let's not tell Mr. Slater that we've never had a real Christmas before. I don't want him to worry that we can't do the job."

She stole a look at Keith again, who just rolled his eyes. "Whatever." He turned his attention back to the view, withdrawing like he had since his father left last year.

"What else you gonna do, Mommy?" Nicky asked.

"Just cook. And…stuff." *Like pretend to be married to him when the owner of Kincaid Toys comes by for a visit.*

She felt like rolling her eyes when she thought of Clay's insane plan. Did he really believe that he could fool David Kincaid into thinking he was a "family" man? He was certain they could pull it off, but in the cold light of day, the idea seemed preposterous.

But last night, in the snow, in the dark, with that man so close and so persuasive…she'd said yes. Of course, once he'd said the magic words—*a Hallmark card of a Christmas for your kids*—she pretty much gave up all hope of rational disagreement.

And, frankly, there was no good reason to say no. She got to keep her promise to Nick and Keith, and she got paid great money. And, as a secret bonus, she got to spend one solid week with the most attractive man she'd ever met.

She could play along with his charade and he didn't seem concerned that Kincaid would eventually find out the truth. He was utterly convinced that after a few races of driving the Kincaid car, the man would be so enamored of his talent, that how Clay got the job wouldn't matter.

Anyway, his future wasn't her problem. Hers was. And five thousand dollars would go a very long way to smoothing the bumpy road that always lay ahead for a single mother.

"What about all your own stuff? When will you have time to do that?" Keith had returned to the conversation with a little more force. He hadn't come out and accused her of reneging on her promise, but he had implied that he thought this sudden plan to go have Christmas at somebody else's house didn't really count as a family Christmas. Although he'd softened when he heard a race-car driver was involved. Even if he'd never heard of Clayton Slater.

"The only thing we have to do is have ourselves a merry little Christmas," she said brightly. "You guys are on school break and we're going to a beautiful home on the water."

"How will Santa find us?" Nicky asked, horror rounding his blue eyes. "I sent him our address! He's never been there before. I told him I'd leave the kitchen window open 'cause we don't have a fireplace."

"Oh, he'll find you," she assured him, with

another glance—this one a warning—to big brother. They'd never done the Santa thing, but this year Nicky decided he believed.

Keith said nothing, just looked out the window.

"Will he find us, Keef?" Nicky urged his brother.

"If he has GPS," Keith finally said.

Lisa worked the busy traffic that had picked up since she'd gotten within a few miles of the vast lake. The winter sun was brilliant enough to bounce off the cars and pavement, sparkling over the man-made lake and luxury homes that surrounded it.

She turned off the main highway, following the directions Clay had written down for her the night before. His handwriting was bold, confident, fast.

Like the man.

At a break in the woods of towering North Carolina hardwood pines that lined the road, she turned toward the water, as his map indicated. The residences grew grander and farther apart as she neared the shore, well-appointed custom homes of brick, flagstone and clean white clapboard, surrounded by sprawling tree-filled lots and rows of fences.

One last turn, a few more houses and she'd be there. Why was her heart thudding?

Because she was the very last person on earth qualified to set up a storybook Christmas? Yes, that was part of it. Because if this blew up in her face it could ruin her kids' first and only real Christmas? Also part of it.

Because the man made her flat-out dizzy?

Let's forget that part.

She slowed the car as she arrived at a terra-cotta brick wall, reading the address on a brass plaque. Burying doubts, second thoughts and what was left of her common sense, Lisa pulled in and drove around a clump of pines.

"Holy crap!" Keith said, sitting up straight for the first time in miles.

"Don't say crap," Lisa chided absently, her attention on the imposing house in front of them.

"Mom, it's a mansion," Keith insisted, as though that called for colorful language.

"Not quite." But two stories of cedar shake, with several gabled rooflines, arched windows and an imposing leaded-glass door probably looked like a palace compared to the apartment they'd been living in since they'd moved from New Hampshire.

"Look, there's the ocean!" Nicky exclaimed, pointing to the sun glinting off an endless blue body of water beyond the house.

"That's a lake, honey. It's thirty-some miles long, so it just looks like the ocean."

As she turned off the ignition, a wave of longing rolled over her. What would it be like to call this home? Before she could analyze the ache that suddenly blossomed in her chest, the front door opened and a whole different kind of longing threatened to cut off her air.

Clay wore a soft blue button-down shirt, untucked over those same tight jeans. Bare feet, long hair and a sinful expression that could be bottled and sold for a million bucks.

"All right, boys." *Here's your daddy for a week.* "Let's meet Mr. Slater. But I'm sure he'll want you to call him Clay." Especially if David Kincaid actually showed up as a one-man audience to their performance. They hadn't exactly discussed how they'd get the boys to play along.

Oblivious to the below-forty temperatures, Clay ambled down the steps of the front porch and walked straight to the driver's side of the van. Lisa unlatched her seat belt as he opened the door and grinned at her, placing one bare foot in the van and dipping his head dangerously close to hers.

"Hi, honey. You're home."

Just as Lisa's world tilted so far she thought she might fall off, he kissed her on the mouth and sent her right over the edge.

CLAY KNEW he couldn't hold out for long, so better to get the lip lock out of the way immediately. That way, he had control. Sort of.

He pulled away from a quick, chaste kiss and

looked at the surprise in her baby blues, her full mouth opened in a sexy little circle and the peaches-and-cream skin turning even peachier. "Man, you're even prettier than I remembered."

"She's not pretty," a small voice announced from the back seat. "She's my mom."

Lisa blew out a quick laugh and Clay slid open the kid-friendly side door to see the owner of the urchin voice. Indigo eyes that matched his mama's stared back out of a delicate face barely out of babyhood. "You're right. She's not pretty. She's gorgeous. Who are you?"

"He's Nick," said the slightly larger carbon copy sitting next to him. "I'm Keith."

Clay offered the younger one a set of knuckles. "Hey, dude."

The little guy tapped him with a closed fist and a lopsided grin. "Hey, dude," he mimicked.

When Clay reached over to give the same greeting to the bigger one, he got an icy stare in return.

"Keith," his mama warned gently.

The boy set his jaw and narrowed his eyes. "You know Austin Elliot?" he asked.

*Okay*, Clay thought. *This would be easy.* "I've met him."

A flicker of admiration was held in check. "Garrett Langley?"

"Had dinner with him a while ago." There were six hundred other people in the room, but the kid didn't need to know that.

"J.C. Fuller?"

"Passed him twice in the last Busch race he ran."

Keith shrugged, fighting to be unimpressed. Clay stepped out of the open door and shifted his attention back to Lisa. "Brought me a NASCAR fan, did you?" he asked softly.

Her eyes glittered a little. "He takes a while to warm up."

Unlike the other one, who was already yanking off his seat belt and scrambling out of the van.

"I wanna see the ocean!" he yelled before his feet actually hit the ground.

Clay scooped him by the jacket as he started to run, his feet continuing to jog in the air like a set of skinny eggbeaters. "Whoa, dude. Hold on there. We'll take a boat ride later. Let's get your stuff—"

"You got a boat?" The question was accompanied by another engaging, toothless grin. "Cool!"

The minute Clay let go of his jacket, the kid took off.

"Don't go near the water, Nick," Lisa called as she climbed out of the car. She shot him her own engaging smile—not toothless and completely sweet. "He's the active one."

"I figured that."

He started toward the back of the van just as slender fingers closed over his elbow. "Are you sure you want to do this?"

Her questioning eyes were as the same color as the skies over Daytona on a perfect, hope-filled race day. And every bit as alluring.

"Yeah." He drew back and gave her a pretend glare. "You think one hyper five-year-old is gonna scare me?"

"He's six." The announcement came from the other boy, who had silently rounded the back of the car. "I'm gonna be nine next month."

Clay looked down at him. "Then you're old enough to drive."

His eyes widened and he gave a quick glance to his mother.

"A quarter midget," Clay explained. "And I happen to still have mine—a Junior Division championship QM—in the garage."

"What's a quarter midget?" the boy asked, unable to hide his interest.

"A kid's race car. A lot of NASCAR drivers started in midget carts, probably younger than you." Clay gave him a hard appraisal, liking that the kid just jutted a defiant jaw under the scrutiny. "But you look strong and smart. We'll check your wheel reflexes later, okay?"

The boy nodded slowly. It would take more than a spin in a quarter midget to win this one over.

Clay lifted the van hatch, expecting a load of luggage, but there was very little tucked into the back of the clean, if worn, mom-mobile. One inexpensive suitcase and a few supermarket plastic bags. "You are going to stay the week, aren't you?" he asked Lisa.

Her color deepened a little. "Yes, we travel light." She reached for the suitcase, but he beat her to it.

"Be careful with that one," she whispered, leaning closer. "It has the you-know-whats in it."

He knew exactly whats. That last trip to Thunder Racing to get those toys had been a stroke of genius. Shelby was waffling a little, and he'd had a reason to see Lisa again. Then he had this brainstorm of an idea.

"This place is stunning," Lisa said, admiring the house.

"You think?" He squinted, seeing the white elephant through her eyes. "My accountant made me buy it. Come on, I'll show you around."

In a few minutes, she'd corralled the younger kid and Clay led them all through the front door. He expected her to look around with an assessing eye, hoping she'd know exactly where to put a tree and what color lights to hang, but he noticed a completely different type of expression on her face. Wonder.

"Wow," she said, studying the curved staircase in the front.

"There's a more manageable set of steps in the back," he told her. "But I bet you can do something with these."

"Do something?"

"You know, hang green stuff and a ribbon or something."

"Oh, yes. Um…garlands?" She sounded entirely unsure.

"Do you think the tree should go here?" He pointed to an empty corner formed by the turn of the stairs. "Or there in the living room? Or maybe we should have more than one? Whatever you normally do."

This time he got a weird look from Keith.

"Oh, wowzarootie!" The exclamation came from the back of the house, where Nick had escaped. "You guys gotta see this!"

The trophy room. What else could make a six-year-old boy drool?

"Come on." Clay tapped the other boy on the back and cocked his head in the direction of the voice. "I'll show you my gold."

But the little one hadn't made it to the trophy room. He was standing in the only other room in the house that Clay had had a hand in decorating. Nick pointed, openmouthed, to the giant plasma screen and the three smaller ones that took up most of one wall. Then he fell on one of the leather seats Clay had installed for watching simultaneous sporting events and race replays, his little body not heavy enough to trigger the recliner.

"Awesomacious!" he exclaimed, bouncing a little.

"Holy crap!" Keith mumbled.

"Don't say crap, honey," Lisa said, coming into the room behind him and laying a gentle hand on his shoulder. "Oh," her voice dropped as her gaze ricocheted from the TV to the boys and back again.

"You don't want them watching TV?" he asked.

"Their shows will never look the same on our little box," she said quickly.

"Oh, is that all?" He scooped up the remote and clicked on the TV, which turned on immediately to the Speed Channel, and squinted at the race. "That's the 2002 Daytona 500," he said. "They play old races sometimes in the afternoon." He handed the remote to the older boy. "Here you go. There's an Xbox 360, too, just open up the table there."

With a look that vacillated between wariness and wonder, Keith took the remote.

Clay put his hand on Lisa's shoulder. "Don't worry. There are only racing video games. I use it to practice. Now, come on, I'll show you the rest of the house. They won't leave this room."

"Ever," she said dryly.

Clay stayed behind her on the back stairs, taking in the excellent rear view. The Opinionated Waitress was one sweet-looking woman. He'd known the minute she gave him her first sunshiny smile, the first time she tilted her head and bounced those blond curls over her shoulders that she was the epitome of the girl next door. Not his type, since he pretty much limited himself to brief encounters with the sexy models who occasionally visited the NASCAR garages.

But for the job at hand, Lisa Mahoney was ideal to impress David Kincaid.

That's why his lightning bolt of an idea seemed so…appealing. Along with that little dip right above her hips. Major appealing.

She turned and caught him checking her out, her warning look as clear as a caution flag.

*Slow down, Slater.*

Not that *slow* came naturally to him. But he had to remember why she was there. Not for pleasure, not for fun, not for keeps.

Regardless of the sizzle he sensed between them, this was not a race to the bedroom because one wrong move would send her right out the door. And he needed her. She was his ticket to the only thing he wanted: a ride in the NASCAR NEXTEL Cup Series. And that was all.

He surveyed her killer curves one more time.

A ticket to the big time, and that was *all,* his brain screamed. But his body definitely didn't get the message.

## CHAPTER FOUR

"YOUR KIDS ARE GREAT," Clay said as they neared the top landing.

"They have their moments. And this—" She swept a hand toward the wide hallway where three landscapey paintings he had never really liked hung side by side. "This is quite a…"

"What?" he prodded.

"New experience for them." She paused as he stood next to her, noticing that she seemed a little taller than she had in the restaurant and the little bit of makeup she now wore enhanced the almond shape of her eyes.

"I hope it's not too much of a drag, taking them away from home for Christmas."

Her laugh was humorless. "Nope. It's fine." At his look, she added, "Their father took off last year around this time. So, this is really a chance to give them a happy holiday. Really."

What kind of idiot would walk away from a pretty woman and two nice kids? Especially at Christmas?

"Sorry to hear that," he said, studying her face. "What did they think about our plan?"

"Actually, it's your plan. And I didn't tell them."

"You didn't? I thought last night you said—"

"I thought I'd wait to be sure you got the meeting with David Kincaid before I inform them their mother is pretending to be married. You know, it doesn't exactly send a valuable message about honesty and ethics in life."

"I hadn't thought of that," he admitted.

"Why don't we see how it goes, be sure you get this meeting set up, and then I'll tell them that it's a game we're playing," she said.

He stopped mid-step. "A game?"

"What would you call it?"

"A strategy. A strategy for getting what I want."

She narrowed her eyes at him. "Do you always get what you want?"

"Usually. Sometimes." *Lately, rarely.* "I sure as hell don't take no for an answer when I can figure out a way to get yes."

There was that warning look again. "You know, we got a little carried away with your idea last night," she said slowly. "Maybe it would be a good time to set some ground rules for the week ahead."

"Ground rules?"

"Yes. First of all, please watch your language around my boys. They're very impressionable."

"No problem."

"Second," she said, looking at him with the same defiance he'd noticed in her older son. "I'll handle telling them what we're doing and why we're doing it, okay? If it even happens."

"It'll happen. I have a call into Shelby already."

She nodded. "When we know that Kincaid is coming out here, I'll talk to the boys. Okay?"

"Fair enough, but they have to know it's not just a game. They can't blow it by telling—"

She held up her hand. "I understand that."

"Good. Anything else?"

"Yes."

Here it comes. *Keep your hands and eyes to yourself, Clay.*

"Just one Christmas tree."

He let out a soft laugh. "Okay. I mean, you're the boss on Christmas."

"Good. It's just that I want to do a good job for you. Two trees, well, that might be too much."

"That's your call." He guided her down the hall. "Anything else?"

She looked up at him, innocence radiating from those incredible eyes. "Yeah. Don't kiss me again."

He *knew* that was coming. "Even in front of Kincaid?"

She half smiled in consent. "Just once. For effect."

"All right," he agreed. "And same with you."

"What?"

"Don't kiss me, unless it's for effect." He kept a serious face as long as he could, then grinned.

She laughed softly. "That's a deal. Now show me the rest of your home."

"It's not really a home," he said, pushing open a door. "More like a four-thousand-square-foot hotel room. I'm not around that much." He indicated a room with two simple twin beds and a dresser. "The kids can sleep in here. Is that okay?"

"Perfect." She nibbled on her lower lip again, then looked up at him. "And what about me?"

"My room's at the end of the hall."

Her eyes flashed electric-blue.

The temptation to tease her was too great. "You can sleep there. You know, for effect."

She tapped him on the shoulder, with a little more oomph than would be considered playful. "Very funny."

"I do have one more guest room," he said. "And an office with a pull-out sofa. I use the other bedrooms for trophies and exercise equipment. Come on, I'll show you."

Downstairs, he led her to the guest suite, where his anonymous decorator had gone a little overboard with violets. "Mathilda was in her purple stage here."

"Who's Mathilda?" she asked, pausing in the doorway.

"Whoever went through this house and put up drapes and pictures and—" he stepped to the bed and fluffed the flowered comforter "—spreads. I don't know who she is, but her touch is so pervasive, I had to give her a name. I picked Mathilda."

She looked confused. "You never met your decorator?"

"This house was a model for the development," he explained. "I bought it furnished. What you see is what I got."

She glanced at the dresser that held nothing but a fussy arrangement of silk flowers. "That explains why there's nothing…personal."

"You haven't seen the trophy room."

"But there are no pictures. Of family. Or anyone."

"My family is really just my parents and sister. They're back in Lexington." He indicated the house with a wave of his hand. "So what do you think, doctor? Kincaid's supposed to be in town on the twenty-second. That's five days. Can you turn this place into a Christmas card by then?"

She nodded, looking around thoughtfully. "Probably."

"What do you need? Money? A truck? Ladders? I guess you'll want to go to Home Depot and…" She gave him that same quick look of doubt he got when he'd suggested they share a bedroom. "Don't tell me you hate home improvement stores."

"No." She dipped her hands into the back pocket of her .jeans, unknowingly stretching her cotton sweater across her bust. He forced himself to keep focused on her serious expression, and not one more leisurely trip over his *wife*.

"I'll take the boys to start shopping right away."

She headed toward the entryway, and Clay stayed back, enjoying the sway of her hips, the swish of curls cascading over her shoulders.

He had fully intended to let her do her job while he went on with his life, taking the boat out, tinkering with the cars, working out. He had plenty to do during his time between rides. It really would be better if he'd just keep his distance and let her do what he hired her to do.

Scratching his neck, he watched her disappear down the hall and then he did the only thing a man trained to reach his destination as fast as humanly possible could do: he followed her, passed on the right and whipped his keys out of his pocket.

"I'll drive you."

"YOU DON'T HAVE A LIST?"

A list? She didn't have a *clue*.

Lisa gave Clay a bright smile and repeated her mantra, not that it had worked for the whole drive to Home Depot. "I know what I'm doing."

Except she hadn't expected an audience.

Fortunately, the boys had been so enamored of the sky-high truck and the nifty back seat they'd been buckled into that they didn't contradict her once when Lisa reassured Clay she was an old hand at setting up Christmas.

"I'll help you get the tree," he announced.

"We'll do that last."

"Last?" He looked like she'd suggested they hit the woods with an ax and chop one of their own. "How will you know what to buy if you don't get the tree first?"

Huh? "Yes, of course." She could do this. How hard would it be?

Next to the building, they found a virtual forest of freshly cut trees, and she had the answer. *Very* hard.

"I like firs, don't you?" Clay moved toward a particularly fat blue-green tree. "But then the pines have longer needles. Were you thinking of big, heavy ornaments or something lighter for a theme?"

"A theme?" She blinked at him and then covered her surprise by looking at the tree. "Did you want something in particular?"

"Well, last night you gave me the impression that when you did your house in the past, you liked it to all sort of go together. I think Kincaid will like that."

Had she said that? Sometime between his announcement of a "five-thousand-dollar professional fee" and "a Hallmark card of a Christmas for your kids"…yes, she might have mentioned a theme. Impulsiveness would surely be her downfall.

"So, what's the theme you have in mind, now that you've seen my house?"

"Uh…let me think."

"Christmas on Lake Norman?" he suggested, then immediately wiped the idea away with a sweep of one hand. "I know. Something more original."

Her brain whirred. *Lake Norman.* Lake… "A Norman Rockwell Christmas," she blurted out.

"That's genius! What could be more traditional and homey than Norman Rockwell? Big fat Santas and freckle-faced kids." His brown eyes glinted with a spark of gold as he slid his arm around her and squeezed, beaming at the boys. "Your mother is brilliant."

Nick nodded; Keith looked dubious.

"So let's get…" She spun and randomly picked a tree. "That kind. It looks just like a Christmas tree in a Norman Rockwell painting." Not that she'd seen any recently, but the tree looked wholesome and traditional.

A clerk in an orange vest came out of nowhere. "The blue spruce is our most popular tree," he assured Clay with a friendly smile. "Your wife knows what she's doing."

Lisa almost kissed the guy, and Clay just laughed

softly and tightened his grip in a far too familiar fashion.

"That's why I married her."

She shot him a look and he winked, doing wild and silly things to every cell in her body, especially the ones in charge of rushing blood to her cheeks.

"Look at that," the clerk chuckled, seeing her blush. "You two newlyweds?"

"Sort of."

"Not really."

Their answers canceled each other out and the clerk laughed again, guiding them to a pile of tightly tied trees. Clay pulled her forward, but Lisa glanced over to check on the boys.

"They're fine," Clay assured her, tugging her into his side, his mouth just a little too close to her ear.

"I'm Bob, by the way," their assistant informed them. "How big a tree are you looking for?"

"I guess six feet," Lisa said.

"Nine or ten at least," Clay corrected.

Bob, clearly amused, slipped his hands into the pockets of the orange workman's vest he wore. "Let's do it this way. How high is the ceiling?"

As they discussed the measurement, Lisa turned to see the boys, who had moved to another Christmas tree display and were laughing together about something. The sappy scent of cut pine and fresh wood permeated the wintry air, and a chorus of "Let

It Snow" trilled from invisible speakers over the buzz of holiday shoppers. Clay stood in deep conversation with Bob, volleying terms like "tarps" and "angle cuts" while Lisa took it all in.

And the strangest, most unfamiliar sensation fluttered through her. Something definitely delightful, something warm and safe and happy.

Was this what Christmas was supposed to feel like?

It never had before. The first one she remembered smelled antiseptic and scary, it was dark and full of an agony so deep she couldn't bear to think of it. Her first Christmas memory had been an endless stream of strange people patting her on the head and saying 'how sad that it happened at Christmas.' And then every year that followed, when the landscape turned red and green and white, her mother turned inward and miserable, and Lisa just counted the days until the world packed up their holiday spirit and moved on to January. Only then could Lisa sleep without hearing the sobs in the next room.

She'd never felt a giddy rush of happiness at the sight of a jolly elf or a child bouncing on Santa's knee. But this…this felt…*okay*. And, after all, she'd promised her boys a Christmas. There was no reason for them to hate the holiday, even though she did and their father had gone along with that approach because it was easy.

She'd promised…and now, thanks to Clayton Slater, she was delivering.

"C'mere and look at this one." Clay waved her over with a heart-stopping invitation in his eyes.

Then again, maybe all the fluttering in her tummy had nothing to do with Christmas spirit.

"Your husband likes this one," the clerk said.

She glanced up at Clay, who just gave her another devilish grin.

"That looks great," she said, barely looking at the tree.

Once again, he slid his arm over her shoulders and eased her into the solid muscle of his side. And once again, her whole being tightened and tingled.

If she had any chance, any chance at all, of figuring out how to buy a whole-house decoration for Christmas—a Norman Rockwell Christmas, no less—she'd have to get away from the distraction of the man who'd hired her to do it.

"I need to do this alone," she said to him. When he gave her a disappointed frown, she added, "It's how I work."

"I just started having fun." For a moment, she thought he was about to argue. But then he shifted his attention to the boys and called them over. "Let's get the tree in the truck and go for ice cream."

"Ice cream!" Nicky hollered, jumping up and down on his invisible bungee cord. "I love ice cream."

Keith shrugged. "'Kay."

"And you," Clay said, turning back to her, "can meet us at the front of the store in…" He glanced at his watch. "How long will it take you to pull together Christmas?"

A lifetime. "Two hours, minimum."

He nodded. "Better idea. Ice cream after the movies."

Nicky's eyes widened to silver-dollar size and even Keith threatened to smile at that.

Forget it. She'd never bring her boys back to earth after this week. "Thanks," she said to him with a smile.

"Here." He reached into his back pocket, pulled out a wallet and handed her a gold credit card. "You'll need this."

"And a budget."

"To get that ride with Kincaid, there is no budget, doll. Spend what you have to." Then he reached out two hands, and each of the boys took one. As if that wasn't mind-boggling enough, he leaned forward and brushed her cheek with a featherlight kiss. "Make Norman Rockwell proud."

Speechless, she watched the trio march away, Nicky practically skipping and reaching out to touch every tree, Keith taking measured but certain steps. She was filled with love for her boys and that foreign, fluttery, giddy sensation again.

But it evaporated the instant she realized that

those three would be alone together for hours, and the boys might very well reveal her secret. She knew *nothing* about Christmas.

Well, she'd simply prove them wrong.

Turning back to the friendly clerk, she looked him straight in the eye and admitted the truth. "Bob, I need help."

## CHAPTER FIVE

CLAY PLACED one finger on the light switch and grinned at his audience of three.

"Lady and gentlemen…" He paused and looked pointedly at Nicky who, as he had for the past two days, waged a constant war to stay still. He usually lost.

"Start your engines!" Nicky screamed so loud it reverberated through the front hall.

As he always did when the words were spoken, Clay flicked the switch. Only this time it wasn't the ignition. It was something an electrical genius from the home-improvement store had installed that afternoon.

There was a small flicker, and a collective intake of breath from the four of them. Then, magically, twenty-five-hundred lights bathed the front of his house in red, white and green.

"Yeah, baby!" Clay exclaimed, scooping up Nicky, who was dancing in a circle.

"Holy crap," Keith murmured, looking out the window at the amazing display.

For once, his mother didn't correct him. Lisa just

beamed at Clay, her blue eyes as bright as the billion watts outside matching her victorious smile.

"Isn't it gorgeous?" she asked Clay.

Her smile? It sure was. He eased Nick back to earth and cocked his head toward the living room. "Next, the tree."

As Clay led the way, he glanced at the curved staircase, draped in loops of evergreen and sparkling with tiny white lights. The newel was wrapped in red velvet, topped off with a giant gold bow. On every table, there were poinsettias, holly berry candles and a few snow globes.

"I still can't believe what you did with this place in two days," he said to Lisa.

"I had help," she said, once again refusing credit for the job.

"But you were the crew chief, doll. And he—or, in this case, she—is way more important than the driver." He picked up the porcelain figurine of two children crouched in front of a fireplace, looking up for Santa. "And I can't believe you found that store."

She took the piece from him and set it gently back on the mantel. "Hey, you wanted Norman Rockwell, Clay."

"But that's practically all they sold there."

"Told you I could do it." She beamed again, then grew serious. "No call from Shelby Jackson yet?"

He shook his head. All this work, expense and anticipation, and he still didn't know if the CEO of Kincaid Toys had agreed to meet with Clay. He'd done a sales job on Shelby, although he didn't tell her he'd basically bought a wife and kids—he just made one more compelling pitch.

She wanted him to drive for her and if he could just get her to agree to set up a meeting with Kincaid, he had a shot. A long shot, but he was good at getting to the front. Real good.

"Turn it on! Turn it on!" Nicky bobbed next to the giant spruce.

"Chill, dude," Clay said softly. "I think your mother should do the honors."

He handed her a remote control. "Mrs. Claus?"

"I haven't quite figured out that thing, yet. And don't we have to put this up?" She lifted a translucent star from a box and handed it to him. "I wasn't sure if you'd want to do this."

"Of course," he said, taking it from her. "Keith, can you get me that step stool from the kitchen?"

"Sure," Keith said, hustling out of the room. Lisa watched him leave, amazement in her eyes.

"He's a good kid," Clay said softly.

"I can't believe the change in him the past two days."

"He's having fun," Clay assured her.

In the time he'd spent alone with the boys, he'd learned a lot about the little Mahoney family. Keith didn't talk as much as Nicky, but his silence said plenty. Clay didn't know why or how, but he knew the kids' father had bailed and was pretty much out of the picture. He was no shrink, but it was easy to figure out why the kid was sullen most of the time.

"All right," he said as he climbed up on the stool Keith brought back. "Let me have it."

Lisa reached up and handed him the star, their hands brushing as he took it. He glanced at her just as she looked up at him.

The eyes said it all. She felt it, too. The spark of electricity when they accidentally touched. The pull of tension when they caught each other's gaze. The buzzing undercurrent that kept his body on alert and blood in a southbound direction.

He'd done a noteworthy job of keeping this professional for two days, but it was getting tougher every minute.

He winked at her, an attempt to keep it light. A soft flush of color to her porcelain cheeks just confirmed that she was fighting the same attraction.

Maybe after Christmas, maybe after this was over, they could…

"Do you know how to do it?"

Did he ever. "Uh, you mean the star?"

Her lips twitched in a half smile. "I think you have to sort of slide it right over the…" She paused, and her color deepened.

"Yeah?" he prompted. "Wanna show me?"

"Come on, Clay!" Nick yelled, oblivious to the flirtatious wordplay going on in front of him. "Just put it on so we can do the lights."

She gave him a pointed but playful look of warning. "You heard the boy, Clay."

Still grinning, he turned to the tree, focusing on one of the dozens of superprecious Norman Rockwell reproduction ornaments that hung from the branches.

The tree was perfect. The house was perfect. The woman who did it all was…

"Any day now," Keith said.

He shot the older kid a look, then plunked the star on the top. "Okay, doll, hit the on switch."

In a flash, the whole tree was washed in pinpoints of red, blue, white, gold and green.

"Ohh, look." The lights dimmed, then turned white at Lisa's touch.

"Mom, that is so cool," Keith said.

"Mommy!" Nicky hopped around the tree, his arms waving. "Look at this. We finally have a Christmas tree for the first time ever!"

Clay froze in the act of stepping down. He didn't actually hear Lisa's intake of breath, he felt it.

"Nick," Keith barked harshly. "Shut up."

Slowly, Clay turned from the tree to look at Lisa. Her skin was still glowing with color, but this was not the result of innuendo and flirtation.

More like embarrassment and guilt.

"You've never had a tree before?" Clay asked.

She glanced at one boy, then the other. "Not… exactly."

"We've never even had Christmas before!" Nicky said suddenly. "Mom hates it."

Clay just looked at her. "Really?"

She managed a tight smile, avoiding eye contact. "It's not my, uh, favorite holiday."

"But you…" He indicated the room, the stairs, the outside lights. "You told me—"

She quieted him with a pointed look. Whatever lies she'd told, it wasn't going to change anything to examine them in front of her sons.

"All right, dudes." Clay eased down the last step on the ladder. "It's late and this has taken all day. To bed. Your mom and I will finish the rest."

"I'll take them up," she said quickly.

"Hurry back," Clay said as he snapped the ladder shut and seared her with a meaningful look. "So we can talk."


LISA SIGHED as she closed the boys' bedroom door. She'd assured them both that it was okay that Clay knew her little secret.

What did it matter if she'd given him the impression she knew how to pull off Christmas? The house looked like Mr. Rockwell himself decorated it—

thanks to the geniuses at the home improvement store and that incredible Christmas shop she'd found.

Still, Lisa delayed the conversation by taking the back stairs to her room, where she brushed her hair and added just a touch of mascara and blush to her pale cheeks. She considered changing from the jeans and T-shirt she'd worn to work in all day, but why? To impress the man she worked for?

From another room, she heard a phone ring and prayed he'd be busy with a long call. Part of her wanted to just chicken out and go to bed. But part of her had been aching to be alone with him all day.

The achy part won.

She tiptoed into the living room, and stared at the magnificent tree.

Had she really done that? She'd been so focused on the job, on making sure she'd gotten every detail the way he wanted, she'd forgotten why Christmas made her sad.

And that, she realized, was a side benefit she'd never expected.

"Guess what?"

She whirled around as Clay ambled into the room and tossed a cordless phone on a chair.

"What?" She barely had the word out when he slid his arms around her waist and lifted her with the ease that he picked up Nicky.

"David Kincaid is what!" He twirled her in a complete circle, her breath catching in her lungs at the mix of muscle and speed and the scent of pine and…Clay. "He's coming on Friday!"

"In three days!" she managed to say, his enthusiasm washing over her in one infectious wave. "We can do it. We're ready."

He set her down but kept his hands firmly on her waist. "I love your attitude."

Just as he dipped closer to her face, she leaned back, out of kissing range. "Not what I expected you to say."

"What?" he asked, not backing away. "You expected me to give you a hard time for telling me you were some kind of expert at Christmas?"

The glint in his eyes took away all her worries. He wasn't too mad. He was too close, too sexy, too big and too fast, but he wasn't mad.

"I just want you to know something," she said, finally managing to wiggle out of his large and possessive hands. "I didn't do it for the money."

"No?"

"Well, the money is going to help, of course." She took one step backward and dropped onto the sofa, looking up at him. "I did it because my kids wanted to have Christmas this year and it seemed like the only way I could give them that."

A little line formed between his eyes as he

frowned at her. "Why would you ever *not* give your kids Christmas?"

She took a deep, steadying breath, then reached over and grabbed one of Mathilda the Decorator's fluffy pillows. Hugging it to her chest, she kept her gaze on Clay.

"I hate Christmas," she said on a sigh. "But it's a long, personal story that you don't need to hear. It doesn't matter. You have Christmas here and we're going to pull off this—"

"I want to know." He came around the coffee table, and sat next to her on the sofa. "Will you tell me?"

There was something in his voice, something so indescribably inviting, something that crumbled a lifetime of defenses.

"I…there was an…something happened when I was a little girl."

Wordlessly, he took her hand, closing it between his much larger ones, the gesture so comforting it brought tears to her eyes. She knew she'd cry, but not because he was so *kind*.

"I can't believe you're really interested in this."

"Why not? You're going to pretend to be my wife. I should know a little something about you, don't you think?"

She narrowed her eyes and looked thoughtfully at him. "You know what, Clay? You're not a bad boy at all."

He grinned. "Depends on your definition of bad."

"Seriously, you're a nice guy."

His thumb made a circle on her palm, sending sparks straight up her arm and a million goose bumps in their wake. "If you tell anyone, I'll have to kill you."

She laughed. "All that stuff Shelby Jackson said in the restaurant is wrong. Or at least, an act."

"No, she's right. I'm bad. Hedonistic. Reckless. And you—" he nuzzled closer, the length of his thigh pressing against hers "—are not going to change the subject." Threading his fingers through hers, he said, "Tell me why you hate Christmas."

She closed her eyes. The faster she said it, the sooner it would be over. "When I was a little girl, my brother and father were..." She squeezed her eyes. *Come on, Lisa. It's been twenty-five years.* "My brother and father went Christmas shopping to get my mom and me some presents. On December twentieth."

His hand tightened on hers. "That's tomorrow."

She opened her eyes, and looked straight into his, the dark brown as sympathetic as his voice. "Yes, it is. They skidded on a patch of ice on the highway and..." The details weren't important. "Anyway, my mother and I never celebrated Christmas. It was just a sad anniversary."

"And after you moved out and lived on your own? After you got married?"

She shook her head again. "I never lived on my own," she admitted. "I got married at eighteen to a man…" How had he just described himself? Bad? Hedonistic? Reckless? Patrick Mahoney had been all of the above and more. "To a man who didn't care for Christmas, either," she said. "He was just as happy to skip the holiday. I'd get the boys a present or two, but we never did a tree or Santa or Christmas cookies or—" Damn, there went her voice.

"I'm sorry, Lisa. Sorry about your dad and your brother."

He squeezed her fingers again and, this time, she tightened her grip on his hand, too.

"It was a long, long time ago. And, this year, since the divorce and the move to North Carolina, I promised them a real Christmas. But it wouldn't have happened if not for you. Once I lost my job—"

"Which also wouldn't have happened if not for me."

"Not really, I told you. Ben was gunning for me ever since I turned him down."

"He hit on you?"

She made a disgusting face and nodded. "He's a worm."

"Certainly not worthy of you."

At the tone in his voice, she looked at him. He was so close, just a whisper away. One inch, maybe two, and their lips would touch.

"Clay," she said softly. "This is really dangerous."

"I like danger," he whispered, closing that space a half inch. "I live for it."

Her throat tightened and blood pumped noisily in her head. She wanted to close her eyes, take that kiss.

"I thought you'd be mad if you found out that I am clueless about Christmas."

He shook his head a fraction. "I don't care that you're a rookie. You got the job done."

"Almost."

"Almost?" He glanced at the tree, then back to her. As if he couldn't stand to look away that long. "It looks done to me."

"I have to pretend to be Mrs. Clay Slater. And the boys…"

"We'll get them to play along."

She gave him a dubious look. "That's teaching them to lie. Couldn't we try and just keep them out of the way while he's here? Playing video games or something?"

"I guess." He suddenly got up from the sofa, leaving Lisa shockingly alone. "I got you an early Christmas present," he said, reaching under the tree skirt she'd bought the day before.

"You did? Why?"

"Because I found this and thought it made the

perfect memory of our Christmas." He handed her a box wrapped in glossy red paper.

"Can I open it now?"

"I want you to."

He snuggled back down next to her as she started tugging at the white satin bow.

"Remember," he said.

"Remember what?" She slipped the ribbon off and slid a finger under the paper.

"That day that you're my wife, when Kincaid comes…"

The box was plain and white. "Uh-huh?" She lifted the lid.

"I can kiss you then."

"Oh!" The polished gleam of hardwood caught the light from the tree. "It's a Norman Rockwell music box. I remember seeing this at the store," she said, grazing the high-gloss top with her fingertip, trailing a line over the profile of Santa studying his list and map of the world. "It's called *Santa at the Map*."

"You remember, right? We can kiss. For effect."

She just smiled and opened the lid of the music box. A Christmas carol played softly. And there, nestled in the dark green felt, lay a gold band lined with a channel of tiny diamonds.

"Oh—" She lifted the wedding ring and stared at it, then looked up at Clay, the most insane exhilaration stealing her breath at that moment. "Look at this."

"Gotta have the right tools for the job," he said, the look in his eyes at odds with the casual tone of his voice. "So, like I was saying, for effect..."

"Yes." She leaned a little closer to him. "In fact, we better practice just to make sure we know what we're doing."

His eyes lit just before she closed the space between them.

The kiss was so warm, so soft, so incredible, she had to open her mouth to take more, to taste him. The tip of his tongue grazed her lower lip, sending the most delicious tension through her whole being.

He let go of her hand, sliding his palm up her arm and nestling his fingers in the hair at the nape of her neck.

Unable to resist, she let out a low, throaty moan of delight. In response, he glided his tongue into her mouth, deepening the kiss, shocking her body with the pleasure of it.

Heat lightning singed every nerve, making her limbs numb, her hands ache to touch him.

She had to stop. *Had* to.

But it felt so—

"Mommy?"

With a gasp, Lisa jerked away and turned to the sound of her younger son's voice. In the hallway, Nick stood rubbing his eyes, still looking around for her.

"What's the matter, baby?" she asked as she stood on shaky legs, grasping the ring in her palm.

"I just realized I never told Santa that we live here now."

"We don't live—" It wasn't worth it. "We'll write him—"

"Don't worry, dude," Clay said, getting to his feet quickly, apparently steadier than Lisa. Maybe the kiss hadn't affected him as much. Which would make him not human.

"I sent him an e-mail before you came," Clay said to Nick.

"You did?" Nicky seemed doubtful as he entered the room. "Are you sure he has e-mail?"

"I already got a response," Clay assured him. "Now," he said as he stepped around the coffee table and lifted Nick in one swoop, "let's get you back up to bed." He glanced over his shoulder at Lisa. "I'll be right back."

She nodded, but knew that when he returned, she'd be gone. Behind a locked door, where she'd probably spend a restless night reliving that kiss. She watched him turn the corner, Nicky's sleepy head already nestled into a spot on Clay's strong shoulder. Nice spot.

She let the frisson of excitement he'd caused die down. Her kids had enough upheaval caused by men who strayed by nature.

Clay might be good as gold on the inside, with a heart so kind she could cry just thinking about it. But he was also a man who couldn't commit to a color scheme, let alone a woman.

She'd be nothing but a notch in his proverbial bedpost. And while that might be a thrill of a lifetime, she was too smart to make that mistake twice.

## CHAPTER SIX

"WHY DON'T YOU MARRY my mom?"

Clay almost dropped the right side of the race car he was holding, his demonstration of a manual tire change in quarter midget racing brought to a red-flag stop.

"What?"

Keith repeated his question. "You like her, don't you? Why don't you marry her?"

Clay lowered the back end of the boxy little frame and placed a hand on the shiny roll bar as he straightened.

"Yeah," Nick said, yanking off the bright red racing helmet he'd been wearing since they'd come into the garage for a look-see at the QM. "Then we could move out of that crappy apartment."

"Don't say crappy," Clay said automatically, his brain still firing away at possible responses to the question.

"You would," Keith chimed in. "If you saw the apartment."

Clay wiped his hand on his jeans, making a tiny grease stain. "I'm sure your mom's doing the best she can."

Nick pulled the helmet back on and flipped the visor down. He held out his hands and turned an imaginary wheel, making muffled motor sounds as he ran around the garage.

Clay picked up a wrench and knelt down to turn the six bolt on the rear wheel. "This is the tricky part," he said to Keith, praying the conversation was over. "You gotta make sure—"

"But isn't that why we're here?" Keith asked.

Maybe not quite over yet. "Isn't what why you're here?" He squinted and got closer to the wheel.

"To see if you two like each other enough to get married."

Clay turned to him and scowled. "Where'd you get that idea?"

"I heard you talking in the kitchen yesterday."

"You did?" God, what had the kid heard? Clay searched his brain and couldn't remember the particulars of the conversation, just Lisa going over what she'd make for dinner and discussing seating arrangements when Kincaid came on Friday. Nothing about getting married. "You mean when we were talking about that sponsor who's coming to see me tomorrow?"

"I mean when you said, 'If you were my wife, I'd

keep you right next to me, not across the table.' Remember?"

He sure did. And no wonder the kid thought they were talking about getting married. They were. But in a totally different context.

"We were just speculating," he said, hoping vagueness and big words would end the discussion.

"What's that mean?"

"Just…you know. Man, these hubs are old. Wanna go get new titanium ones?" Anything, just about anything, to change the subject.

Keith shrugged. "Sure. What's specu…what's that mean?"

"Bet you make a good driver, kid." Clay grinned at him. "You're relentless." At Keith's frustrated frown, Clay held up a hand. "Speculation means to guess what something would be like."

"Like being married to my mom."

"Really, in that conversation, it was just a…" What was it? At the time, it was a compliment, delivered with sincerity and acknowledged with one of those sunny Lisa smiles, mixed with raw terror in her eyes. Oh, she liked him all right. And she wanted him just as bad as he wanted her. But something was holding her back and he didn't want to scare her off trying to find out what it was.

"It was a what?"

Clay'd forgotten what they were talking about.

Something that happened with far too much frequency since that woman had come into his life. "Um, hand me that axle nut, will ya?"

"This?" Keith held up a metal ring.

"Yeah. Where'd your brother go?"

"He's right outside." Keith pushed himself off the tool chest he'd been sitting on and plopped right down next to Clay, half-startling him.

"Does he have a coat on? It's getting cold and we're going to get some snow."

"It's already started," Keith noted. "What's that?"

Clay held the wrench toward the child. "Here, twist it right like that."

Keith followed orders, biting his lower lip as he concentrated. Then he set down the wrench and looked hard at Clay, the mask he'd been wearing now completely replaced by a beguiling, open expression. "I don't think you ought to marry her just 'cause you're rich or famous."

Clay felt a smile pull at his mouth. "Good, 'cause in the scheme of things I'm not either one."

"Not like Austin Elliott or J.C. Fuller."

He had to laugh. "Hell—heck, no. Not like Austin Elliott or J.C. Fuller."

"And it's not 'cause she misses my dad so much, because most of the time he was really jerky and yelled a lot and was never home."

They were definitely getting into the Too Much

Information area that guys, as a rule, should avoid. "Is that right?"

"You want to know why I think you should get married?"

Clay had a feeling he was about to find out.

"'Cause my mom laughed yesterday."

Clay just looked at him. "Your mom laughs all the time, kid. Every time Nick opens his mouth, I noticed."

"Not yesterday. I mean, not on that day. That's always the day she cries and calls Grandma and they cry some more."

He'd tried very hard to keep things light the day before, after Lisa had confessed why she'd never liked Christmas. And the day had been a success, with more laughter in his house than he could ever remember and a big spaghetti dinner with the kids where all *three* boys in the room demonstrated their noodle-sucking finesse. Clay had gone to bed congratulating himself on making the day a happy one for her.

After all that time with Lisa, he'd also gone to bed in desperate need of another hot kiss, but settled for one more cold shower instead.

"Well, I'm glad she laughed," Clay said. He stood, brushing his jeans again. "We gotta hit the auto-parts store."

Keith looked up at him, those eyes so much like

his mother's that Clay's heart actually did something really stupid and kicked up a gear. "So are you going to marry my mom?"

"You are relentless," Clay repeated, tapping the platinum-blond hair lightly. "I got to get you behind the wheel of a car. Fast."

But Keith didn't move. Maybe this was the opening he needed, the move he had to make to win the race when Kincaid showed up. Plus the kid already suspected something was up.

Clay crouched down again, getting eye to eye with Keith. "Listen, kid. I am going to marry your mom."

Keith blinked and his jaw slackened.

"For one day. She didn't tell you yet?"

The boy just shook his head, rapt.

No, she didn't. But Clay had to, or else it wouldn't work. "Tomorrow, this man named David Kincaid is coming to see me."

"The owner of Kincaid Toys?"

"The very one."

"Holy cr…crud."

Clay gently explained what they were doing and why they were doing it. The whole thing sounded much less outlandish, when presented to a nodding, smiling, encouraging almost-nine-year-old.

"So, you see," Clay said when he'd finished. "When your mom and I were talking about getting—"

Nicky came barreling back into the garage, one loud and fast human engine. "Watch out, I'm a-racin'!" he yelled.

"Nick! Guess what?"

The little guy whipped off his helmet and stared at his older brother, obviously alerted by the sound of excitement in his voice. "We're going to drive that thing?"

"No. Mom and Clay are getting married!"

Nick dropped the helmet. "No way! Our dad's going to be a sort of famous race-car driver?"

Clay didn't know what was more of a kick in the stomach, "sort of famous..." or the look on Lisa Mahoney's face as she stepped into the garage.

"THAT'S HER MAD LOOK," Keith whispered to Clay.

"Ya think?"

*How dare he be sarcastic?* Lisa clenched her fists, digging deep for the self-control necessary not to pick up the closest tool and fling it at Clay.

"We agreed," she said tightly. "Or did you forget the ground rules we set when I got here?"

Clay opened his mouth but before he launched into some pathetic rationale of his behavior, Nicky sidled up next to her and slipped his hand into hers. "It's okay, Mom. We like him. You can marry him."

She felt the air escape from her lungs as she shot a look at Clay. Was he *smiling?* That sent her blood up a few more degrees. "I'm not going to marry him, honey." She finally pulled her gaze from Clay and focused on her sons. "We were just going to—" she brushed a silky strand of hair behind Nicky's ear "—play a game of pretend. But it wasn't supposed to involve you."

Granted, she'd told Clay that she'd inform the boys and yesterday had been so…so nice, of all unimaginable things, that she'd put it off.

"We can do it, Mom." Keith bounded up from the floor, his eyes as bright and animated as she could remember. "We can pretend with you. Clay told me the whole thing and we can even call him 'Dad' if you want."

"No!" She was way too emphatic. She stood slowly, keeping a protective hand on Nicky's head.

"That won't be necessary," Clay said, pushing himself off the cement floor. "I don't want you kids to lie."

"No?" Lisa urged. "I think that's exactly what we've set up here."

"They're your boys, Lisa. I'll be their stepfather."

"Forever?" Nicky asked, his little fingers grasping Lisa's hand as he looked up at her. "Really?"

Oh, God. See what she'd done? She'd set up unreal expectations and lies.

"Listen, dude," Clay walked across the wide garage and Keith, Lisa noticed, was no more than two steps behind them. "All I wanted to do was make a really good impression on Mr. Kincaid and—"

"Is he the guy who makes the toys?" Nick's fingers squeezed tighter. "The Mighty Flight and Mighty Motor?" His voice almost broke with shock and excitement.

"He sure is, and he's going to pay a lot of money to put his name on the side of a race car. I want to drive that car, Nick. And, in order to do that…" He glanced at her for help.

But Lisa just shook her head. "This is insane, Clay. And wrong. We're not married and I can't ask my boys to lie and—"

"Why don't you get married?" Keith asked. "Then we won't be lying."

Lisa looked at her son. "People don't just get married for a day."

"Come on, Mom," Nick pulled her arm so hard it almost came out of the socket. "It'll be fun."

Lisa nearly laughed at the innocence of her son but then she saw the serious glint in Clay's eyes.

"It would be fun," he said.

Her heart stuttered, then just about stopped. "He's coming tomorrow…" Was she actually having this conversation? She put up her hands to stop them all, including herself. "This has gone too far."

"You agreed," Clay said quietly, echoing her earlier accusation.

"Not to have my sons lie."

"Mom, it's okay. We can lie," Nicky said seriously. "I did when you asked me if we fought when the babysitter was there."

This time she did laugh, softly, unclasping Nicky's hand to stroke his head again. "I don't want you to lie, honey." She looked at Clay, her heart not quite back to normal. "Somehow, I just thought we could fool Kincaid and not involve the boys. I just should have thought this through."

"I shouldn't have told them," he said quickly. "But now that I have, you need to decide how you want to handle it." He shoved his hand into his pocket and yanked out a set of car keys. "I'm going to take a drive."

"Where are you going?" Keith asked. "To the auto-parts store? Can I come?"

Clay reached over and tousled Keith's hair. "Not now, kid. I'm just going to give your mom some time to talk to you guys and think things over. You're a family and you have to do what the whole family wants."

Lisa tried to swallow and cursed the golf ball that had formed in her throat. "This is all my fault, Clay. I'm so impulsive. I do things without thinking."

He shook his head. "I told you, I like impulsive. And this was my wild idea, anyway. If you're uncomfortable, I'll handle Kincaid when he gets here."

"Do we have to leave before Christmas?" Nicky

asked. If the golf ball in Lisa's throat hadn't done the trick, the heartbreak in her son's voice nearly choked her.

"Of course not," Clay said quickly. "I'll just tell him you're my…" He paused and looked at Lisa. "Friends."

He hustled out of the garage before any of them could argue that.

"Mom, don't you want to help him?" Keith asked.

Yes, yes, *yes*. "If we do what he wants, then I'm teaching you to tell a lie."

"We'll forget you taught us that, I promise," Nicky assured her. "Won't we forget, Keef?"

Keith shrugged. "We'll just remember that you helped him."

Well, there was that lesson. "I just wanted to give you guys a real Christmas," she said, her explanation suddenly sounding hollow. "And make extra money." Even hollower. "And he seemed so…" Her attraction to him was the hollowest reason of all. "But I don't want you to lie."

"Tell you what, Mom," Keith said. "We won't ever actually say anything that's a lie. He can do all the talking and we'll just not say anything."

"A technicality," she pointed out, sighing and looking from one to the other. "I really got us in a pickle, didn't I?"

"Don't feel bad, Mom," Nicky said. "I like pickles."

"I like Clay," Keith said quietly.

"So do I," she admitted.

"So you gonna marry him?" Keith asked. "It's the only solution. Then you can help him and you won't be lying."

A slow, sneaky smile broke over her face. "You know something, Keith Patrick Mahoney? I think you're on to something."

## CHAPTER SEVEN

DARKNESS DESCENDED quickly on the shortest day of the year. Clay glanced at the clock in his truck and saw that it was just four-thirty and he'd been driving around Lake Norman for almost two hours, enough time for a remarkable three inches of fresh snow to cover the town, more than he'd seen since he was a kid.

Enough time for Lisa to talk to her sons. Enough time, in fact, for Lisa to pack up the few belongings she'd brought to their charade and leave.

His gut constricted at that thought. Not because she be reneging on her promise. He'd already punched the steering wheel a few times over that. But because he didn't want her to leave.

He wanted to punch the steering wheel over that, too.

Instead, he swore softly and pulled into his driveway, the wheels of the truck crunching the freshly fallen snow and the headlights shining on flakes that danced in front of the house's new Christmas lights. Much more snow and Kincaid might not even be able to get here tomorrow.

Wouldn't that be the perfect twist to an already twisted story?

Something hit the windshield with a resounding splat and Clay tapped the brake. As the wiper cleared his view, Clay could see the victorious grin on Keith's face while Nicky worked hard to pack another snowball.

In a flash, Clay was out of the truck and scooping up a handful, leaving on the headlights to illuminate his target. "Wanna play hardball, eh, kid?"

In the light, he could see the littler guy bouncing and bopping like a Mexican jumping bean. Dipping behind the truck, Clay threw his snowball just hard enough to make it across the lawn, purposely aiming for Keith's legs. The kid jumped and escaped a hit with a shout of laughter and surprise.

Nicky tossed a loosely packed grenade puffball that barely made it to the truck. To play fair, Clay stepped out from behind the truck and got in the headlight beam, grabbing a handful of snow and packing it as he maneuvered into a place where they could hit him.

"Two against one!" Keith called out, waving his snowball like a mad warrior.

A double set of snow grenades came flying at Clay, hitting him in the shoulder and leg. He fell to the ground in a dramatic tumble, secretly packing a snowball while he played hurt.

"Clay!" Nicky hollered, running toward him. "Are you all right?"

Clay rolled and fired right over Nicky's head to clock Keith in the upper arm. "I'm great." He leaped up and gently tackled the tiny boy to the snow. "But you are my prisoner!"

"Noooo!" He half giggled, half screamed as Clay lifted him, barely dodging the wild kicks of his unstoppable legs.

"You can keep him," Keith offered, gathering ammunition.

"Oh, no, you can't." At the sound of Lisa's voice, Clay almost dropped the bundle of boy he held, turning to see the reflection of golden Christmas lights glisten off her snow-dampened hair.

She didn't look mad anymore. In fact, she looked radiant.

"I'll pay any ransom," she offered with a musical laugh.

He raised his shrieking prize higher into the air, looking past the squirming body into Lisa's blue eyes as she approached.

"Any ransom?" he deliberately let the innuendo into his voice.

She laughed softly and came closer, reaching out for her son. "I'll never let him go." She wrapped her arms around the little boy and tried to squeeze him, but he squiggled and scampered away.

"He never lets me kiss him anymore," she said wistfully, watching him go and tackle his brother.

"Then he's nuts."

She looked up at him, her eyes bright. "You're not mad at me anymore?"

"Did I act mad?"

"Well, you kept it in check."

"Occupational hazard," he said dryly. "If I let my reactions get ruled by emotions, I'd spin out in every race."

For a moment, they said nothing, as the boys wrestled in the snow a few feet away.

"I forgot my cell phone," Clay said. "I thought you might be gone when I got back."

"No, no." She glanced at the boys, then back at him, her eyes sparking with a mysterious look. "As a matter of fact, we decided that…"

*We're leaving.* Clay braced himself for the words.

"That you and I…"

Ought to forget this whole thing.

"Should get married."

He stared at her.

Both the boys descended on them, as though they might have been listening instead of fighting.

"We'll marry you right here and now!" Nicky said.

# An Important Message from the Editors

Dear Reader,

Because you've chosen to read one of our fine novels, we'd like to say "thank you!" And, as a **special** way to thank you, we're offering you a choice of <u>two more</u> of the books you love so well **plus** an exciting Mystery Gift to send you — absolutely <u>FREE</u>!

Please enjoy them with our compliments...

*Pam Powers*

Lift here

Peel off seal and place inside...

## The Reader Service — Here's How It Works:

"I'm the marrying guy," Keith added. "Like the judge or priest."

"Hey! I'm the marrying guy!" Nicky said. "You told me what to say."

Lisa tucked her hands into the pockets of her ski jacket and winked at him. "You said you liked impulsive."

He must have looked as unsure as he felt, because she laughed and punched him lightly in the arm. "It's not real, Clay. It's for…them."

He couldn't hold back the slow smile. "Will it make you feel better about this?"

She nodded and Nicky started dancing around the two of them. "Ready? Are you ready?"

"Come on," Keith nudged his mother closer. "Quick, before you change your mind."

"Or he does," she added.

"No way," Clay said, stepping closer so that together they were right in the direct beam of his headlights.

"Okay, okay!" Nicky exclaimed. "Do you take Mommy for your awfully wedded wife?"

At Clay's choking laugh, Nick looked offended. "That's what you're supposed to say."

Clay managed to look serious. "I do."

"I'll do Mom," Keith said, pushing his brother gently aside. "Now, Mom, do you take Clay Slater for your *lawfully*—" he looked pointedly at Nicky "—wedded husband?"

She grinned at him. "Why not?"

For some reason, her cavalier quip hurt. "Why not?" He reached for her hand, tugging her closer. "What kind of vow is that?"

"Temporary." Her eyes glimmered with playfulness.

He pulled her into his chest, unable to resist for one more second. He lowered his head to kiss her just as Keith stuck his hand in between their mouths.

"Not yet! You gotta wait till I say the man and wife part."

"Then say it," Clay said gruffly, inches from the mouth he wanted. "Fast."

"I now pronounce you…"

Clay didn't hear the rest. Blood rushed through his head as he captured her mouth and took the kiss he'd been thinking about for two days. In the distance, he heard the boys hooting and hollering, but every brain cell he had was focused on the soft, sweet, willing mouth against his. She made a little rumble in her throat and walloped his whole body with desire.

Or was that the clump of a snowball on his back? Then one hit his knees, and slid off Lisa's shoulder into his chest. Icy white fluffs exploded around them, oddly reminiscent of rice.

Lisa giggled, and Clay pulled her tighter, wishing the down jacket—and maybe the kids—would disappear.

"One more," he urged. "Just for effect."

Laughing, she lifted her face to him, her lips parted, her eyes closed. Just as he put his mouth on hers, a wet grenade hit his head and their teeth bumped.

He eased his mouth to her ear and whispered, "Someone has to die."

"Someone small," she agreed.

Instantly, they parted and started scooping and packing and bombarding the boys, who nearly choked with hysterics. Clay's fingers burned with numbing cold, but he hardly felt the pain. It didn't take long for the battle to become every man for himself and after Lisa lobbed one right at his face, Clay managed to get her back as she ran around the darkened side of the house.

She went down laughing and he was kneeling over her in a second, grasping her narrow hips between his knees. Snow clung to her hair as she twisted and breathlessly fought him, grabbing handfuls of snow and pathetically trying to fling them at him.

"Now, you're my prisoner," he said, tightening his lock on her hips. "Say uncle."

She just shook her head and flipped some snow at him.

"Say it," he insisted.

More snow flipped as she laughed. "No."

"Say it."

Suddenly, she stilled. Her whole body stopped moving, but he could feel the pulse jump where he pinned her wrists. "Kiss me again," she whispered.

He needed no more encouragement. He dropped lower, holding her smoky gaze, and relaxing his legs enough to let their hips press against each other.

Easy, slowly, he kissed her mouth again, holding himself back, forcing himself not to let go, lie down and give in to the need for full body contact.

"Uh, Mom."

Clay jerked up at Keith's voice. This wasn't the place, or the time. But later…

He slid off of Lisa, ready for a snowball shot, but froze at the look on Keith's face.

"What's the—"

Behind Keith, a tall, imposing shadow of a man blocked the moonlit clouds.

"Hope you don't mind, Slater. We decided to come early to beat the snow. I tried calling your cell, but there was no answer." The man leaned over and looked at Lisa. "And this must be Mrs. Slater." He patted Keith's shoulder. "This nice young man tells me you're newlyweds."

Clay managed to kneel and reached out his hand to help Lisa do the same. "As a matter of fact, we just got married, Mr. Kincaid."

"I WOULD KILL my husband if five people showed up a day early." Sasha Kincaid settled into a bar stool at the kitchen counter and trained deep brown eyes on Lisa. "I think you're handling the disruption with aplomb."

The woman had no idea just how much aplomb—whatever that was, exactly—Lisa was demonstrating. "I'm just glad you made it in before the snow," Lisa said. "And delighted that Mr. Kincaid decided to bring the whole family."

Okay, *delighted* might be pushing it. But, so far, Sasha and David Kincaid and their three daughters, had been warm and classy and extremely apologetic for arriving unannounced and with more people than had been expected.

"Still, you're being quite gracious." Sasha folded her arms and leaned forward, her arresting, dark looks mesmerizing Lisa. "I'd planned to stay in Asheville and shop with the girls while Dave came over here, but the weather was getting so ugly and our cell phones didn't work in the mountains. We didn't want to get separated or stranded."

"It's no problem, Mrs. Kincaid," Lisa assured her.

"Please, I just invaded your house with three kids. You'll have to call me Sasha."

Lisa poured the hot water into the cups she'd lined up for five hot chocolates, and glanced up at her guest. "Your daughters are beautiful." They were all carbon copies of their exotic-looking mother, although they all wore their hair down, while Sasha's was slicked back to accentuate her striking cheekbones and wide eyes. "I always wanted a girl."

"Until they started rolling their eyes and hitting me with 'whatevers,' so did I." Sasha laughed lightly, then lifted one perfectly arched eyebrow. "Perhaps now that you've remarried, you can get that little girl."

Lisa splashed some hot water over the rim of a cup. "Maybe."

"Careful, doll." Clay blew into the kitchen, sliding a cordless phone on the counter as he seized a dish towel to blot her spill. "Don't burn yourself."

In one smooth move, he wiped the water, then pulled Lisa into a far-too-familiar hug. "We're in luck," he announced with a wide grin. "Pizza Man is still delivering." He looked at Sasha. "Not exactly the Christmas dinner my wife had planned, but—"

Lisa blinked at him, startled by the "my wife" and the nearness of him. She covered her reaction as quickly as she could. "Pizza?"

"My girls love pizza," Sasha told them, looking from one to the other. She tilted her head and gave them a sly smile. "You two seem very happy. How long have you been married?"

"Not very," Lisa said. "About five—"

"Weeks," Clay finished quickly.

Lisa smiled up at him, fingering the diamond

wedding band she'd remembered to put on when the Kincaids arrived. "It just seems like five minutes, doesn't it?"

He laughed and cuddled her closer. "Time flies when you're this much in love."

Lisa almost choked, but Sasha let out a soft sigh. "I remember when Dave and I were first married. We couldn't stand to be in different rooms."

"Speaking of rooms…" David Kincaid's booming voice suddenly filled the kitchen, along with his six-foot-four frame and shock of prematurely gray hair. "Did you see the living room, Sasha? You'll love the Norman Rockwell theme."

Clay and Lisa shared a quick look of victory.

"He's my wife's favorite," David told them.

Clay winked at her. "Funny, he's my wife's favorite, also."

Her heart rolled around helplessly for a second time when he called her "my wife." She sure better get a grip on that if she was going to make it through this evening.

"I'll tell the kids that hot chocolate is ready," Lisa said, easing out of Clay's arm. "Are they still outside?"

"They've all moved into the TV room," David said. "I think they're becoming fast friends."

Lisa placed the last of the hot chocolate cups on a tray. Fast friends? How long could Nicky be trusted not to burst out the truth? She scooped up the tray and started for the door. The best place for her to be was with the kids, making sure they didn't blow the cover.

"Here, I'll take that," Clay took the tray from her hands. "I'd like to see how they're doing."

She gave him a pointed look as they turned the corner, out of earshot. "This could get dicey," she whispered.

"Are you kidding?" he asked. "You're amazing."

"Thanks, but I'm not worried about me. What about Nicky? I thought the boys would be hiding in their room all night, not playing with other kids. How long do you think he'll last before he announces that he just 'married' us on the front lawn?"

"He's cool. I talked to him."

"What did you say?"

"The two most powerful words known to control the behavior of a child."

She frowned. "Time out?"

"Santa Claus."

In the family room, the *Polar Express* DVD was blaring from the main screen, while Keith and the oldest Kincaid girl, a nine-year-old beauty named Renata, were already dueling over a video game. The other two girls, who were just about seven and five, were comfortably curled on the sofa, ready to get lost in the Christmas movie.

"No one seems very concerned about who married whom and when," he whispered to her.

"Yeah, let's hope we can keep it that way," she said, taking in the scene.

"Lisa." The serious tone of Clay's voice pulled her attention back to him.

"What is it?"

"Thank you," he said softly, leaning over the tray to drop a single kiss on her head. "I couldn't have invented a better wife."

That made her laugh. "Thank me when we get through this."

He singed her with a meaningful look. "I will."

Her stomach did the roller-coaster dip again and she managed to find her voice to announce the arrival of hot chocolate to the kids.

While Clay handed out the drinks with plenty of teases and jokes, Lisa headed back to the kitchen to the adult guests. Absently, she touched the spot on her hair where Clay had just kissed her. For a second, she let herself remember the way he'd kissed her out on the lawn and the way her whole body had responded.

She could barely resist the guy. Hadn't she kissed him right back? Hadn't she loved it?

Hadn't she learned her lesson from the first bad boy she'd married—for *real*—and the heartache he'd caused her?

All she had to do was get through this evening, this one little pizza party, give him a chance to impress the potential sponsor and then...

Then what? She wasn't going to leave—Christmas wasn't until Monday, and it was only Thursday night. No, she'd stay and let the boys have their Christmas. They were enjoying themselves more than they had in ages.

She'd just have to keep her distance from that man and his soul-melting kisses. That's what she'd do: she'd play her part, do her job and then *keep her distance*.

As she neared the kitchen, she heard Sasha Kincaid moan in frustration. "Oh, I don't believe it!"

Lisa froze. What didn't she believe? Was the jig up already?

"Believe it," David Kincaid boomed. "This storm is going to sock us in."

Relief poured through her. They weren't talking about the pretend marriage; they were discussing the weather.

"How bad is it?" she asked conversationally as she breezed back into the kitchen.

"Bad," David said, holding his cell phone. "I'm afraid we're here for the night."

*The night?*

"No problem." Clay made the comment from behind her, following her into the kitchen and easing those husbandlike arms around her waist, this time from behind. "We have plenty of room."

"I hate to impose," Sasha said.

"It's not an imposition," Clay replied. "The girls can sleep in the pullout and on an air mattress in my office and you can have the guest room."

Which would leave Lisa…

Clay's embrace tightened imperceptibly as he eased her back into the granite of his chest.

Which would leave Lisa exactly where the guests would expect *Mrs. Slater* to sleep.

In *Mr. Slater's* bed.

So much for keeping her distance.

## CHAPTER EIGHT

CLAY OPENED THE CLOSET door with one eye closed. Could she have done it? He'd kept the kids busy outside with another snowball fight while the Kincaids took a walk down by the lake. Lisa's job, they'd secretly agreed, was to get her stuff out of the guest room.

The room looked completely abandoned. She'd done it. She'd fluffed up Mathilda's violet comforter and even stocked the bathroom with fresh towels.

"I think you'll be comfortable here."

"Thank you, Clay," Sasha said. "I'm sure we'll be able to leave by tomorrow afternoon."

"There's no rush," he reassured her.

"I have to tell you, son," David said with a friendly hand on his shoulder. "I'm mighty impressed with your home life."

Clay could barely keep from raising a fist and hissing "Yes!" David Kincaid's beaming smile was as welcome as a checkered flag.

"Thank you, sir."

"Seriously," Kincaid continued. "Your stepsons are obviously well loved by you and your wife is a gem."

"That she is," he agreed heartily.

"I can't understand Shelby Jackson's reluctance in having me come out here," Kincaid added. "I know she thinks you're an excellent driver and more than ready for Cup racing, but she did seem wary of my visiting you."

"Your decision to sponsor a second team for Thunder Racing is very important to her," he said, hoping the noncommittal answer would work.

Kincaid nodded. "It's important to me, too," he said. "If and when we put the Kincaid colors on the side of a race car, I want the right man driving it."

"I know you do, sir," Clay admitted. "And I hope that I'm that driver."

Kincaid just nodded. "I'm mighty impressed," he repeated.

That was as close an offer of sponsorship that Clay could hope for. Shaking Kincaid's hand and giving Sasha a friendly hug, he left them in the guest room and practically catapulted down the hall to his bedroom to share the news with Lisa.

The room was empty.

Clay stood in the doorway, punched by disappointment.

"Lisa?" When she didn't answer, he entered and closed the door behind him, and then peeked into the bathroom, but it was completely dark. His bed was made, and there was no sign of her. Where had she put her stuff? Where had she gone?

And, why, he wondered, did it matter so damn much.

"Lisa?" he called again.

Then he saw the shadow. On the balcony that overlooked the lake. Had he ever even gone out there? He jiggled the handle of the French door and it opened easily.

She was nestled into the corner, her down jacket pulled around her, her hands deep into the pockets.

"What are you doing out here?"

"Just enjoying the view."

He followed her gaze to the black water, lit by a streak of moonlight, and the ice-covered trees that surrounded it. "It's pretty," he agreed, approaching her. "But you're prettier."

She smiled and finally shifted her focus to him. "How are our guests?"

"You mean my new sponsor?"

Her eyes popped open. "He said yes?"

"Not in so many words, but real close." He couldn't help it. He had to touch her. He slipped his hand in her pocket and swallowed her chilly fingers with his much warmer ones. "All because of you."

She gave him a doubtful look. "I won't be driving that car, Clay."

"I know, but you…" How could he say this? "You give me confidence."

She looked as surprised as he felt. "What do you mean?"

"I don't know," he admitted. "I just feel so…sure of myself with you here."

"Clay, you're very sweet, but I doubt that there's ever been a time in your life when you weren't sure of yourself. I can't believe confidence has ever been a problem for you."

He frowned. "Believe me, when you're in my business and you have no ride, no contract, no sponsor, no team, self-confidence is a fake to psyche out the competition."

She regarded him for a moment, the released her hand from his grip. "Well, it looks like you're about to have a ride, a contract, a sponsor and a team, so you can be confident again."

Her dry tone caught him by surprise. "What's the matter?"

"Nothing," she said quickly. Much too quickly.

"Are you upset about sleeping in here? The boys don't even know, they are having so much fun and I promise…" What did he promise? He couldn't promise anything. All he wanted to do was get her inside, undressed and…

*Hit the brakes, Slater.* She wasn't his wife, girlfriend or a one-night stand. "I'll sleep on the floor." His offer sounded magnanimous…and stupid.

She gave him another look, but he still couldn't decipher what was going on in her head.

"That's not necessary," she said. "I'll be asleep in five minutes. It's been a long performance tonight."

"You were really something," he said, following her as she opened the door. She didn't respond, just slipped out of her down jacket and dropped it on a chair.

"I mean, the way you handled everything, I was…" He was what? Proud of her? Enamored with her? Enchanted by her? All of the above. "The way you made them so comfortable and got the kids distracted so easily." And the way she'd stayed near him, held his hand, laughed at his jokes and looked at him like she was…

Like she was in love with him.

Who was he kidding? In love with him? That was an act. A performance, she'd just called it.

At the bathroom door, she tapped on the light and looked over her shoulder at him. "Just doing my job," she said softly.

Yeah? Well she was doing it really, really well.

She closed the door with a thud that matched the way his heart landed in his stomach.

Exactly when had this game become *real?*

LISA SQUEEZED HER EYES and leaned against the cool wood of the bathroom door. Who knew she was such a consummate actress?

Not that acting like Clay's wife had been difficult. No, that role had come pretty naturally.

But acting like she didn't care that this was a job, that she didn't mind that she was being paid to pretend, that he hadn't wormed his way under her skin with that seductive smile and that boyish charm—now *that* was Oscar-worthy.

But she could do it. Taking a deep breath, she slipped out of her clothes and rummaged through the bag she'd left on the bathroom floor. She found a long T-shirt and flannel sleep pants and slipped into them, then brushed her teeth, combed her hair and took a hard look at herself in the mirror.

*Come on, Lisa. It's a king-size bed.*

And he was a king-size man.

*This is business, not pleasure.*

At the very thought of pleasure, her heart slammed against her ribs and she had to wet her lips they had become so dry. Slowly, she opened the bathroom door. The only light was from the moon, slipping in through the sheer curtains on the balcony doors.

The sheets rustled. In the dim light, she could see the outline of a body and it seemed that Clay had positioned himself dead center in the middle of the bed.

She tugged at the corner of the comforter and pulled it back. He was definitely mid-bed. And bare chested. And…not asleep.

"Good night," she said in a tight voice.

He just laughed softly and patted the pillow. "Don't worry, doll. I don't bite. Unless you want me to."

She'd gone way past *want*. Seconds crawled by. She could feel his gentle breath, smell the musky scent of him and only imagine how incredible his solid muscles and hot skin would feel under her fingertips.

"Good night," she repeated, with a little more force than necessary.

She shivered against the icy sheets.

"You cold?" His voice was low, provocative.

"Just my feet."

Without warning, warm, bare toes closed over one of her numb feet. "I'll just help thaw them."

"Ohhh," she sighed as the warmth of his skin penetrated her cold toes. "That feels good."

"Anything else need thawing?"

Yeah. Her *heart*.

Why was she fighting this? Right now, this close, this intimate, this moment, she couldn't remember the reason she needed to keep her distance from

Clay Slater. Even if she could, she'd ignore reason right now.

Unable to stop herself, she rolled over, only half surprised to find him right there, just inches from her face.

"As a matter of fact," she said softly, "my mouth is cold."

She could feel him smiling just before his lips covered hers. The kiss was easy at first, almost tentative, then he opened his mouth and she did the same, shivering at the first touch of his tongue.

"Better?" he whispered.

She murmured softly.

He kissed her cheek, her eyes, her hair, her ears and Lisa arched closer to him with each bolt of electricity that zipped through her.

"Anything else?" he asked again, his voice husky with the passion she could feel humming through his body.

It was all up to her. He was letting her make the call, letting her tell him what was okay. Should she keep her distance and protect herself, or take the warm, silky pleasure he was offering?

His hands stayed firmly on her back, their legs not quite touching, their bodies suspended as time ticked away while he waited and she decided.

"I'm cold all over," she finally said on a whisper.

"I can take care of that."

THE FIRST GRAY-WHITE FINGERS of dawn slipped through the flimsy curtains that the ever-present Mathilda had chosen and the never-present Clay hadn't bothered to change.

He opened his eyes long enough to register that it was almost morning, but kept them open when his attention fell on a tangle of blond curls framing the woman sleeping in his arms.

*Lisa.*

He lifted his head to look at her. As heavy as his eyelids were after his interrupted night's sleep, he managed to keep them open and study her face. Long, wispy lashes brushed the delicate, pale flesh under her eyes, and her lips—oh, those magnificent, delicious lips—parted as slow, even breaths slipped in and out.

He lowered his head onto her pillow, letting her hair tickle his face while sliding his hands over her stomach. Her skin was like warm satin, her curves and dips as feminine as anything he'd ever touched.

He couldn't remember ever, ever feeling this content.

*Lisa.*

Funny, impulsive, sexy, smart, sweet Lisa. His pretend wife.

He could still see the beaming smile of David Kincaid. *I'm mighty impressed. Your wife's a gem.* Man, that was an understatement.

"Lisa," he whispered, not even aware he was talking out loud. "We did it. We really did it."

"Three times."

He drew back from the mess of her hair and choked a laugh. "Who's counting?"

Smiling, she twisted around to face him, blinking sleep from her blue eyes, a tiny smile tipping her lips. "Wanna make it four?"

"Yes." He kissed her forehead and she moved sensually against him. "But I was thinking that we'd done something else. We fooled Kincaid."

She jerked back, her eyes suddenly wide. "Oh, God, I forgot about the Kincaids."

"That's sort of how we ended up here." He reached under the sheet and found her hand, jiggling the wedding ring. "Mrs. Slater."

"Yeah, I guess we got a little carried away with the whole pretend marriage thing," she said.

Slowly, carefully, he stroked her back easing her closer. "I don't know about you, honey," he whispered, "but I wasn't pretending a thing last night."

"Me, neither."

For a moment, they didn't say anything, but searched each other's eyes.

"No regrets?" he finally asked.

She shook her head. "No."

"No second thoughts?"

"None at all." She reached out, tangling her

fingers into his hair. "Anyway, we're married. Or did you forget I'm your awfully wedded wife?"

"No," he said softly, "I didn't forget. In fact, I thought about it a few times last night." When she lost control in his arms, when she touched him with a tenderness that took his breath away, when she fell against him, spent and satisfied. All night, actually, the word *wife* had rolled around his head, making the whole experience somehow more satisfying. Wasn't that weird?

"Don't worry," she said, patting his cheek like he'd seen her do to one of her sons. "Today we go back to make-believe."

For some really insane reason, that disappointed him. He curled his leg around her. "Can we play make-believe again tonight?"

Her eyes flashed and then she trilled the sweet laugh that usually preceded one of her more impulsive moves. "You bet." She tapped his arm gently. "But now I gotta get up and make-believe I'm the woman of the house."

She rolled away and in one move, slipped on the T-shirt he'd disposed of last night, covering up what he longed to see and touch some more.

Turning toward him, she blew him a kiss and climbed out of bed. He rose on his elbows just to watch her walk across the room and disappear into his bathroom, then fell back onto the pillow with a sigh of exhaustion and desire.

In what seemed like five seconds later, she was nudging him awake. But it must have been more than five seconds and he must have fallen sound asleep because his sexy morning mistress had been replaced by a showered, made-up, nicely dressed mother of two, ready to take on her role as his wife again.

"I'm going downstairs to start coffee and breakfast," she said. "You want to sleep longer?"

He did, but he wanted to be with her more. "Gimme a second," he said, "I'll get dressed and help."

When he came out of the bathroom, in jeans and a T-shirt, she was just putting the finishing touches on the bed. He froze, watching her in the domestic act, a sudden, totally foreign lump forming in his chest.

She turned, a tiny frown creasing her forehead. "What's the matter?" Her words eerily echoed his thoughts.

What *was* the matter with him? Why did the sight of a woman making his bed give him the same sinking sensation as a wreck on the track dead ahead? Or maybe it was a different feeling—the white flag. The "so close I can taste it and it" feeling?

Either way, he couldn't explain it.

"I don't know why you're bothering to make the bed." He reached for her hand and pulled her close enough to whisper in her ear. "We're just going to mess it up again tonight."

She shivered slightly. "So we are."

He was still smiling—and holding her hand—when they reached the bottom of the stairs and stopped at the sound of sudden laughter.

"They're up already?" she asked.

"That sounded like more than two boys. They're *all* up."

"Let's go." She tugged at his hand, pausing when they heard a young voice shriek.

"It's the truth!"

Lisa sucked in a little breath at the sound of frustration and desperation in Nicky's tone, shooting a worried look at Clay.

"I don't believe you!" one of the younger girls replied.

"Nick, cool it." That warning came from Keith and the ominous tone made Lisa and Clay step up their speed to a near jog as they passed the dining room and headed in the direction of the voices.

"The game is Truth or Dare and I don't want to dare!" Nicky said furiously. "I want to truth. And that's the truth."

"They're not really married?" The question made Renata Kincaid's voice rise an octave, and made Clay's gut clench.

"He's lying!" This from one of the younger girls who jumped up from the sofa right as Clay and Lisa reached the doorway.

"I am not!" Nicky yelled back.

Renata spun on her heel, jammed her hands onto narrow hips and stared at Clay as he entered the room. "This kid is a liar and you can't play Truth or Dare with a liar."

"I am not!" Nicky bounded toward the door, directly at Renata, propelled by his need for self-defense. "They are not married. They made the whole thing up. My mom is his personal assist... assist...helper and we're just visiting for Christmas week and pretending so that your dad will let him drive a race car! Isn't that true, Clay?"

Nicky's face had turned red, his little fists clenched in righteous, childlike indignity, his mouth poised to stick his tongue out and sneer *I told you so* victoriously at his enemy of the moment.

When Clay didn't speak, Nicky's red face deepened a shade or two and his eyes flashed. "Isn't that true, Clay?"

Five sets of eyes—and probably Lisa's—bored into him and waited for his answer. A collective breath was held. The room, and time, stood still while he braced himself to smear the child, save his own butt and continue the lie.

He swallowed. "That's true, dude."

"What?" Renata blinked at him.

"What Nicky said is true," Clay said firmly.

Lisa's slender fingers tightened around his hand and he turned to look at her, but over her shoulder all he could see was the burning glare of a man who didn't like to be deceived.

# CHAPTER NINE

*AWKWARD* TOOK ON A whole new meaning. But Clay didn't know how else to handle the situation, so he waited in the entryway after the girls and Sasha had left for their car and David had gone back to the guest room to retrieve his wife's handbag.

Little had been said. Explanations had sounded empty and had been met with looks that ranged from dubious to stunned. However, David Kincaid was not the type to blow a fuse, give a lecture or offer a piece of his mind. He'd simply confirmed what Clay suspected: nothing about the charade they'd played amused or impressed him and the roads were clear enough for them to leave. Now.

And before a pot of coffee could be brewed, they were out the door.

"Uh, David…Mr. Kincaid," Clay rose from the bench where he'd been waiting for his guest. "Can I speak with you for a moment?"

Kincaid's look was steely-gray. "I'm in a hurry,

son. I have another driver to interview not far from here. For another team."

Clay nodded. "I understand. And I understand why you're leaving. But before you go, could you at least give me an opportunity to explain?"

"Your actions speak louder than your words, Slater."

Slater? Oh, he had fallen in the older man's estimation.

"I consider what you did a form of cheating," Kincaid continued. "And that just makes me wonder how you'd race if the pressure is on and you're in a tight spot. I don't condone cheating. I don't condone lying. I don't—"

Clay held up a hand. "I get the idea, sir. I don't cheat." Not normally. "Shelby Jackson told me the only thing keeping me from driving a race car in the NASCAR NEXTEL Cup Series with your sponsorship was my lifestyle. My lack of ability to commit to something or someone."

"So you got creative."

He smiled, hope stoking him. "I like to think of it that way."

Kincaid regarded him for a long time, saying nothing, his wheels spinning. Clay waited, praying for a break, for a second chance.

But Kincaid just shook his head. "My family is waiting."

"I understand, sir—"

"No." Kincaid froze him with that silver gaze again. "No you don't, Slater. You have no idea what family means. You think you can buy it, rent it, use it for your own good. You know…" He took a breath and glanced at the stairs, dripping with garlands and festive bows. "What I really hate is that you're cheating yourself, not me."

"Excuse me?"

"You can't manufacture contentment. What I saw here last night was a genuinely contented family. Newly formed, yes, I could tell that. But the spirit of unity was there, between parents and children. That's what impressed me, not your Norman Rockwell decorations or your fancy lights. I saw you laugh with your…with Lisa. I saw the boys look at you with respect. I saw a family."

He stepped away and pulled open the front door, his eyes still on Clay.

"So I happen to know that the kind of man I want driving my logo around in circles really does live right here." He tapped Clay's chest. "But you chose to cheat instead. And by doing that, you're selling yourself short, Slater. Not me. You."

The accuracy of that statement hit Clay like a sledgehammer to the heart.

"Now," Kincaid continued, "if I know anything about children—and I do—you have a little boy curled up on his bed upstairs sobbing his heart out."

Clay closed his eyes at the thought of Nicky's misery. "I'll talk to him."

Kincaid nodded. "You do that."

He was out the door and down the steps before Clay could say goodbye. He stayed in the doorway long enough to watch the rental car navigate his driveway and disappear into the trees that lined the property.

Then he pivoted on his heel and took the stairs two at a time to get to Nicky. But he stopped dead cold when he saw a few plastic bags outside his own bedroom door. Was she packing?

The door to the boys' room was closed, so Clay continued to the end of the hall, where he found Lisa in the bathroom, stuffing toothpaste and cosmetics into another plastic bag.

She didn't turn to look at him, so he stood in the doorway for a moment, saying nothing.

Finally, he cleared his throat. "I should get you a nice set of luggage for Christmas."

She looked up into the mirror and caught his gaze there. "Don't bother. I don't travel often. We'll be out of here in ten minutes."

He blew out a long, slow, pained breath. "Don't."

She ignored the order and continued packing. Maybe she didn't understand.

"Don't leave," he said, taking a step into the bathroom. "Please stay for Christmas."

She tied a knot with the bag handles. "Don't be crazy."

"Crazy? I want you—that was part of the deal. The kids would have Christmas here."

She let out a humorless laugh. "I'm sure they'd have a blast now. You'll probably never speak to Nicky again and—"

"What?"

She turned to him. "He blew it."

"Lisa," he said, exasperated. "He's six years old."

Her eyes widened just enough to reveal the moisture gathering in the corners. "You're not really mad at him?"

"I'm mad at me," he said softly, looking away and scratching his neck as he combed his brain for the right words. "The idea was nuts to begin with, and foolhardy. I just got in too deep too fast, moved without thinking things through."

"Welcome to my world," she said. "I'm usually the one doing something impetuous and, in this case, my act-without-thinking gene was not only monumental, it was clearly passed on to my little boy."

"Stop." He put his hands on her shoulders and gripped firmly enough to keep her from shoving past him. "That was too much on his little shoulders, and we should have known it. I never expected Kincaid to bring family, or show up a day early and spend the night."

She closed her eyes. "We're both guilty here, Clay. Now let me go so I can get the boys home and out of your way."

"You're not in my way."

She shimmied out of his grasp and slipped past him into the bedroom. "Stop it."

"I mean it." He reached for her again, turning her slightly to face him. "I want you to stay. I want you to be with me."

Her eyes flashed.

"Not just…like that." *Slow down, Slater.* He could hear his inner spotter shout in his head. *You're blowin' it, man.* "I really like you, Lisa. I want you to stay with me."

She blinked just hard enough to release that tear she was fighting. "Oh, please, I beg you, don't do this to me."

"Do what?"

"Don't…don't." She shook her head furiously and jerked her arm out of his fingertips. "Don't make me like you. Don't make me fall for you. Don't…hurt me."

The last two words were spoken so softly he wasn't sure he understood. "Hurt you? Why would I do that?"

She stepped back and looked at him. "You can't help it, Clay. You are who you are. You don't commit, you can't settle down, the last thing you want is a…person in your life who comes with—" she lifted the plastic bag she held "—no luggage but plenty of baggage."

He stared at her, half-wondering if she was right.

Or was Kincaid right? Did a man who could know contentment live inside of him, waiting for the right woman, the right family?

Before he could answer, she slid the one suitcase she'd brought out from under his bed. "I can't keep these," she said, unzipping it to reveal the purple and yellow toy boxes.

"Why not?" he asked, incredulous. "They certainly earned them."

She sighed. "I guess I'm being stubborn and stupid."

"Ya think?"

"Okay," she agreed. "But I won't take anything else." As though to prove her point, she reached into the corner of the suitcase and pulled out the Norman Rockwell music box. Wordlessly, she placed it on the nightstand. And then she slid the wedding ring off her finger and put it on top of the box.

The sledgehammer was at work on his heart again. "I owe you five thousand dollars," he said, more gruffly than he should have.

"I didn't get the job done. Don't you see, Clay? I failed. Again. I tried to do the one thing I thought I was really good at—be a wife—and I failed." She blinked at him, fighting tears. "I don't want your money. I don't want your ring. I don't want Christmas here. I didn't earn it and I don't want to stay because you feel sorry for me." Then she scooped up the suitcase and swept by him.

Sorry for her?

He followed her out the door, but this time the boys' door was open and, when they passed the room, Clay could see their beds neatly made and no sign that a human, let alone two little male humans, had ever stepped foot inside.

Seems they all wanted to leave. In a matter of minutes, all evidence of his "family" would be gone.

Nicky and Keith were waiting patiently at the van tucked next to the garage. Keith looked as stoic as the day he'd arrived, except for the one arm he held protectively over his little brother.

Nicky's eyes were red rimmed and his little body shook with the occasional shudder.

Clay paused as he approached, taking them in. Sure, he wanted Lisa to stay and warm his bed. And, God knows, he wished he could celebrate a new ride in the NASCAR NEXTEL Cup Series with all three of them.

But the thing he was going to miss the most was seeing the look on their faces when they opened those Mighty gifts. Or the first time one of them drove a quarter midget. Or hit a home run. Oh, man.

*Slater, that was the wall you just hit, buddy.*

"Bye, Clay. I'm really sorry this didn't work out." Lisa's voice pulled him out of his thoughts.

He looked from her to the boys. "I think we had fun."

Nicky blinked at him. "I'm really sorry, Clay."

Clay resisted the urge to take the boy in his arms. "Hey, don't worry about it." He crouched down to Nicky's height. "I'm sorry I got you in a Truth or Dare bind."

Keith patted his brother. "And he coulda let you hang, Nicky. But he didn't."

Clay looked up in appreciation. "It's never a good idea to lie, kid. Even when it seems like an easy way to get things done."

"Come on, guys," Lisa slammed the van hatch door and ended the conversation with a bang. "Let's hit the road."

Slowly, Clay stood and held his knuckles out to Keith. "See ya around, kid."

Keith tapped him and turned to climb in the car.

Tiny arms clasped Clay's leg and he reached down to ruffle Nicky's silky blond hair. "Take care, Nicky."

Nicky looked up, the bloodshot eyes overflowing with unshed tears. "I'll miss you, dude."

The endearment sucker punched Clay in the solar plexus. "Me, too, dude." Then he helped him into the back seat, buckling his belt without looking into Nicky's miserable blue eyes.

Instead he turned and met his mother's, just as blue and just as miserable.

Was it only six hours ago those eyes were fluttering with pleasure and satisfaction? How did they go from that…to this?

"Bye, Clay," she said simply.

He started to reach for her, but the warning look she shot him was loud and clear. "Bye, Lisa."

She was in the driver's seat, buckled and backing out before he even had a chance to try again.

He stood there a long time, blinded by winter sun and something else that made his eyes blurry. Then he reached down, scooped up some fresh powder and blasted a snow ball as hard as he could across his lawn.

It broke apart against a pine tree and disintegrated in the air.

"I CAN'T THANK YOU enough, Valeen," Lisa hugged her closest friend and former coworker one more time. "This is really above and beyond the call on Christmas Eve."

"Oh, don't you worry, darlin'." The older woman tugged at Lisa's jacket, like a mother making sure her child was warm. "All my presents are wrapped, and my daughter and her husband won't show up until noon tomorrow. I don't mind babysitting for a few hours."

"They should stay asleep until I get back," Lisa assured her. "I just have to do this, Val."

Val took her hands. "Of course you do, dear. They'll be thrilled to see a tree here tomorrow morning."

"If there are any left," Lisa said. "I'm pretty sure the supermarket had a few trees when I was there yesterday."

"They might even be on sale."

"That'd be great. But I have some cash and this is important. It's bad enough Nicky thinks Santa has to climb through the kitchen window. I can't have him leave presents on the coffee table, too."

Val glanced at the two wrapped presents and a few other smaller gifts in the living room, then back at Lisa. "I still think you're plum crazy for leaving that racer man."

Lisa gave her a weak smile. "So you've said."

"The boys told me an awful lot, Lisa. Told me all about the *wedding*." With two fingers, she made exaggerated air quotes and lifted one eyebrow suggestively.

Lisa rolled her eyes. "Please. That was one crazy game of pretend."

Val nodded, but her look said she didn't agree. "The boys told me you kissed the groom. And weren't no pretending going on from what I hear."

Lisa felt heat burn her cheeks. "The groom kissed me." *A lot. All over.* "It was all just for effect."

Val chuckled and brushed Lisa's face. "Yeah, I can see the effect, all right."

"Bye, Valeen. I'll be back in an hour."

She navigated the apartment steps carefully, although they'd been brushed since that morning's light dusting of snow. The roads were nearly empty, but then, it was eleven o'clock on Christmas Eve. No one but Santa was out.

At the twenty-four-hour supermarket, the huge space where they'd been selling Christmas trees was dark and empty. A clerk informed her that all the trees had been shipped out that afternoon.

"But I just got finished tagging the artificial trees for half price," he said, pointing toward the far back of the store. "Not a whole lot left, but you might find a small one."

Thanking him, she headed to the corner where all things Christmas—or what was left of them— were lined up, bright half-price stickers drawing her attention.

The choice was limited, but she found a small tree with lights already on it and several boxes of not so pretty but functional ornaments. Kneeling on the ground to see the very back of the bottom shelf, she felt a shiver of déjà vu.

Of course she'd done this before. Once in her life. About a week ago, in a precious Christmas store stocked with Norman Rockwell reproduction ornaments. She'd bought so many they'd filled an eight foot tree. And garlands and bows and candles and…

She swiped a tear. What was the matter with her? She hated Christmas. And those boys wouldn't care about the quality or quantity of the decorations. They probably wouldn't even care if there was a tree, once they saw the Mighty Flight and Mighty Motor Remote Control toys.

Hopefully, the sight of the Kincaid logo wouldn't send Nicky into another crying jag.

Gathering up as much as she could afford, Lisa took her packages to the front, paid cash, wished the clerk a Merry Christmas and rolled a wobbly shopping cart toward the door.

Light, lacy swirls of white danced around the parking-lot lights. Lisa paused for a moment, taking in the sensation of Christmas cold. She turned her face up to it, and closed her eyes.

Would she ever see or feel snow again and not think of Clay Slater?

She blinked away the tears and launched her cart down the small ramp toward her van.

Where a man stood brushing away the flakes as they hit her windshield.

She froze mid-step and stared. Was she imagining this? Was her pain-numbed brain playing tricks with her?

Or was Clay Slater waiting for her, his familiar down vest not nearly warm enough and his familiar cocky grin burning hot?

"Merry Christmas," he called, just loud enough for her to hear him.

She pushed the cart an inch. "What are you doing here?"

"I was in the neighborhood."

She narrowed her eyes in distrust as she wheeled closer.

"I was," he insisted. "I was over at Thunder Racing all afternoon and most of the evening. Then I stopped by your apartment." At her look, he added, "The boys told me your address. You're smart to make sure they have it memorized."

She shook her head and half laughed. "I can't believe you're here."

"The nice lady at your apartment told me where to find you."

She would. "I…I decided to get the boys a tree."

He put one hand on the cart and eased it closer, pulling her with it. "Not quite what they left."

"Don't rub it in."

When she unlocked the minivan back door, he lifted it for her. "Let me help."

She nodded, watching him unload the bags and tuck the box for the artificial tree in place. When he finished, he closed the door and brushed his hands on his jeans, leaning against the minivan with an oddly expectant look on his face.

Lisa took in an icy cold breath, the chill hurting

her lungs. Or maybe that was just the agony of looking at the man she…really liked.

"Aren't you going to ask what I was doing at Thunder Racing?" he asked, cocking an eyebrow.

She hadn't even thought of it. She'd been so busy trying to reconcile the fact that he was there, in the parking lot, in her town.

"Why were you there?" she asked.

"I had some papers to sign." A maddeningly slow grin broke across his handsome face. "Aren't you going to ask what kind of papers?"

She shook her head and a cloud of white came out as she laughed. "Okay, Clay, what kind of papers?"

"Contract…ual things."

She frowned at him. "What kind of a *contract?*"

He nodded, still grinning.

"You got a contract to race for Thunder?"

He reached both arms out toward her. "I sure did, doll." Before she could take another breath, he embraced her and lifted her right off the ground and turned her around. "You are currently in the arms of the new driver of the second team for Thunder Racing."

She was currently in the arms of the most fascinating, sexy, appealing man she'd ever met. She drew back just enough to look at him. "I'm so happy for you!"

She didn't even think to stop from kissing him. It was natural, right and oh so perfect. As they kissed, he eased her back to the ground, not that her shaky legs could stand so well.

"Wait a second," she said, suddenly pulling away when a question popped into her head. "Who's the sponsor?"

"Kincaid Toys."

Her jaw dropped. "No."

He pulled her closer, warming her with the look in his eyes and the strength of his body. "Kincaid told Shelby Jackson everything that happened and I would love to have been a fly on the wall at that meeting."

"Was Shelby furious?"

He laughed. "She was blown away. She told me she convinced Kincaid right then and there that I was made of the same stuff her father was." His eyes widened. "Can you imagine? Thunder Jackson? My all time favorite driver in NASCAR history?"

Lisa giggled, his excitement infectious. "But how did she get Kincaid to change his mind?"

"She told him that her father would have loved that *stunt*—her word, not mine. And she persuaded him that anyone who wanted a ride that bad should have it."

"And you should," Lisa agreed.

"And I do." He tightened his hold on her. "Thanks to you and the boys. You should have seen how excited they were when I told them."

Once again, her jaw went slack. "Excuse me? When did you tell them?"

"About twenty minutes ago. I must have just missed you."

"You went to my apartment, woke up my boys and told them this before you told me?"

He chucked her chin. "Chill out, Mom. They're psyched. They're packing right now."

"They're...*what?*" Disbelief—or something—made her dizzy.

"I hope you don't mind. I brought them some suitcases." At her look of sheer incredulity, he added, "You, too. I thought it would be easier for the trip to Lake Norman tonight."

"Tonight?"

"Of course. So we can wake up there on Christmas morning."

All she could manage was a soft laugh. "You're crazy."

He closed the space between them and put his lips on hers. "Crazy is having a whole Norman Rockwell model home just sitting empty on Christmas morning. And who knows?" He kissed her quickly, then buried his fingers into hair, sending endless goose bumps down her back. "Santa might even stop by."

"Aw, Clay." She closed her eyes. "Don't do this to me."

"Don't do what?"

She could barely speak. "Don't torture me."

He tightened his grip just enough to raise her face to his. She opened her eyes and met his dark, determined expression.

"I don't want to torture you, Lisa. I want to make you happy. I want to wake up next to you and go to sleep with you in my arms. I want to laugh and cry and dream and race and do everything with you. I know you think I'm exactly the man you don't want. But I just proved Shelby Jackson and David Kincaid wrong, and I can prove you wrong, too."

"Clay, I don't want to play any more games."

"This is no game, Lisa." He lowered his face and brushed her mouth with his lips. "Give me a chance. Shelby did. Kincaid did. Will you?"

She drew back and looked into his eyes. "Just this once. For effect."

"Not for effect," he insisted. "Forever."

# EPILOGUE

*One Year Later*

"IF YOU JUMP ANY higher, dude, you will knock that tree over."

Nicky grinned at Clay, then Lisa. "Think I could?"

"You might." She scooped up the wrapping paper that littered the living-room floor. "Okay, you got your out-of-town gifts and your special package from the Kincaids. You better get to bed or Santa won't be down that chimney."

"He's not real," Nicky announced.

Keith burned his brother with a deadly glare but said nothing.

"Keith told me."

Lisa looked at her older child. "Did you?"

"Yeah!" Nicky said, bouncing again. "And he told me that he wants to marry Renata Kincaid."

"Cool," Clay said quickly. "Free toys for life."

Keith just closed his eyes in total disgust. But, Lisa noticed, he did not argue the point.

The kids had spent plenty of time together at various races over the last year, and if Keith and Renata had a budding ten-year-old romance, so be it. She loved Renata—all of the Kincaids had been wonderful to them.

They'd never again mentioned the debacle of the pretend Christmas, and simply accepted her for what she was: Clay Slater's girlfriend.

Clay knelt in front of the fireplace and stabbed the crackling logs with a poker. "I think it's time for you kids to go to bed, or the bearded man will not show."

Keith and Nick exchanged a look, then, smart boys that they were, disappeared upstairs.

"I'll be up in a minute to kiss you good night," Lisa called after them, cozying up next to Clay near the tree.

"Me, too," Clay promised, then he winked at her. "Just as soon as I kiss your mom for an hour."

In one smooth, fast move, he had her in his arms and halfway on his lap.

"You're fast, Slater," she teased. "But then you did make the Chase in your rookie year of NEXTEL Cup."

"Thanks to you."

"Me? I just cheer. And close my eyes when you pass on the outside." She demonstrated by closing her eyes, half-waiting for a kiss.

When nothing happened, she looked at him and sucked in a tiny breath at the wrapped box he held.

"Well, look what Santa just dropped down the chimney."

She slipped off his lap, eyeing the gift. "I recognize the wrapping paper." The Christmas Store, where once again, she'd selected more adorable ornaments and decor for the house. All Norman Rockwell, of course.

He held it toward her. "Merry Christmas, Lisa."

She gingerly took the box. It wasn't small enough to be what she really had hoped for, but she tamped down any disappointment. The past year had been the happiest of her life, and she and Clay didn't need a formal agreement to solidify their love.

She slipped off the bow and scraped a nail along the bottom of the paper. This box was precisely the size of the one he'd given her last Christmas, and when she lifted off the lid, she smiled.

"Another Norman Rockwell music box. Thank you, Clay." Her fingers touched the edge, ready to open it and listen to the song, when the unfamiliar painting reproduced on the top caught her eye.

It was classic Rockwell: a young couple peering over the massive old-fashioned desk of serious-looking clerk, watching him do paperwork. The young lady's yellow pump heels rose off the floor in anticipation, while her man wrapped a protective arm around her waist.

"I've never seen this one before," she said.

"It's called *Marriage License*."

Her heart stuttered and her fingers quivered. *Marriage License.*

"Open it, Lisa."

She looked up at him, her heart slamming against her ribs. His eyes were warm and intense, and full of expectation.

Slowly, she lifted the lid of the music box and heard the first few notes of a classical piece. There, tucked into the dark green felt, was one very familiar diamond wedding ring.

"Clay." She could barely speak. "Oh, Clay."

"Told you I could prove you wrong."

She let out a soft laugh that was far too thick with tears. "Yes, you did."

In front of her, he lifted himself to one knee. "For the second and last time, Lisa Mahoney, would you marry me?"

"For real this time?"

He laughed. "Unless you want Keith and Nick to come down and perform the honors outside again." He picked up the ring from the box, took her hand and slid it on her ring finger. "I love you, Lisa."

Blinking back tears, she looked from the ring to him. "I love you, too, Clay."

He held her hand to his mouth and kissed her fingers, never taking his eyes from her. "You know," he said, "I think I was half in love with you the first time we got married."

"Me, too. But then, I'm impulsive like that."

"I love impulsive." He lowered his face to hers, sliding his arms around her and easing her to the floor, just under the low branches of the Christmas tree. "And I love you."

Never had pine smelled so good. Never had her heart been so certain of where it belonged. Everything seemed so alive and full of joy that her whole being shuddered with happiness.

So *this* is what it felt like.

She broke the kiss and looked into his eyes. "Merry Christmas, Clay," she whispered.

For the first time in her life, she truly understood what that meant.

\* \* \* \* \*

*Turn the page for a sneak peek at
Roxanne St. Claire's next romance in the
NASCAR Library Collection
THUNDERSTRUCK
Coming in February 2007*

SHELBY JACKSON STEPPED though the door of Thunder Racing and sucked in a lungful of her favorite scent—motor oil and gasoline tinged with a hint of welding glue. No double espresso or honey-laden pastry could smell better in the morning. But there was something different in the air today. She sniffed again, drawn into the race shop by her nose and sixth sense.

There was something pungent, a little bitter and…fresh. Her heart jumped and her work boots barely touched the gleaming white floor as she hurried toward the paint and body shop. With a solid shove, she flung open the double doors and they smacked the walls with a satisfying, synchronized clunk.

And then she drank in the prettiest sight she'd seen in eight long years.

Number fifty-three lived again.

"Oh, Daddy," she whispered as she approached the race car, the hand over her mouth barely containing her delight. "You'd love it."

In truth, Thunder Jackson would roar like an eight-hundred-horsepower engine at the sight of a screaming yellow "fifty-three" surrounded by a sea of purple as painful as a fresh black eye. Then he'd calm down and throw his arm over her shoulders with a mile-wide grin and a gleam of approval in his eyes.

"Shelby girl," that gravelly voice would say, "you done good."

And she had.

She took a few steps closer, nearly reaching the driver's side. The insignia—and openmouthed, wide-eyed clown—may not be the sexiest logo to fly at two hundred mules an hour around a superspeedway but Kincaid Toys was a damn good sponsor. And Thunder Jackson would have known that, too.

"I didn't quit, Daddy," she whispered again, almost touching the glistening paint. Unwilling to risk a smudge, she held her fingers a centimeter from the cool metal, imagining the power surge that would sing through the carburetor and make this baby roar to a heart-stopping victory. "Just like you always said, Daddy. Never, never, never quit."

"Winston Churchill said that." A voice. Deep. Male. Nearby.

Shelby scanned the empty shop.

Then slowly, as if she'd conjured him up, a man

rose from the other side of the car. "Unless Winston is your daddy."

"Huh?" Lame, but it was all she could manage in the face of the eyes as green as the grass on the front stretch of Daytona, all she could say as she took in the sun-streaked hair that fell past his ears and grazed a chiseled jaw. Below that, a white T-shirt molded to a torso that started off wicked, slid right into sinful and braked hard over narrow hips in worn blue jeans.

"Which I highly doubt since Winston's children are—" his eyes gleamed, took a hot lap over her face and body and then returned to meet her gaze "—quite a bit older than you are."

He straightened to what had to be six feet two, judging by how he dwarfed the race car. "Not to mention," he added, a melodic British accent intensified by the upward curl of generous lips. "There's not a redhead in that whole family."

"Who…" *Are you?*

"Winston Churchill."

"You are?"

He laughed and Shelby felt the impact right down to her toes. Which, at the moment, were curled in her boots.

"No relation, I'm afraid. But since we're fellow countrymen, I feel the need to preserve history. To be perfectly honest, the quote was 'never, never, never give in' but it's been messed with over the years. And the man who said it was not your daddy."

Actually, it was. But who was she to argue with…perfection?

# UNBREAKABLE
## Debra Webb

## CHAPTER ONE

RUSSELL JACKSON, better known as Rush to his friends, was in trouble.

It wasn't the first time he'd been called onto the carpet for a minor misstep. He was only human after all. But it was the absolute first time in his career that his team owner had looked as somber as if his race car had been disqualified on a technicality.

*This was bad.*

Buck Buchanan heaved a lungful of frustrated air, his penetrating gaze staring straight through the man in front of him. "You're the best driver I've seen in a long time, Rush. The crowd loves you. You're the underdog everyone wants to see win."

Guilt immediately started its climb onto Rush's already sagging shoulders. "Thank you, Buck. Your opinion means a great deal to me."

Buck Buchanan was the top team owner in the business as far as Rush was concerned. He was a hands-on kind of guy who didn't mind getting greasy to get the job done. The whole team respected him—idolized him, really. Rush vividly remembered Buck's heyday as a driver. He was a legend, one in whose footsteps Rush had always dreamed of following. Three years ago that dream had come true for him. He didn't want anything to screw it up.

"So you understand," Buck said, steering Rush's attention back to the issue at hand, "when I say that this could take you down, son. No one's going to care how great your stats are if your honor is in doubt. NASCAR is more aware of its image now than ever. This could get ugly fast."

"I understand." Rush took a deep breath of his own. "The pictures are a hoax." He'd said this already, but Buck evidently needed to be sure he wasn't slanting the truth to suit his own best interests. Another first. Buck never questioned his word. Further proof just how serious this situation was.

"All right." Buck leaned back in his big leather office chair. This was where the unpleasant side of team business took place. *The office*. No one ever wanted to get called into the office. Racing strategy was never discussed in the office. Buck preferred doing team business in the family-style den he used as a conference room. He wanted everyone to feel right at home.

The owner's office was reserved for sorting out problems. And the pictures of Rush at a topless joint just over the state line were a *major* problem.

Despite the implications of these fabricated photos, the bottom line was he'd never set foot in that establishment. Never had and never would. Not only to keep his reputation untarnished, but more importantly, to keep his family happy. The fact that Rush had turned twenty-five this year didn't matter one little bit to his momma's way of thinking. If she thought he was going to strip clubs, she'd yank him up by the ear and drag him before the minister faster than a tailspin on a damp track.

"I guess it's a good thing then," Buck allowed, "that I have connections with the *Huntsville Times,* otherwise you'd be front page news this morning."

Relief flooded through Rush and weakened his knees. Thank God. "So this story won't be in the papers?" He held his breath, hoping he'd understood right.

Buck shook his head. "Not this time." That piercing gaze leveled on Rush once more. "But we need to find out who wants to see you go down badly enough to doctor photos. The *Times* has a huge circulation, Rush, and this could have done some real harm. Gossip rags are one thing, but the *Times* is a well-respected press."

"Yes, sir, I'm very much aware of that. But how do we find who's behind this?" Nobody wanted to do that more than Rush, but involving the police would only draw in more people and allow additional opportunity for leaks.

Buck took a moment to look over the items on his desk. A couple of major papers had reported sightings of Rush with different women, including an actress who'd recently separated from her husband. None of those stories had been as explicit as these latest photos. Still, Rush hadn't even been in Las Vegas when one of the rendezvous was supposed to have taken place. Another tabloid had reported his involvement in a bar brawl over yet another woman. That time he actually *had* been at the location, but none of the negative reports were anywhere near accurate.

Rush understood that with success came fame and with fame came a certain amount of unsavory attention. He'd been prepared for that. But this was different. These were flat-out lies that seemed targeted at his reputation, a reputation he'd worked especially hard to keep squeaky-clean.

"Whoever's coming up with these rumors is close, Rush." Buck tapped a picture accompanying one of the reports. "Someone in the room shot that photograph of you."

The sour taste of betrayal rose in Rush's throat. Buck was right. That picture had been taken at a private party for a crew member's birthday. Anyone there could have taken it. With practically all cell phones equipped with cameras these days, it was next to impossible to guess who. Or why. That alone wasn't the worst of it. The worst part was that all of the recent negative publicity was cloaked in just enough truth to be damaging. This seemed to indicate that whoever had leaked the photos had done so purposely, since some details were only known by those close to him.

But Rush wasn't ready to accept the possibility that a friend wanted to harm his image.

Yet.

"I know every single person who was there, Buck. So do you. The team, their families. Surely we're not accusing one of our own?" Rush had spent the past three years of his life with these people. He knew them as well as he did his own family. How could he even think such a thing?

"We're not accusing anyone," Buck allowed. "What we're doing is eliminating possibilities. The person who took the picture may have passed it on to someone, a friend maybe, who used it for this purpose. We have to find the source to find the culprit."

As nasty as this business was, Rush had no choice in the matter. These ugly rumors had to stop. "What do you want me to do? Whatever it takes, I'll make this right." The media liked playing up his bachelor status. That was one reason he'd sworn that he wouldn't get in too deep with any woman at this stage of his career. His focus needed to be on driving…on the race. Sure, he had the occasional date, but he kept it simple.

That was the most aggravating part of all this. *Someone* wanted the world to believe that Rush Jackson was a womanizing playboy, but the idea couldn't be farther from the truth. That didn't stop the tabloids from reporting it as gospel, though.

Bad, bad business. And it was up to Rush to help get to the bottom of it.

Buck surprised him then. He smiled.

"That's what I like most about you, son. You're the real McCoy. You just keep being you and focus on being the best damned driver in every lineup. I'll handle this problem."

Rush wanted to insist that this was his problem and he should take care of it, but Buck was right. This was the team's problem, and Buck was the boss.

"I *will* need your cooperation on a related venture, though," Buck said.

"Name it." Anything that would quash this mess here and now was all right by Rush.

"I've been mulling over an idea," Buck started off. "When I learned about this—" he tapped the photos on his desk "—I made my final decision and got on the horn to make it happen."

Anticipation burned through Rush. Whenever Buck Buchanan came up with an idea, it was a winner.

"There are still plenty of people out there," Buck reminded, "who don't consider what we do a real sport. Folks who don't want to look at our drivers as true athletes."

Unfortunately, he was right, but that misconception couldn't be farther from the truth. Most drivers these days, as well as crew members, stayed on top of physical fitness. Rush ran ten miles every other day, rain or shine. The other days he biked twice that many miles. He worked out at the team's private gym on the first floor of the Buchanan Building four times per week. No smoking, no drugs. He ate right, even stayed away from alcohol except on very rare, special occasions, and he got plenty of sleep. Probably a lot of folks would think his life was pretty boring except for those precious adrenaline-filled hours on the track.

"We're working hard to change that image," Rush said. Buck knew how far they'd come in that arena. He'd witnessed the changes over the past decade. "The people who really understand NASCAR know better."

Buck nodded. "But I want to reach the rest," he tacked on. "I want the world to know that we're every bit as athletic as those going for Olympic gold."

Now that might be pushing it. Rush felt sure getting that point across would be impossible, even if his training and commitment were as rigorous as any Olympian's. Some folks just weren't going to change their minds.

"I contacted the New England Institute for Independent Experts a few weeks ago and put a bug in their ear." Buck's expression beamed with excitement. He loved racing. Some folks swore that racing fuel ran through his veins. He lived and breathed the sport. Case in point—he'd be hitting forty in a couple of months and was still single. Single, and totally focused. "I suggested that a study on the athleticism of our drivers and crew members should be conducted to settle the question once and for all. I want an independent conclusion as to NASCAR's authenticity as a true sport. The board of directors agreed. When I called this morning, they were more than ready to jump at the chance."

Rush wasn't sure exactly where this was going, but he had a sneaking suspicion he wouldn't particularly like his part in it. "So they're going to do a study on the Rocket City Racers?" He purposely didn't say *on me*.

"The main thrust of the study will be on you," Buck explained, "but the whole team will be involved."

That was what he'd been afraid of. "So when do we start?" No one could ever accuse him of not being a team player. Especially considering the cloud currently hanging over him, pure gossip or not.

"Right away. We were very lucky that the Institute could move on this so quickly. They're sending down one of their best, a Dr. Max Gray. The analysis will take three or four days and I've assured your full cooperation."

"But it's only four days until Christmas." Rush hadn't really intended for the statement to sound quarrelsome, but who in their right mind would want to come all this way to do this now?

Buck lifted his broad shoulders in a shrug. "Apparently Dr. Gray has no problem with the timing. Do you? This is the only shot we've got at getting results back in time to use them before the season kicks off."

There was that. Rush shook his head slowly, though a part of him still resisted. "No problem. Whatever will work for Dr. Gray will work for me." His family was large and accommodating. His mom would love the opportunity to convert a Yankee with her home cooking, especially a holiday meal.

"If this report turns out the way I expect it will," Buck went on, "I'm going to launch a preseason promotional campaign called *Go for the Gold*. After last year's win at Daytona, I want to herald this year's season with a hell of a roar."

If anyone could do it, Buck Buchanan could.

"When do we start?"

Buck shuffled all the unflattering material on his desk into a pile and tucked it away in a drawer as if he'd already taken care of the problem. Rush hoped it would be that easy.

"You'll pick up Dr. Gray at the airport this afternoon at three o'clock. I've made hotel arrangements at the Embassy Suites. We'll have formal introductions with the rest of the team first thing in the morning."

Three o'clock…*today?*

"I know this is short notice," Buck said, taking Rush's silence for hesitation, "but it was the only way to ensure we had results by New Year's. I want this campaign off the ground with the New Year."

"Today is great." Determined to show proper enthusiasm, Rush took it a step farther. "As a matter of fact, I'm thinking maybe Dr. Gray should just stay at my folks' place. There's plenty of room and that way he could monitor my schedule starting when the rooster crows. You know everybody loves my momma. Let him see my life firsthand. I've got nothing to hide."

"You're sure your mom won't mind?"

Rush could see the thinly veiled enthusiasm for his idea. Buck wanted this Dr. Gray showered with Southern hospitality, and the Jackson family wrote the book on Southern hospitality.

"She won't mind at all. The whole brood's married off now. I'm the only one still living in that big old house anyway. There's lots of room." The more Rush thought about it, the better the concept sounded. "We'll show this Dr. Gray what we're made of down here in Alabama." Shoot, yeah.

"Outstanding." Buck pushed out of his chair. "I'll brief the rest of the team, you check in with your folks and welcome Dr. Gray."

"Yes, sir."

Rush headed for the door with a much lighter step than when he'd arrived.

Buck would handle the situation with the leak, intentional or not—most likely not—and Rush would take care of impressing Dr. Gray.

Rush Jackson might not have an Ivy League education but he had a reputation for being a nice guy, a *charming* guy. He'd never met a soul he couldn't win over.

Buck was a genius. This idea would be a real attention grabber for the sport.

For Rush, it would be a piece of cake.

## CHAPTER TWO

MAX GRAY STARED out the window as the plane bumped down onto the tarmac.

This was her first trip to Alabama.

Actually, it was her first trip south of the Mason-Dixon line.

Already she missed the snow she'd left in Boston. How could it be fifty-nine degrees in Huntsville, Alabama, this far into December? Not natural. As projected by the Weather Channel, it was ten or so degrees above average. The forecast looked much the same for the next five days. She had packed accordingly, although she didn't expect her observations to take a full five days.

While the plane taxied to the gate, she pushed her glasses up the bridge of her nose and opened the folder on her lap. Russell Jackson. Twenty-five, the same age as she. Never went to college. Every single job he'd held since graduating high school was related in one way or another to NASCAR.

Personally, she simply didn't see the appeal.

Roaring engines, screaming fans and drivers doing nothing more than driving in circles.

Perhaps that was harsh. She recognized that some amount of skill was required, certainly. But how hard could it be? In her estimation the whole concept boiled down to merely outmaneuvering the competition. Whether or not driving a race car required the same rigorous physical endurance requisite of a true athlete was yet to be seen.

A frown tugged at her brow as she considered the head shot and the list of physical characteristics Jackson's team owner had faxed to the Institute.

Russell Jackson had unusually pale blue eyes, contrasted sharply by coal-black hair. A handsome man by any standard. Six feet in height. One hundred and seventy pounds. Great cholesterol numbers, according to his last physical. Nonsmoker. No drugs. Conservative drinker, or so he claimed.

She sifted through the contents of the file and considered the reports she'd printed from the Internet. Evidently there were a number of unsavory newspapers who thought otherwise when it came to Jackson's drinking and dating habits.

Giving the man credit, she acknowledged that he was a celebrity and not everything printed about him could be presumed correct. But it was her job to find out if he was the clean athlete he professed to be.

He looked fit, but looks could be deceiving.

The next few days would provide the facts, which were all that counted in Max's book. Nothing more, nothing less, only the facts.

She placed the file into the leather attaché her father had given her for her last birthday and glanced at her wristwatch—2:51 p.m. Central Standard Time. Her father would be arriving in Bermuda about now. He preferred to spend his holidays in a more tropical setting.

Her mother, on the other hand, would already be ensconced in her cabin at Lake Tahoe. Skiing was on her agenda, and intimate dinners for two in front of a roaring fire—with her new, much younger boy-friend. At least when her mother was in the throes of a new passion she stayed out of Max's love life…or lack thereof.

Divorce turned adults rather childish, in Max's opinion. Her parents in particular, who quarreled whenever they shared the same airspace for more than ten minutes. Holidays had never been a particularly noteworthy occasion for the Gray family, but since the divorce ten years ago they had gone all but unnoticed.

Not that it mattered. Max was inordinately busy with her work. She didn't actually have time to get involved with lengthy dinners and formal parties. Take now, for example. If she and her family had made plans, she would simply have had to cancel them to take this assignment. Things were far better this way.

The seat-belt light went out and passengers started to move about as the pilot announced their safe arrival in the Rocket City.

Max remained seated until the first mad dash had passed. It was impossible for everyone to deplane at once, but that never stopped most passengers from attempting the feat.

Once the aisle was clear, she got up, careful not to bang her head. She always requested a window seat, not because she cared to take in the view, but because she preferred not to be constantly bumped and brushed by passersby.

Something else she always did was pack lightly and efficiently so that she didn't have to check a bag. Her bags consisted of her briefcase, her purse, of course, and one Pullman that met the carry-on restrictions.

"Here, ma'am, let me get that for you."

Surprised, Max turned from the overhead storage to the man behind her who'd spoken. "Thank you, but I'm fine."

Despite her assurance that she needed no help, the man reached past her and hefted her bag as if it weighed nothing at all. He placed it, wheels down, in the aisle and pulled the handle into position.

"There you go." He smiled broadly. "You have a nice day now."

Max pushed a polite smile into place. "Thank

you." She pivoted and started down the aisle, her Pullman right behind her.

She had to keep in mind that she was in the South now. People were different down here. The man who'd retrieved her bag probably felt compelled to do the heavy work for the opposite sex.

Quaint.

The journey from the gate to the main terminal exit past the security checkpoint took only three or four minutes. The crowd was minimal. Once beyond security she found it odd that no one was waiting with a sign indicating her name.

No one was waiting, period.

Strange.

At Logan, Kennedy, LAX or any of the other airports she frequented, there were always drivers waiting to pick up arriving VIPs or business travelers. Apparently that wasn't the case here.

She had committed Mr. Jackson's image to memory. She would certainly recognize him if she encountered him looking for her. A sign wouldn't actually be necessary.

On the first floor she moved through the baggage-claim area just in case he was waiting there for her. She didn't find him, so she continued through the terminal until she reached the exits. In this small airport, all three doors opened to the same area, so it didn't really matter which one she took.

A number of taxis waited at the curb. That, she recognized. Across the lanes that took the sparse traffic past the pickup and drop-off zone was a temporary parking area where more recent arrivals joined those waiting with open trunks and hatches.

That was where she found him.

Russell Jackson leaned against the back of his truck, one foot propped on the rear bumper. He wore a pair of faded jeans, what appeared to be cowboy boots and a denim jacket. Like her, he scanned the crowd. His attention landed on her, lingered several seconds, then moved on.

In that moment, to her utter dismay, she stopped breathing. Certainly not her typical reaction to the assessing gaze of the opposite sex.

Irritation zipped along her nerve endings, whether from her uncharacteristic reaction or from annoyance that he didn't bother to acknowledge her, she couldn't precisely say.

When he made no move to cross to her side of the thoroughfare, she squared her shoulders and headed his way. Apparently not all Southern men still clung to the old rules. Mr. Jackson showed no signs of caring whether she handled her own bag, which she generally did anyway.

She wouldn't hold that against him. His chivalry or lack thereof was irrelevant.

His gaze landed on her once more as her destination became obvious. This time he surveyed her quite carefully, top to bottom and back actually.

She squared her shoulders, resisted the urge to adjust her glasses and strode straight up to him. "Mr. Jackson?" she asked, in an effort to prompt his recognition and give him an opportunity to save face. Evidently he had not been provided with enough relevant information regarding her identity.

Confusion claimed his expression, affirming her theory.

"I'm Dr.—"

"Where's Dr. Gray?" he cut in, easing off the truck and coming to his full height. He glanced past her as if expecting someone else to come along.

Now she saw the whole picture. He hadn't realized the person he was meeting was a woman. "I'm Dr. Gray."

Surprise flickered in those uncommonly light blue eyes. "Er…okay." He immediately reached for her bag. "Sorry, I thought—"

"That I was a man," she offered, trying quite genuinely not to be amused by his befuddlement.

A smile that could only be called dreamy slid across his lips. "Oh, no, ma'am, I would never in a million years think *you* were a man." He surveyed her again, taking the journey even slower this time, unabashedly inventorying her black slacks and blazer as well as the soft charcoal sweater beneath.

Her cheeks burned for the first time in too long to remember. She suddenly wished she hadn't bundled her long hair into a French braid so that perhaps it would hide her foolish reaction. Too late for that, however.

"Well." She offered her hand. "I am Dr. Max Gray, the Max is for Maxine, and I presume you're Mr. Russell Jackson." She never made apologies for the fact that she was usually presumed to be a man. Presumptions were the bane of human existence. If people learned to operate on fact, as she did, life would be far less complicated.

Long fingers, much softer than she'd anticipated, closed around her hand and gave it a quick shake. "Call me Rush, ma'am, everybody does."

"Rush." That the single word issued so smoothly from her lips annoyed her further. This was not like her. At all.

"You look like you could use a good meal," he said as if he'd noticed something about her that made him say as much. "Dream Land Barbecue makes some mean ribs. We could stop in on our way home. Dinner's at seven, but the ribs'll tide you over."

While he loaded her bag into the bed of his truck, she deciphered what he'd said. Suggesting that she could use a meal was probably his way of asking her if she was hungry—either that or he considered her too thin. "Mean ribs" surely meant tasty.

The one point that left her curious—no, not curious, *concerned*—was the last...*on our way home.*

"Where are we going?" she asked, suspicion nudging out etiquette.

"The first place we're going, little lady," he said as he ushered her around to the front passenger door "is to get you something to eat."

He opened the door and waited for her to climb aboard. She stalled. "Mr. Jackson—"

"Rush," he reminded.

"Rush," she amended. "I had an early lunch before I got on the plane. So, I'm fine. Why don't you take me to my hotel and we'll discuss our agenda en route." With that settled she climbed into the seat and reached for her safety belt.

When her gaze bumped into his once more she knew it wasn't going to be as simple as that.

Another of those wide grins spread across his face, lighting up his pale blue eyes. "Mr. Buchanan and I didn't want you stuck in some generic hotel, ma'am. Besides, the house is plenty big. You won't even know we're there until mealtime."

He was serious.

Before she could argue, he closed the door and strode quickly around to the driver's side.

When he'd fastened his own safety belt and started the engine, she inquired, "Are you suggesting that I stay in your home?"

"Absolutely." He shot her a wink. "We want you to feel right at home. That's the way we do things down here, ma'am."

This was definitely a first. Unfortunately, it was never, ever going to work.

# CHAPTER THREE

DR. GRAY WAS A WOMAN.

Thin as a rail, to be sure, but every inch female.

As he took the North Parkway exit headed toward home, he glanced over at her. She stared out at the passing city that probably looked like a hole in the wall compared to Boston.

He hated to pass judgment too quickly, but she acted a little uppity to him. Or maybe she was just one of those uptight big-city women. He'd met a few. None who looked like her, he had to admit.

Dr. Maxine Gray was different. Pretty, in a sweet, girl-next-door way. He just didn't see why she would want folks to call her *Max*. Maybe that was her way of putting distance between herself and people she didn't know.

She wore her dark brown hair back in a long, loose braid, little wisps escaping here and there. Glasses, the accountant type with narrow black frames, added to the uptight theme and attempted to hide her brown eyes. Didn't work too well, though.

Her eyes were wide and expressive even behind those all-business glasses.

When he'd shaken her hand, she'd been ready to let go in an awful big hurry. Small hands. Very delicate. Truth was, she *looked* delicate. Fragile.

His gaze slid down to the briefcase she carried. She probably had a file in there on him. Not that he hadn't expected her to. It just felt a little weird being analyzed by a complete stranger.

Of course, he should be used to it by now. Tens of thousands of folks assessed him pretty darned closely on race days. But that was different. Those were the fans, his extended family. He tried hard not to disappoint them. Well, he would try just as hard not to disappoint this little lady.

And he'd have to remember not to call her "little lady." He'd let it slip at the airport, but big-city women didn't like that kind of thing. It wasn't like he meant anything by it. Still, she wouldn't like it and he'd have to try not to step on her toes.

"So what's our agenda?" he ventured when she didn't.

She swung her attention back to him. "Oh…yes." She looked straight ahead and cleared her throat. "I'll observe your workout routine as well as your race-day preparations, whatever those might be. I'm looking for your normal routine, Mr.—Rush, that's all." As she spoke she seemed to draw her shoulders up a little straighter. He wondered if that was her way of shifting into work mode.

"Sounds like a plan," he noted when she didn't say more.

She glanced at him before turning her attention back to the street. "As long as we understand each other there won't be any glitches."

"I'm certain we won't have any glitches, ma'am." He tried to sound reassuring, but she sounded less than convinced.

He hadn't really expected to get a feel for where she stood on the subject of his athleticism. After all, she was supposed to be an *independent* expert. But, admittedly, he had hoped to be able to read her just a little.

She was about as easy to read as a closed book written in Greek.

Oh, well, he'd have to wait and see like everyone else.

Just outside the Huntsville city limits he took a right onto Medford Road. The Jackson home place was one of the few farms still left this close to the city that hadn't been turned into a subdivision. As long as he was alive he intended to see that it stayed that way, and his four sisters and one brother felt the same.

He picked up on the subtle change in Dr. Gray's posture when he turned left onto Jackson Lane. She was curious about his home. His mind quickly wandered into forbidden territory. She had a nice nose. Small and cute. And she kept pushing her glasses up the bridge of that slender little nose. He smiled, couldn't help himself. If he blocked out the fancy black suit, she looked exactly like a girl headed for her first day of high school. That was the other thing about her, she looked young. Really young.

"Is there something you'd like to say, Mr. Jackson?"

Well, damn. She'd caught him sizing her up? He snapped his eyes front and center. "I...I was just wondering how long you'd been doing this independent expert study stuff." A bald-faced lie but it could work...if he was lucky.

"Four years."

Now wait a minute. He parked his truck, shut off the engine and shifted his full attention to her. "How old were you when you graduated college? Twelve?"

She turned her head and stared directly at him. "Sixteen. Then I spent four years in medical school and one year on a fellowship before receiving the offer to join the Institute."

Yep. She was really smart. A genius, from the sound of things.

He figured that was already one strike against him in her eyes. He'd never even gone to college. He'd done all right in high school. Hadn't been Valedictorian or anything, but he was damn good at what he did. Nothing wrong with being proud of hard work. This wasn't a competition, anyway.

Now he was analyzing himself.

"That's amazing, Dr. Gray," he said with all sincerity. "Your folks must be real proud."

She looked surprised at his comment. Before she could say anything, if she even intended to, his mom was on the porch waving madly.

"Is that your mother?"

He smiled. "Yes, ma'am."

Rush hopped out and skirted the hood to open Dr. Gray's door. She was halfway out before he reached her. He'd figured she'd do that. "I'll get your bag," he offered.

"I can take care of it," she countered firmly.

He held up his hands stop-sign fashion, then pointed to the house. "Not in front of my momma, she'd have my hide. You go on, I'll be right behind you."

Max glanced toward the house and the woman waiting there. Rush's mother smiled and waved. Max lifted her hand and waved back.

She needed a hotel.

No ifs, ands or buts.

The Jackson family home was nice. A two-story white frame house with a corner-to-corner front porch. Well maintained. Not the first sign of chipping paint or neglect of any sort. Large trees loomed close by, their branches bare for the winter. She imagined the huge oaks and maples provided sufficient shade in the summer. All nice, homey details anyone would appreciate. Just not in this particular situation.

"No need to be shy, Dr. Gray," Rush said as he walked up beside her. "You'll like her. Everybody does."

"Of course."

Max followed him across the spacious lawn. Keeping up with his long, confident strides took two steps to his every one. Moving alongside her he seemed somehow taller than his file had indicated.

He gestured for her to take the steps to the porch before him. She did. Getting this over with as quickly as possible was necessary. It wasn't that she didn't appreciate the invitation, but a hotel would be much more comfortable for her. She spent a great deal of her time in hotels. Hotels she understood, knew what to expect. But this? She faced Rush Jackson's mother. This was outside her comfort zone. She needed neutrality and distance.

"Dr. Gray, this is Evelyn Jackson." Rush moved to his mother's side. "Momma, this is Dr. Maxine Gray from Boston."

The abrupt reach toward Max was so sudden, so completely unfathomable, that for several seconds she couldn't respond in an appropriate manner.

Evelyn Jackson hugged her. Not the cheek-to-cheek air hugs to which she was accustomed, this was a full upper-body-contact embrace.

"Welcome to our home, Maxine." Evelyn gave her one last squeeze before drawing back. Even then she didn't let go, but held on to Max's arms. "You sure are a pretty thing," she added with a bright smile. "We're so glad to have you." She turned to her son. "Rush, take her bag up to Ashley's old room."

"Yes, ma'am."

Before Max could argue, he'd walked right past her, snagging her briefcase as he went, and disappeared through the front door.

That wasn't supposed to happen.

Evelyn hooked her arm around Max's, drawing her attention back to the other woman. "Come on into the kitchen and we'll have tea."

Despite her trepidation, that sounded like an excellent idea. "Thank you, Mrs. Jackson."

"Call me Evelyn, darlin'. No need for formalities around here. We're just plain folk."

Max managed a nod. "Evelyn."

Her hostess kept talking as they entered the house, but Max was too busy taking in the details of Rush Jackson's home to actually listen.

The front entrance opened into a center hall. To the left was a large living room that had earned its name. Two overstuffed sofas and three chairs were arranged around the room with a big-screen television as the focal point. The furnishings showed the wear and tear of everyday use.

Before a large front window stood a grand Christmas tree. As large and full as the tree was, it remained undecorated. Perhaps the family hadn't gotten around to that part yet. Max couldn't remember the last time she'd had a Christmas tree in her home...maybe before she went off to college.

*Before the divorce.*

Banishing the unexpected thought, she followed Evelyn across the hall to a more formal room that Evelyn called a "gossip parlor." A wood-burning fireplace with an intricately carved mantel captured her attention immediately. Framed family photographs lined the rich wood of the mantel. The furnishings in this room looked scarcely touched and were probably family heirlooms. Definitely antiques. Yet it was the photographs that drew her attention again and again as she considered the room.

"This," Evelyn said as she picked up one of the frames, "is my Robert."

Max studied the photograph of a much younger Evelyn and a handsome man from whom Russell— Rush—had no doubt inherited his good looks.

"He passed away three years ago, just before Rush ran his first big race."

"I'm sorry for your loss, Mrs.—Evelyn."

The older woman pressed the photograph to her chest as if she could hug the man pictured there. "There isn't a day goes by that I don't miss him."

Evelyn Jackson then went through the framed memories, giving Max a detailed history of each, some of which would be useful in Max's analysis. After all, family history played a significant part in who people became.

She learned that Rush had four sisters and one brother, all older and married. He was the baby, as Evelyn called him, and still lived at home. Max had to wonder about a twenty-five-year-old man who lived with his mother. But she would reserve judgment for now.

When Evelyn placed the final framed photograph back into its special position on the mantel, she urged Max toward the door. "Let's have that tea now."

Just down the entry hall beyond the staircase was a massive kitchen and a large dining area, all in one big room that claimed at least half of the downstairs floor space. The kitchen smelled like fresh bread. Rush was already there, peering into the refrigerator.

"Come keep Maxine company," Evelyn ordered. "I'll take care of that."

"She likes being called Max," he said to his mother, since Max hadn't bothered to correct her. He winked at Max as he said this.

To her utter dismay, Max found herself holding her breath as Rush walked her way. Why would she do that? Admittedly there was a grace about the way he moved, a fluidity that fascinated her on some unconscious level. But he certainly wasn't the first good-looking man with appealing body language she'd ever met. Maybe it was that silly wink he'd tossed so casually in her direction.

He'd shed the denim jacket. The navy flannel shirt he wore beneath served as a sharp contrast to those pale, pale blue eyes. Did he do that on purpose, she wondered? Or was blue simply his favorite color?

He gestured to a chair at the long dining table. "Make yourself at home, Max."

She started to mention that keeping things a bit more formal between them would be for the best, but that very well could be construed as rude considering his mother had already used her first name repeatedly. And he *had* insisted that she call him Rush. She needed these people cooperative, not defensive.

With his assistance, Max settled into one of the chairs. For himself, Rush chose the one at the end of the table next to where she sat. "I guess you got the family photo tour."

"Yes. You have a large family." She glanced past him, out the windows to the open pastures that rolled out in every direction. Maintaining eye contact was too uncomfortable just now. The wide-open space of his home and the surrounding land made her think that her tiny apartment back in Boston would easily fit into this room.

"You have brothers and sisters?"

Reluctantly, her gaze reconnected with his. "No."

His eyebrow drew together as if her answer puzzled him or concerned him in some way. "This is awfully close to Christmas to drag you away from your folks. I feel kind of bad about that."

If she hadn't been looking directly into his eyes, she might have considered his comment merely idle conversation. But clearly he meant what he said.

"No need," she assured. "We rarely celebrate the holidays together." In reality, they rarely celebrated, period. Holidays had never been a priority. Their schedules had always been too busy. Her father's research as well as his teaching at Harvard kept his calendar quite full. As an archaeologist, her mother traveled most of the time. Now that she thought about it, Max couldn't actually remember the last time they'd all been together in one place.

"It's against your religion?"

Max blinked. What was he asking her? "Excuse me?"

"You don't celebrate holidays because of your religion?"

Oh. "No, it's not that." That he genuinely looked

concerned surprised her all over again. "We're all very busy, Rush. Holidays are simply something we don't take the time to do."

"Don't you worry none, darlin'." Evelyn placed a tray on the table, barging right into the conversation. "We'll show you how it's done." She placed a tall glass with a lemon wedge perched on the rim in front of Max. "If we're lucky the good Lord will bless us with a little snow for the occasion."

Iced tea. Max stared at the glass. She'd forgotten about that. Southerners liked their tea sweetened and served over ice. She pressed her lips firmly together to prevent a frown.

Evelyn settled into the chair across the table from Max. "We'll have stew for dinner tonight," she announced. "And fresh-baked bread."

Rush made a sound that indicated this was good news, indeed.

Max tried to look pleased as well. She wasn't a vegetarian but she was quite selective in the meats she ate and how they were prepared.

Evelyn then launched into stories about her son's childhood. Rush pretended to be embarrassed, but Max wasn't so sure that was an accurate assessment. The more she listened and watched, the more certain she became that the man simply adored his mother and anything she said was okay with him.

Strange. She and her mother had lengthy conversations occasionally, but theirs lacked this familial hierarchy, and, to Max's displeasure, usually revolved around her ongoing single status. Her mother firmly believed that her daughter should get a life, as she put it.

The iced tea wasn't so bad. A little sweet, but quite refreshing. As much as she enjoyed listening to Evelyn's tales about her son and his siblings, Max was glad when Rush showed her to her room.

She needed quiet. Distance. She needed to find her footing in this new environment and to analyze what she'd seen and heard so far.

Mainly, she just needed to be alone.

"This was my sister Ashley's room. I hope it's okay."

Pink walls and a white canopy bed. Cheerleading and dance trophies filled a number of pristine white shelves. Posters of some celebrity Ashley had apparently idolized still adorned one wall.

"This is nice." Max turned to face the man. She really needed to make him understand this point without offending him. "A hotel would really be better, Rush. I don't want to intrude like this."

"Whoa there." He held up his hands and shook his head. "You're not intruding at all. We won't have you staying at some hotel all alone. It's almost Christmas. It's not right for anyone to be alone at Christmas."

Again she was surprised by the sincerity in those eyes that continued to throw her off balance.

"Besides," he went on, a smile toying with one corner of his mouth, "my momma's just tickled to death to have you here. She loves company."

And there was her dilemma. Max certainly couldn't insist on going to a hotel and risk hurting Rush's pride—or his mother's feelings.

How scientific was that?

"Besides," Rush suggested, "I was thinking that this way you could get firsthand knowledge of my training." The smile spread into a full-fledged grin. "I apologize in advance, but I like to start at the crack of dawn. I'd love for you to join me, if you're up to it."

If she was up to it? Please.

Something else he said filtered through that competitive layer she was never quite able to suppress as well as she'd prefer. Firsthand knowledge. He was right. She'd have time to explore his home, his room. His mother loved to talk, so getting her to spill her guts wouldn't be a problem.

Oh, yes. This was actually quite good.

This was the perfect way to assess from the inside out how Russell "Rush" Jackson lived.

"You're right," she relented. "Staying here is an excellent idea. And I'll be happy to join you for a run."

All she needed to know was his estimation of the time that constituted the crack of dawn.

## CHAPTER FOUR

SHE KEPT UP FOR THE first four miles.

Four miles at his pace and Dr. Max Gray had hung in there just like one of the boys.

Rush was impressed.

She might look delicate, but she darn sure held her own in a full-throttle run.

At least for a little while.

The last six miles had gotten the better of her. He'd slowed down out of respect, but she'd insisted that he keep going at his usual pace. She would catch up.

So that was what he'd done. He resisted the impulse to look back and see how far behind she was at this point. That would only rub in the idea that she was way behind him.

When he hit the ten-mile mark, he slowed to a walk for his cooldown.

The pavement was no longer damp from last night's rain. He drew the clean air into his lungs. Another mile and the route would bring him back to his starting point, the Buchanan Building. His training didn't include an indoor track. Nope. He used the environment as part of his workout, especially the scorching summer days. It was hotter than Hades inside the car on the track most of the time during racing season, might as well train under the right conditions. Most folks thought he was crazy to run in the middle of the day, especially in July and August, but he needed the heat to mimic the interior of the car during a few hundred laps. That was another reason for selecting this particular route. The city's concrete and asphalt radiated heat in the summer.

She was catching up to him now. He heard the slap of her Nikes on the asphalt.

He still didn't look back.

"What's next?" she asked as she came up beside him, synchronizing her movements with his.

Rush bit back the urge to ask her if she really wanted to know the answer to that. She had to be dog tired.

"Now, I hit the gym for a little weight training, then the shower. After that," he said with what should have been a quick glance at her. "We have lunch."

He told himself not to keep looking...but he just couldn't resist. Her chest rose and fell rapidly as she fought to catch her breath, but that wasn't even the part that rattled him. It was the whole outfit. Not sweats like he'd worn, not shorts, either. Nope, she had on some kind of sleek formfitting bodysuit like a competitive cross-country runner. If there had been a single doubt about what kind of curves existed beneath that black business suit she'd arrived in, there wasn't any now.

She paused at the door that would lead into the lobby of the Buchanan Building. "I'll need to take your vitals again."

He nodded. "No problem."

Shifting his attention to anything other than her petite form, he opened the door and followed her inside. He led the way to the gym and right back to the small examination room used for routine exams with the team's personal-fitness trainer. Rush didn't wait to be told to strip off the sweatshirt. He'd been through this routine with her once already. Only this time sweat had plastered his T-shirt to his chest. Probably nothing she hadn't seen before.

As he leaned against the exam table, she entered more info into the handy-dandy minicomputer that fit right in her palm, or into the case clipped to her waist. She'd already entered his height and weight and a dozen other details he hadn't even known about himself before they got started that morning.

When she'd finished entering data, she reached into the bag she'd left in the exam room earlier that morning and retrieved her stethoscope and BP monitor.

Strapping the cuff around his bicep, she checked his blood pressure. After recording that data in her little computer, she took his pulse rate and then prepared to listen to his chest.

She hesitated as she reached for his T-shirt. He imagined that she didn't look forward to touching the sweaty shirt. "Sorry." He peeled off the tee and waited for her to do her thing.

That she still hesitated made him frown. Maybe she would rather wait until after he'd showered.

Then she reached for him, the stethoscope's shiny metal disk in her hand.

The metal was cold against his skin. He shivered. Her fingers trembled. He pretended not to notice since she was clearly uncomfortable.

She listened. Moved the disk to a new location and listened some more, intently focused on her work.

He held as still as possible, tried not to breathe. He would have made it through the whole ordeal just fine if she hadn't licked her lips. Air rushed out of his lungs so suddenly that her head snapped up.

"Sorry," he muttered again.

She tore off the stethoscope and tucked it back into her bag. "You move on to weight training now?"

Those big brown eyes peered at him through the unflattering glasses.

"Yeah. Not to bulk up, just for endurance. Staying

lean is important," he added in case she didn't know that already. He dragged his T-shirt back on. "I work on overall muscle tone and endurance." He'd said that already, hadn't he?

She nodded. "I noticed your body fat percentage is lower than average for a man your age, twelve percent maybe."

She said this matter-of-factly but somehow she wouldn't hold his gaze…as if she didn't like looking at him or that the subject embarrassed her. Impossible. He had to be making too much out of this.

"Leaner is better," he clarified, steering his thoughts back on target. "Bulking up would make me heavier and less agile."

More information went into her little computer and then she followed him over to the free weights. His routine took only a half an hour, during which time she silently watched and entered more notes. He had never been more thankful than when it was over. The whole situation was crazy ridiculous and somehow he couldn't get a hold on his runaway reactions.

"That's it." He scrubbed his arm across his forehead to keep the sweat from dripping down into his eyes. He didn't usually get this overheated but for some reason today he'd felt on fire.

She lifted her eyebrows in what he took to be surprise. "That's it?"

"You think there should be more?" That one sneaked out on him. He hadn't meant to ask the question, didn't want to open up that can of worms, but there it was. Now she knew for certain he was anxious about her assessment. About *her*, if truth be told.

"My question wasn't intended as a measure of what I've seen so far, Mr.—Rush. I was merely verifying that you were finished for the day."

He felt pretty sure that was a "no comment," except he wasn't sure since she kept her tone real neutral. No use borrowing trouble. Besides, he had no reason to be worried about this evaluation. His workout was plenty grueling—she'd learned that firsthand.

"Now I head for the showers." He gestured to the door that led into the men's locker rooms. Several of his crewmates had already headed that way. Most of the team had the same workout schedule, but the length of the run and the biking differed for everybody.

"Excellent." She slipped her little computer into its holster. "I'll do the same."

*No way*, Rush thought. Even he had his limits. Doctor or no, she wasn't going into the locker room with him.

"I'll see you in twenty," she told him as she headed for the ladies' side of the locker rooms.

He was pretty sure his face was fire-engine-red, considering the smile on hers. She'd known exactly what he'd been thinking.

"Yeah. Sure." He meandered off in the other direction.

*Dumb, Rush. Real dumb.*

He hesitated, peeled off his T-shirt and fought the need to kick himself for being such an idiot. For some totally insane reason he'd spent a good portion of the morning doing some observing of his own. He'd kept looking for Dr. Max Gray to show signs of being attracted to him.

There he'd said it…if only in his head.

Maybe he was letting all the fame and glory go to his head. Not every woman had to see him as handsome and charming.

Especially not this woman. She was doing a job. She probably didn't even like racing. She was a scientist. A genius. She most likely thought he was just some dumb hick who didn't know how to do anything but drive a car around a track.

Why the heck was he so bent on finding some spark where one couldn't possibly exist?

Because he'd lost his mind, that was why. Here Buck was doing everything he could to turn this negative media attention around, and Rush had to go looking for trouble.

From this second on he would do better. He would treat Dr. Gray the same way she treated him—like a lab specimen...a test subject.

Maybe there was still a chance he could get through this.

MAYBE THERE WAS STILL a chance she could get through this.

There had to be a logical explanation for her reactions.

Max had almost made it to the locker-room door. *Almost*. She would have gotten away without incident if she just hadn't looked back.

But she had.

He was nearly to the men's locker-room door before he did the one thing she would have been far better off not to have witnessed twice in one day.

He paused briefly...just long enough to peel off his T-shirt.

Had she not been a trained physician and known that the feat was impossible—considering she hadn't dropped dead—she would have sworn that her heart stopped.

Since the crack of dawn, which had turned out to be five o'clock, she had observed and assessed every flex and extension of dozens of muscles... all belonging to Rush Jackson. He'd worn sweatpants, a tee and a sweatshirt over that. And still she'd observed the languid ripple of well-honed male muscle beneath the layers. Even the skullcap he'd pulled over that thick dark hair hadn't detracted from his appeal.

For hours earlier that morning he had played video games especially developed to sharpen eye-hand coordination. He'd watched dozens of race videos focused on the competition to study the maneuvers of the other drivers. His keen focus had impressed her, but nothing about those long hours had prepared her for the actual physical workout to come.

The run she'd gotten through, barely. Not that she wasn't physically prepared for a ten-mile run; she simply wasn't accustomed to his pace or his stride length. As if watching him from behind all those miles hadn't been troubling enough, then he'd stripped off his T-shirt right in front of her—not once but twice. While listening to his heartbeat she'd actually trembled just touching him. Trembled! Her! It was wholly ridiculous.

Adding insult to injury, she'd watched every flow of sinew beneath all that sweat-drenched skin as he'd lifted weights for what had felt like an eternity.

When he finally disappeared beyond the doors marked Men, she blinked and finally found the wherewithal to push through the ones marked Women.

She had examined dozens of human bodies, male and female, she reminded herself as she made her way to the locker where she'd stored her things.

How could she lose her objectivity so frighteningly fast?

Max sank down onto the closest bench. Not once in her entire life had she been so obsessed—and that was all she could call this—with a male physique.

The impulse to call her mother was suddenly overwhelming, but she chased it away.

Her mother had warned her this would happen one day. She said avoiding men was like a chocolate addict neglecting her craving. At some point, there was bound to be a breakdown in discipline.

Was *this* her breakdown?

Certainly she'd never experienced such an uncharacteristic attraction before. Most assuredly not when the subject of her distraction was also the subject of her work.

And it wasn't that she never dated. She'd had a couple of short-term relationships. She was twenty-five, for goodness' sake. It had simply been a while...quite a while. Her mother's words echoed in her ears. But Max didn't purposely avoid men. She was on the road more often than not and she absolutely refused to become physically involved with strangers. She would leave that up to her mother.

Her thoughts shifted from men to mothers so

abruptly the room spun just a little. Evelyn Jackson
was nothing at all like Vivian Gray. Max's mother
was ultramodern and completely uninhibited, a true
forward thinker. Evelyn, on the other hand, was extremely conservative. She spoke frequently of
church and God and family, pretty much in that
order. The sheer number of events the Jackson family
had planned around the coming holiday astounded
Max.

Like Rush, his mother had been up at the crack
of dawn. Before, actually. The coffee had already
been brewed when Max came downstairs. Evelyn
had promised a full breakfast and she hadn't failed
to follow through.

If last night's meal was any measure, the Jackson
family never went hungry. Though red meat had
been on the menu, Max had to admit she'd been surprised at the lack of fatty seasoning Mrs. Jackson had
used. Other than the sweetened tea, the meal had
passed muster for an athlete's regimen.

So had the workout. No question.

And he hadn't faked one second of any of it. An
athlete who worked out regularly maintained a
slower heart rate during physical exertion. Anyone
who didn't work out regularly was busted the
moment their blood pressure and heart rate were
measured. You simply couldn't fake those statistics.

Max showered and slipped on black slacks and a

matching sweater. Her trouser socks and leather flats were black as well. A coat wouldn't be necessary with this heavy pullover. Mrs. Jackson thought maybe there would be snow for Christmas. Max had wanted to warn her not to count on it, but opted not to. Surely the local news provided a seven-day forecast similar to the Weather Channel's. There would be no snow in north Alabama for Christmas.

Max quickly dried her hair and twisted it into a hasty braid. She'd lost some time with all that woolgathering.

Rush waited for her in the corridor outside the locker rooms. "I thought I'd show you how we log in our workout hours."

Max slung her bag over her shoulder and followed him to the desk in the gym's lounge. A large white board on the wall listed every crew member and the days of the month. Each one had checked off his or her completion of a workout on a given day.

"Once a month," Rush explained, "we rate each other just to make sure we're achieving the next level of fitness. Every other month the physical trainer comes in and does the same. This way we stay on track."

Several of the names on the board she recognized from people he'd introduced her to that morning. She checked her watch. "What I've seen today is your typical workout?"

"I alternate running and biking, but I only come to the gym four days per week. So, yeah, I'm usually finished about this time every day. Some days we have practice runs or other driving-related tasks first thing in the morning. On the days we don't I work on eye-hand coordination like I did this morning."

Rush watched her enter more data into her handheld computer. She would make a great poker player. No way could he get even a hint of what she was thinking. Since it wouldn't do him any good to obsess about that, he surveyed her petite form instead.

Black and black. He wondered if she always wore black. Before he'd picked her up at the airport he'd imagined a white lab coat. But then, he'd thought she was a man, and he'd been wrong about that part, too.

She wore her hair in one of those long, loose braids again. Though he knew she'd just fashioned it, because her hair had been in a ponytail before her shower, her hairdo had that slept-in look. Silky wisps had slipped loose to hug her face and neck. He liked that she wasn't one of those women who spent hours ensuring everything was perfect. As far as he could tell she didn't wear any makeup at all. He liked that, too.

Other than the fact that she didn't talk a lot and she didn't appear to have any close family ties, she seemed real nice...real likable.

His mom called her shy. Too early for Rush to tell about that. He glanced at the ring finger of her left hand. No sign she'd ever worn a wedding band. He wondered if she had a boyfriend and, if she did, why he hadn't put up a fuss when her job took her so far from home this close to the holidays.

And absolutely none of that was any of his business. Not to mention he'd just made up his mind to be objective about her. So much for self-discipline.

"What happens the rest of the afternoon?"

Those wide brown eyes peered up at him through those very businesslike glasses. He wished she would take them off…just for a little while.

"When the weather doesn't cooperate, like now, for a test or practice run, we work on other aspects of training. Training videos related to the competition, sort of like I did this morning. Safety updates from manufacturers. There's always an update to regulations that we need to become familiar with and—"

She held up a hand. "Wait. Did you say when the weather doesn't cooperate, *like now?* It rained last night but the sun is shining now."

"That was an hour ago, ma'am."

Confusion drew her eyebrows together and she looked as cute as all get-out. "It's ten degrees above average out there. It's practically summer."

He lifted one shoulder and let it drop. "Bo Pike

said this morning that a cold front was moving in with some rain this afternoon. Bo always gets it right."

"Who the hell is Bo?"

Now she looked downright flustered.

"The weatherman on Channel 31. He's got a hundred percent track record. If Bo says it's gonna rain, then it's gonna rain."

Max pivoted on her heel and strode out of the lounge. Puzzled, Rush followed her. She pushed her way through the double glass doors that led into the first-floor lobby. She didn't stop until she'd reached the front entrance and its wall of windows overlooking Williams Avenue.

Just like Bo had forecast, the sky had turned gray and rain drizzled steadily down.

"We have a team meeting this afternoon," he offered in hopes of making her feel better. He didn't exactly understand why the idea of a little rain tore her up so badly, but she was definitely not a happy camper. "Buck—Mr. Buchanan—wants to officially introduce you to the rest of the crew. Everyone's anxious to make your job as easy as possible."

She faced him, her expression someplace between annoyed and impatient. "Fine. Where will this briefing take place?"

"Upstairs." He gestured upward. "In the den."

"Den?"

"You'll see," he said, grinning.

Max had visited numerous corporate offices, from those of the Fortune 500 to the tiniest mom-and-pop operations. Not once had she ever seen a conference room like the one in the Buchanan Building.

Sofas, overstuffed chairs and lots of ottomans were scattered around the room. Coffee, bottled water and juices, energy bars and various fruits sat atop a serving bar. The coup de grâce was the fireplace, its flames flickering against the growing chill even she had started to notice.

George Farley was the crew chief, she learned, and Tom McElroy was described as Buck Buchanan's right-hand man. There were others, from the mechanics who kept the car's engine in order to those whose sole purpose was to stay on top of the tires to spotters who monitored every aspect of the race and kept the driver informed via a very sophisticated communications link.

"Dr. Gray," Buchanan offered, "you feel free to jump in any time you sense the need to ask a question."

"Thank you, Mr. Buchanan."

She listened as David Mason announced the changes to the car's setup for the next time trials. Farley discussed regulation changes expected before the season opened. Every person in the room paid close attention to each speaker. Notes were taken, questions were asked.

Rush asked more questions than anyone else. Max decided that made sense, since he was the one with the most to lose if anything went wrong.

Her attention lingered on him as she mulled that over. Was Rush Jackson just another adrenaline junkie who gladly risked his life for the fun of it? Certainly she understood the competitive aspect of all this. But was how he and his car performed—one couldn't be judged without the other—really as important to this man as winning? Or was the real reward the fans, or just the surge of adrenaline related to driving speeds equal to the momentum of some aircraft?

The team appeared quite dedicated to their work. Was this the same type of dedication one saw in a true athlete? She couldn't be sure about that yet. Max had observed Olympic athletes before. In fact, that had been her very first assignment, to determine if some were the same kind of athlete as others. Skiers, for example, as opposed to gymnasts. They were, as it turned out.

But could the same be said of these people?

She surveyed the room. Each member of the team, even the owner himself, looked quite fit. Not the slightest indication that a single one was a beer-guzzling good old boy, as lore would have it. There were even two female crew members, Charlene

Talley and Lori Houser. One was a spotter, the other a public relations representative for the team.

"I'll be supervising the installation into Number eighty-six this morning," Mason said.

Max tuned in to the conversation again.

"Then we'll resume this meeting at the shop," Buck announced. "And you can walk us through it. I'm sure Dr. Gray will be interested in seeing that."

They were going to the car.

To her surprise, excitement fizzed inside her. She didn't understand it. She'd never even watched a NASCAR race before. But suddenly the idea of seeing Rush in or near the car made her…giddy.

And just like that, her objectivity was in doubt all over again.

## CHAPTER FIVE

RUSH WISHED THEY WERE loading the car into the hauler and driving over for that practice run. That would sure have made his life a lot easier. At least then he'd give Max Gray something to study while giving himself a little distance.

Less than twenty-four hours and he was already having trouble figuring out a way to keep Max entertained without getting any closer. How could something like that happen so blasted fast? Women hung around the track, and every other place he frequented, all the time. Fans waited before and after every race or media appearance for an autograph.

In three years he hadn't had the first problem keeping all of them at arm's length when it came to personal involvement. Not once had he let his deep respect for the sport or the fans falter.

Buck had advised him well on getting involved. If becoming the top driver in the sport was his goal, there were certain measures he had to take to protect himself. First and foremost, never take advantage of those who love the sport or you. Some fans, in the heat of the moment, might just do anything to say they'd been close to a NASCAR driver. To cash in on that adoration was as much a sin as any other stated in black and white in the Good Book.

Secondly, Buck impressed upon him the importance of a healthy, balanced relationship with a woman. It was, in Buck's opinion, impossible to have that kind of relationship with any woman outside NASCAR. If she didn't get racing, she didn't get Rush. Racing was not only what he did, it was who he was.

Dr. Max Gray didn't get it. Furthermore she didn't *want* to get it. This was her job, nothing more. Maybe he was judging her a little prematurely, but he suspected she felt about the sport of racing the same way she did about Christmas—she didn't see what all the fuss was about.

Who didn't love Christmas?

This part greatly troubled him, because he wanted so badly to connect with her.

Even when a yellow flag was waving madly right in his face.

*Dumb, Rush. Real dumb.*

He glanced over at his passenger. She was busy reviewing data or something on her little computer. She hadn't said two words since they left the office. At first he'd thought she seemed a little excited at the prospect of going to the shop, but he must have been mistaken.

He probably just wanted to see excitement in those big brown eyes.

"Number eighty-six is special," he said, breaking the long, long silence. "There are great cars," he added, "and there are *great* cars. This one is a *great* car."

She stopped doing whatever she was doing and glanced at him. "Is this the same vehicle you've driven since the beginning of your career as a driver?"

Victory kick-started his heat in anticipation of having a real conversation with the lady, one that didn't include questions related to her study of his athleticism.

"No. I've had the same sponsor from the beginning, but we alternate the actual cars from track to track. And, of course, a car doesn't always make it through a whole race. I remember the first time I didn't finish—it was midseason my very first year." Not his best day. He remembered worrying that the rest of the team would see hiring him as a mistake. He'd been an unknown, after all. But Buck stood by him and the others had as well.

"Oh, yes, I recall reading something about that when I looked you up on the Web." She immediately turned back to her electronic notes.

So much for thinking she wanted to talk. Her Googling him was just another part of her job.

Okay, he had to get his head on straight here. This lady doctor was only here to assess him as an athlete. Her final report was extremely important to the team. Buck wanted some real teeth to his *Go for the Gold* slogan.

This wasn't personal, this was business. Rush needed to keep that in mind. Max Gray wasn't here to be impressed by him as a man. This was about racing. Only racing.

Usually he didn't have any trouble with that. Somehow this time was different. It might have had something to do with his last single sibling having wed this year—lately his mom had really been pushing the whole settling-down thing.

Maybe his overreaction to the doc here was some knee-jerk response to what the family expected of him.

At least at the shop it wouldn't be just the two of them the way it had all morning. Even at the gym, though other folks were around, he'd felt alone with her. And he was definitely obsessing way too much on the subject.

He'd lain in bed last night and thought about her across the hall. Did she like his mom? What did she think of his family home? Did she get enough to eat? Lame stuff like that.

Then, in preparation for the workout, she had appeared in that running suit. As petite and delicate as the good doctor was, she had a definite feminine shape. One that had kept him slightly off balance for the first half of the run. He'd had a hell of a time not staring at her. Good thing she'd fallen behind or he might have made a real fool out of himself.

Thankfully she'd changed into her standard business attire.

That was the thing, his mom had told him many times, with Cupid, you couldn't ever tell when he was going to strike. And now was *not* a good time.

All the rumors popping up about his tawdry love life had made him even more cautious than usual. Maybe he'd neglected that part of his personal life a little *too* much. That had to be the problem. He and Max didn't have the first thing in common.

Nada.

Zilch.

How could he be obsessing over a woman he scarcely knew and who had no appreciation for a single thing he held sacred?

Maybe this was God's way of showing him that he wasn't nearly so in control as he thought. Rush might be a rising star in NASCAR, but he was still just a man with the same weaknesses as every other member of the species.

He'd always heard that if a man got a little too big for his breeches the good Lord would give him a humbling experience to take him down a notch or two.

Church was just another thing he'd neglected lately. His ego could use a good rattling by a fire-and-brimstone sermon. The other drivers, who clung so staunchly to superstition, said so all the time.

Rush didn't have a superstitious bone in his body. So what if a black cat crossed the road or if he walked under a ladder or broke a mirror? The sun would still come up in the morning. About the only thing he did before a race, besides the typical preparations, was say a heartfelt prayer for protection. He didn't pray for a win. He figured if he couldn't do that part with the help of his team, he didn't deserve to win.

He'd just about reasoned himself into a ball of nerves by the time they reached the shop. The rest of the team arrived about the same time.

Thank God.

Two more minutes alone in the silence with her and he might have said something he'd regret. He would not ask her any private questions. Not only would it likely give away his interest, poking his nose in her business might very well influence her opinion of him. He would not take that risk.

No way.

MAX COULD FEEL his tension vibrating inside the vehicle. For some reason Rush Jackson seemed out of sorts today. She felt reasonably certain that his apprehension related to her study of his sport-related habits, but some aspect of his uneasiness kept nagging at her.

She had to admit that he was in prime physical condition. This she had seen with her own eyes. And if observing all those bulging muscles firsthand weren't evidence enough, she had his vital statistics as confirmation. The man could run ten miles while maintaining a heart rate most would kill for. There was no denying he was as fit as the proverbial fiddle.

She had spot-checked a number of other crew members and decided they were equally fit. In all honesty she hadn't doubted what her findings would be. These men and women took physical health seriously.

The next question was whether the so-called sport itself actually met the basic definitions associated with the term "sport." That definition had been listed as part of her overall assessment in comparing NASCAR performance to Olympic athleticism. There were some who believed that a ball or puck must be involved for an athletic endeavor to actually be a sport. For others, the true measurement was the essential ingredient of death-defying fearlessness. Without doubt, car racing met the latter criteria. NASCAR was also competitive and strategic. Training was required, as well as skill and dedication if a driver expected to win.

In reality, the definition boiled down to personal interpretation. The Olympic Committee recognized three dozen sports and hundreds of events and that number was constantly expanding to include additional competitive contests.

With that in mind, Max saw no reason not to interpret NASCAR racing as a sport in the purest definition of the term.

Rush parked his truck in front of the sprawling building that basically sat in the middle of a field. The shop or garage was actually several miles outside the city and might have passed for a storage facility for hay or farm equipment were it not for the guard shack and containment fencing through which they'd had to pass.

"You have round-the-clock security?" she asked, breaking the silence for the first time. She'd spent most of the journey lost in her own thoughts.

"Twenty-four/seven."

She opened her door before he bothered with his own. Not really because she was in a hurry but because she wanted to save him the trouble of dashing around to open her door. He attempted to do so each time they rode anywhere together. His chivalry was charming but totally unnecessary.

"That's the hauler," he said as he pointed out a big rig, the kind that carted goods across the nation. "It's pretty much a garage on wheels. Number eighty-six doesn't go anywhere unless it's inside that hauler."

The shiny, massive vehicle was painted with a racing scene that emphasized his sponsor's logo, the car, number eighty-six, speeding past its competition in a blaze of crimson and white.

"I'd like a tour of the hauler if that's okay." She didn't want to overlook any aspect of how the team prepared for an event.

"Sure thing." Rush opened the door to the building for her. "We can do that when we're finished here, if you'd like."

A buzz of activity had already started inside. Lori Houser, the PR rep, showed Max around the shop while Rush joined the others at the car.

The car.

The machine kept distracting Max from her tour. Lori patiently explained what every gray storage cabinet and worktable was designed for, despite Max's lack of attention.

When they moved into the storeroom, which was quite large and housed every imaginable replacement part the vehicle might need, she finally had to speak up.

"I'm sorry, Lori," she interjected, butting into her ongoing presentation, "I'd really like to observe the regulation update with the car."

"Oh." Lori looked startled. "Well sure, Dr. Gray. We come back to this later."

Max smiled. "Thank you."

Back in the main part of the garage, Rush had settled behind the wheel of number eighty-six. From what Max ascertained, the safety-regulation update had to do with the harnessing system for the driver. Crew Chief Farley explained that once the update was completed it would have to go through NASCAR inspection prior to each race.

"NASCAR's rules are very strict, Dr. Gray," Mr. Buchanan offered. "Safety is the absolute top priority. The slightest infraction can cost a team a big fine, and depending upon the severity, an entire race. We follow the guidelines to the letter. That's one reason our team is one of the best. We don't take risks."

Max nodded and turned back to the goings-on in the car. Buck Buchanan reminded her of the coaches she'd observed in the Olympics. He was as much cheerleader as boss. From what she could ascertain so far, Buchanan not only oversaw the team's work, he stayed in the thick of getting things done. Despite his gung ho spirit and undying support, she also saw the traits of an exacting taskmaster—and the marks of a good coach.

She was also impressed with the way the team members worked together, though she doubted any dissension would be permitted in her presence. Still, the easygoing camaraderie came too naturally to be faked. The team members were like old married couples, they finished each other's sentences, as if mind reading were a prerequisite to joining the club.

Though her attention was ostensibly focused on the smooth workings of the team, a large part of her awareness remained fixed on only one man. *Rush*.

Simply the way he snaked his way in and out of the car was quite an interesting display of fluidity and strength. The way he touched the car with such reverence made her curious, drew her closer. He'd removed his belt and his shoes before climbing in and out, a precaution against scratching, she supposed.

"That's it," Farley announced.

"Great." Rush slapped his teammate on the back. "You expect any more changes before trials?"

"I think that'll be the last one," Farley said after a moment. "Unless there's an unexpected manufacturer's alert."

"Dr. Gray!"

Despite having watched Rush turn his head toward her and his lips form her name, Max jumped.

Rush motioned for her to join him at the car. "Come on over here, Dr. Gray."

She glanced around at the others, who had dispersed into different directions, Farley with his clipboard, the others with their various duties.

Feeling totally out of place, Max walked over to where he stood next to the car. "Yes?"

"I thought you might like to climb on in and see how she fits?"

For a moment she was distracted by the glitter of excitement in those unusual blue eyes. "What?"

He reached out to put word into action.

She took a step back. "That's really not necessary." She glanced at the car. There was no need for her to climb inside.

"Don't be afraid, Doc. It's just a car." He took hold of her arm and tugged her back the step she'd taken as well as another. "Come on, how will you know how it feels if you don't climb on in there?"

The softness of his voice…the heat in his eyes mesmerized her.

The next thing she knew he'd placed his big, wide hands on either side of her waist.

"Say when and I'll give you a lift."

She toed off her shoes and took a breath, trying her very best to ignore the feel of his palms burning her skin through her sweater.

"When."

He chuckled, the sound deep and rich as if it had come from way down inside his chest.

As he lifted, she threaded her legs and then her upper body into the vehicle. His fingers trailed up her sides as he let go. She barely managed to suppress the shiver that kindled along the flesh he'd touched.

And then all other thought vanished.

She was in the car.

So many gauges and knobs and buttons. The quarters were closer than she'd expected and totally unluxurious. She held her breath as her fingers wrapped around the steering wheel and tingled at the texture. The expanse of hood that stretched out in front of the windshield was emblazoned with the number of the car.

This was his whole world during those long hours as he wound around and around the track, pushing the engine for every mile per hour it would produce. If he made a mistake, this was where he would pay the price.

The awe that rose up inside her was so profound that she felt entirely overwhelmed. She tried to take a breath, but there didn't seem to be enough air in the car.

Where was her objectivity?

She scrambled upward, poking her head out in an effort to draw in some air.

"Whoa there." His hands were on her again, lifting her out of the vehicle and then settling her onto her feet against the cool garage floor. "Pretty awesome, huh?"

Irritation at her own reaction whipped through her, making her want to stomp off somewhere until she'd regained control of her emotions. She never, ever let her ability to remain detached slip like this. What was wrong with her?

She faced the man who clearly waited for some profound response. She refused to give him the real one. Not in a million years. Then he would know, as she already did, that her ability to be impartial had abandoned her today.

"It's different from what I expected. I don't see how you stay awake." She settled her gaze on his as she stepped into her shoes. "It must get boring sitting in that small space and making all those left turns."

And just like that his exuberance morphed into disappointment.

Good. She didn't want him to be so friendly to her. All she wanted from him were the facts.

## CHAPTER SIX

SHE HADN'T PREPARED FOR THIS.

No one had told Max that her observations of Rush Jackson would include a cocktail party. She'd had no choice but to have Rush's PR rep, Lori Houser, recommend a local boutique. Then, of course, she'd had to beg a ride from Lori since she hadn't bothered renting a car—another mistake. This assignment appeared to be a catch-up session on how much she could do wrong, given enough rope to hang herself.

A dress required shoes, which meant another stop.

And here she was. In the requisite little black dress with three-inch heels, which she hated. She didn't care for the rare social functions required at the Institute. But independent funding depended largely on grants and philanthropic donations. To that end, a certain number of social appearances were necessary.

Still she didn't fit in here.

Lori should have warned her that Southern women didn't stick to the rules of black. And if she'd ever seen this many blondes in one room before, she had no recall of the event. Something in the water here apparently induced lighter manes and heavier bosoms.

Red, royal-blue, hot-pink, emerald-green, you name it, every imaginable color of dress was there…except black.

As if the flashy colors weren't enough, Max was certain she hadn't seen so much flagrantly displayed cleavage since she'd done that report on Victoria's Secret lingerie. Was the famous line of undergarments as comfortable as it was sexy? (Incredibly, the answer had been a solid yes.)

That was the one thing Max would wager not a soul in this room would guess. Beneath her conservative black clothing, she wore the sultry chain's most risqué panties and bra.

It was Max's one naughty little secret. Even her own mother didn't know.

A smile tickled the corners of her mouth. She liked feeling womanly and sexy. That no one else knew in no way detracted from her enjoyment. She was, in spite of her usual ironclad objectivity, only human.

One who had an undeniable problem with her current subject.

Max watched as Rush worked the room. He was

careful with the use of his hands. A cordial handshake or a chaste touch to an arm. Quite surprising, since most of the females in attendance—reporters and various sponsor representatives as well as a few chosen fans—were only too happy to touch the handsome driver as intimately as they could get away with.

Shocking.

Well, not really, she backtracked.

Calculating the measures for true superstardom in one study had thrust her into the very center of the music and movie world. The bigger the celebrity, the more desperate the moves of those who wanted to be a part of their world. Even the most professional woman or man would stoop to wholly unprofessional means for a few seconds of fame. Forget the whole fifteen minutes thing, fifteen seconds were quite sufficient for most.

Tonight's roll of VIP guests proved no different.

In fact, of the celebrity athletes she had observed, she had to admit that, from what she'd seen so far, the fans who trailed in the shadow of this NASCAR driver were in a league of their own. Their loyalty and idol worship set a new standard.

Before coming here she had watched several races borrowed from Motorsports Images and Archives' official library. As tense and exciting as seeing a gold-medal performance in the Olympics was, the roar of the engines and the thunder of the crowd at a NASCAR race took the moment to a different level.

Though she had not experienced a race firsthand and wouldn't before completing this study, she had watched the close-up shots of fans over and over. The palpable connection with the participants was acute. All five senses appeared to be in tune with the cars and drivers flying around those tracks.

The idol worship of the fans, judging from the lines to enter a race and in the autographing sessions, ranked right up there with superstardom in any other entertainment field. And wasn't that what any sport was really about, whether it be gymnastics or football?

Entertainment.

Most would argue and say it was all about the competition, but in her opinion, whenever money was involved, it was as much about entertainment as competition.

That aspect of NASCAR racing she had to give full marks. It met every definition, in her opinion. She had seen that the driver and his crew members were seriously into physical fitness and, considering all the other aspects involved in the actual competition, NASCAR certainly met the definitions of a sport. Yet, she needed to see more to form a full evaluation. First impressions could be impulsive.

That was the perfect word for the way she'd behaved practically since her arrival...*impulsive*.

Max Gray was never impulsive.

Surely a mere man—albeit a celebrity athlete—couldn't have her falling this far off her usual mark.

*Focus, Max. There's more to do here.*

One glaring question remained in her mind: did the attitude of sportsmanship follow through with the rocketing stress and extreme physical endurance required to finish a race? As far as Max was concerned, an athlete could be amazingly physically fit, highly trained and inordinately gifted, but if he fell down in when it came to displaying true sportsmanship, he didn't fit the bill. That part she still needed to measure on this assignment, and she couldn't rely on some show Rush and his team put on for her benefit. Her judgment would need to be based on performance at the track in the heat of a competition.

The attitude appeared to be in place. The entire team put forth a demeanor that indicated the sport, first and foremost, came before winning. But that was an easy thing to do in a noncompetitive setting.

Measuring the attitude in a competitive setting would be far harder to accomplish.

Tonight might very well turn out to be an opportunity to gauge a sampling of how well the attitude stood up to a test, she decided as she watched Rush continue to fend off blatant female advances with unflagging deftness and style.

Max would be watching closely the whole night, that was certain.

Perhaps too closely.

If Rush Jackson looked handsome in jeans and flannel or sweats and tee, he looked incontestably stunning in crisply starched khakis and a crimson pullover sweater. The cowboy boots had been replaced by leather loafers.

But she was relatively certain it wouldn't matter what he chose to wear. The ladies flocked to him as if he was the last man on the continent.

"These things do get tedious."

Max glanced up to see Tom McElroy standing next to her.

The entire team was present for the occasion. Max had to admit she was impressed with how the whole lot cleaned up. Very nice, including Mr. Buchanan and his closest confidant, Mr. McElroy. McElroy had a beer in each hand. The one in the left he offered to her.

"I imagine they do," Max agreed, taking the beer though she wouldn't drink it. Simply accepting it was far less trouble that explaining that a nice white wine was her only alcoholic indulgence. Just another thing to make tonight less than comfortable.

"Am I allowed to ask how your study is going?" McElroy asked. "If there's anything you can tell me without telling me anything," he added with a grin.

Her eyes sought and found Buck Buchanan across the room doing his own brand of networking with a number of the reporters on hand. "Did Mr. Buchanan order you to ply me with drink and then question me?"

"Absolutely not," McElroy said with a firm shake of his head. Then he winked. "He was hoping my Southern charm would do the job."

She'd met more Southern charm since her arrival than she would ever have imagined existed in one town.

"How long have you been involved with Mr. Buchanan?" The best way to avoid questions, she had learned, was to ask some of her own. People liked talking about themselves.

"That's going back a mighty long ways. Twenty years or a little better as colleagues. A whole slew before that as school chums."

McElroy's gaze turned distant, as if her question had awakened old memories.

"You must know all his secrets, Mr. McElroy." That should surely throw him off the scent of how her study was going.

To her surprise he shifted his gaze back to hers and smiled, but oddly, his expression wasn't entirely pleasant or genuine. "We all have secrets, Dr. Gray. I'll bet even you have a few."

*Touché.* Mr. McElroy was quite adept at evading questions as well. "Secrets are not my style, Mr. McElroy," she countered. She didn't mention the lingerie. "I deal purely in facts. It's my one and only rule. No others are necessary."

"The world would be a better place if everyone operated that way, Dr. Gray."

The words weren't particularly telling, just a comment meant to muddy the waters. It was where his attention shifted as he said the words that proved strangely forthcoming. He planted his gaze squarely on Rush Jackson as if he'd meant to refer to him.

"Enjoy your evening and let me know if there is anything at all I can do for you."

With that he swaggered off.

That was another thing about Southern men, Max noted. They swaggered. Young, old, whatever. Every one she'd met poured on the charm and swaggered away when he was finished.

Putting McElroy and the odd conversation out of her head for the moment, she watched Rush. He'd been nursing that same beer all evening. She might have thought otherwise since she'd been distracted briefly from time to time herself, but the label had a little tear in the upper right side. It was the same bottle.

The gossip rags had recently gone off on a tangent about Rush's behavior, the women and the drinking. From what she'd seen so far, neither was true, but that could be what he wanted her to see.

She surveyed the crowd until she located McElroy once more. Perhaps that was what he'd been talking about. The question was, why would McElroy tell *her?* Or maybe he'd spoken without thinking. He had moved on rather quickly after that.

All athletes faced temptation. She surveyed the ever-changing crowd that surrounded Rush. The real test of an athlete was how he handled temptation.

And temptation was all around him.

If she got through this night without seeing him slip, she would really be impressed.

IF HE GOT THROUGH this night without a bruise on his backside, he'd be damned lucky.

Rush had had his derriere patted and pinched a dozen times tonight. Man, some of these ladies were bold.

His face hurt. He'd smiled and laughed so much already and the night wasn't half-over. This was his least favorite part of the business, but keeping the press and the fans happy was extremely important. Fans won the opportunity to attend one of these events and it was Rush's job to make sure they enjoyed every minute of it.

Just now, what he really wanted to do was waltz over there to Dr. Max Gray and ask her if she wanted to dance. Not that anyone was dancing. But there was music. His jaw had hit the floor this evening when she'd come down the stairs in that little dress.

It was still black, like everything else she wore, but this dress served as a complement to her compact little body rather than a shroud.

She'd even left her hair down. But the glasses were perched right there on her nose. Still, considering the way all that wavy dark hair looked hanging over her slender, bare shoulders, he could forgive most anything else.

Then there were the legs. Very nice. Shapely and also bare, they looked smooth as silk. A hankering to touch them had started the instant he saw her. His mouth went bone dry at the thought. He took a sip of his beer. He'd been holding it so long it was past warm. People expected you to have a drink in your hand at these occasions, but discipline was the key. Take one beer and nurse it all night.

"Rush, can I get a picture with you?"

Sheila. A fan who came to every race and always brought all her friends.

"Why, sure, Sheila." He gave her a wink and a smile.

She nestled up close to him and he draped his arm around her shoulders. She snaked hers around his waist and, of course, patted his backside. Cameras flashed. Before he knew it a half-dozen others crowded up to have their picture taken.

The idea that someone in the room might take advantage of the situation gave him a second thought, but this was part of the job. These people had certain expectations and he had no intention of letting a single one of them down.

By the time the photo session was over he'd had several kisses on each cheek and, of course, a couple of phone numbers slipped into his pocket.

If he'd kept them all over the past three years he could start his own phone book. But he always turned them over to Buck. He knew the rules. Buck was firm about getting involved with the fans or the media. Bad business, any way you looked at it.

He was right.

Rush hadn't totally understood his firm standing on the matter until recently. Now, with the rumors flying about him in spite of his close attention to the rules, he could only imagine how nasty things could get if he even once stepped over the line.

First chance at escape he got, he wandered across the room in Max's direction. She was busy talking to Buck, but when her gaze suddenly tangled with Rush's, he hesitated. She seemed to falter as well. By the time he'd shoved into forward motion once more someone had caught up with him.

"Rush!"

He turned to see which of the reporters had called his name. He remembered the voice and the face but not the name. An automatic smile slid across his lips.

"How are you going to be spending Christmas, Rush?" she wanted to know, something suggestive in her expression.

"The same as always, ma'am," he assured. "Christmas with the folks."

A dozen other holiday-related questions were thrown at him and he tried his best to answer them all. By the time he'd gotten through that patch and turned back to where he'd last seen Max, she was gone.

Weaving through the crowd and hoping no one else would launch a new barrage of questions, he made his way around the room. No sign of Max. Where the heck had she gotten to?

Buck was still in the same spot, working his magic with the sponsor representatives. Rush scanned the crowd twice more. Maybe she'd taken a break in the ladies' room. He'd just have to wait until she reappeared.

"You hanging in there?"

Rush turned to face Lori Houser, his PR Rep. "You betcha." He smiled. "How 'bout you? This is your show as much as it is mine."

She rolled her eyes. "I don't think so. Nobody wants my autograph."

Rush wondered sometimes if living in his shadow got to the others now and then. He wished it didn't have to be that way. Winning was a joint effort. He couldn't do what he did without every single member of this team, but they didn't get nearly as much credit as he did. It wasn't fair.

He leaned down and whispered in Lori's ear. "If these folks were smart they'd be interviewing you guys, not me. I'm just the driver. You guys make everything happen."

She shoved at his chest. "Get outta here, you big dummy." But her smile was a mile wide. "Thanks, though, for saying so."

He gave her a quick, one-armed hug. "I meant every word."

"Watch out," Lori warned, "there's Dr. Gray. She hasn't taken her eyes off you all night."

He found Max in the crowd. "That is her job, you know." The doc looked away when his gaze met hers.

"Nah." Lori shook her head. "This isn't about her job. It's about her having the hots for you."

Rush laughed out loud.

"Seriously," Lori challenged. "I've watched enough awestruck fans to know. The woman is more than a little attracted to you."

She was serious.

He scanned the room until he found Max again. She stood all alone, watching no one in particular, the way she had most of the night when she wasn't watching him.

Lori had to be wrong.

Totally wrong.

Just then Max looked directly at him, then jerked her eyes away just as abruptly.

Lori leaned closer. "See, I told you. Now close your mouth before someone sees you gawking like that."

He snapped his mouth shut and shook off the whole ridiculous idea.

*No way.*

## CHAPTER SEVEN

THE WEATHER CHANNEL had gotten it wrong.

The temperature had dropped more than twenty degrees by sunrise the next morning. Not that Max wasn't accustomed to weather far colder than this. After all, she lived in Boston. The problem was she wasn't properly prepared.

She'd packed her bag for travel using the Weather Channel as a guide for years. That was her routine. She'd not once regretted it…until now.

Nor had she ever regretted her behavior on an assignment as she did this time.

Rush had caught her looking at him a couple of times last night. Probably he considered that a part of her study, but she still felt uncomfortable about it.

Fortunately, they had arrived at the press reception in a limo and had departed the same way, ensuring that she and Rush weren't alone. But there had been those few minutes inside the house around midnight before they'd gone their separate ways to bed. He'd offered to make a pot of coffee, she'd declined.

Too risky.

How in the world had she let this happen?

She and Rush Jackson had nothing in common. Not a single thing. And yet, she wanted to know him better.

How could she write an independent study on the man when she couldn't stop thinking about how cute and charming and just plain nice he was?

If she believed in voodoo—which she did not because she had done a study on it and found absolutely no reason to—she would be convinced that her mother had cursed her.

Her mother wanted a wedding to plan.

Her mother wanted grandchildren.

At twenty-five Max had plenty of time for both. Yet something had abruptly changed in the past forty-eight hours. But how and why, she didn't understand.

*Stop it*, she ordered. *Focus on the assignment*.

Today she needed to see the collaborative efforts of the team and their reactions to both victory and failure. The only way to get that was from previous races. She didn't sense that a show was being orchestrated for her benefit, but she needed to be sure.

Motorsports Images and Archives had recordings of all races, but she needed the race from the team's perspective. Surely Mr. Buchanan kept recordings of his races, either video, audio and/or digitally photographed history. That would help tremendously—*if* he was willing to allow her full access.

That would be asking a lot, since she'd hear the team's every unguarded moment. However, if he had nothing to hide he would gladly go along, wouldn't he?

That would be her first point of attack this morning. If she got what she needed she might just be able to tie this up more quickly than she'd first thought. She needed to get this done and return to Boston.

If they hurried they could be at the office well before anyone else and she would have a chance to speak privately with Buchanan.

"Good morning, Maxine."

Evelyn Jackson waited for her at the bottom of the stairs.

"Morning, Evelyn." The first-name-basis thing still felt a little odd, but Max was adjusting.

"I was just about to come up and tell you that breakfast is ready, darlin'. I've herded Rush into the kitchen already. Come on—" she prodded with a wave "—before it gets cold. Grits aren't too tasty once they cool off."

*Grits.* Well, how could she come to the South and not try true Southern grits? Her mother would be proud. Except she would never tell her mother any of this.

"Sounds great." She'd rarely visited any city

without at least trying something for which the location was famous. Might as well be grits.

In the kitchen Rush was pouring coffee. "Just in time, ladies."

He placed a steaming cup at each place setting. The smell alone had Max practically floating to the table. Evelyn Jackson knew how to brew a cup of coffee.

As Evelyn spooned out helpings of scrambled eggs and grits onto three plates, she explained how she used olive oil and butter substitutes. Her biscuits, she admitted, were her one concession to eating on the edge, but she rarely baked those. She explained that Rush's father had died of a heart attack and that she'd made a conscious effort since to eat healthier.

The grits, as unpalatable as they looked, were quite tasty. The first bite of biscuit melted in Max's mouth. She moaned, hadn't meant to, but she did.

Evelyn and Rush had themselves a major laugh at her unexpected reaction.

As they ate, Evelyn launched into a quick listing of her other children's marital status and procreative feats.

"Carol, my oldest, is married to an engineer at NASA. They had their second child last year." Evelyn pushed away her barely touched plate and sipped her coffee. "Helen is married to a professor, but no children yet. Elizabeth is married to a doctor and they have one child who, let me tell you, is a little genius." She took a deep, satisfied breath. "Anna married earlier this year, he's a car salesman," she added with a knowing look in Max's direction, "but he's very nice. They're pregnant. Robert and his wife, the piano player at our church, have three little ones."

That left Rush, unmarried and childless. Like her, Max mused.

As if picking up on Max's thought, Evelyn shot a look in Rush's direction. "We're all waiting for him to find the right woman. He just needs to slow down and take his time."

"Now, Momma," he warned. "You know I don't have time for that kind of commitment."

Evelyn made a scoffing sound. "Lots of NASCAR drivers are happily married, so don't hand me that excuse."

Max had to bite her lips together to hold back a grin. She was enjoying this maybe a little too much.

"Don't forget we're decorating the tree tonight," Evelyn reminded, turning her attention back to Max. "It's a family affair, Maxine. We hope you'll jump in and join us."

TO RUSH'S ETERNAL thanks the heat was off him for the moment. He had to poke a forkful of eggs into his mouth to keep from laughing out loud at Max's horrified expression. If the lady was expecting to get out of this one, she had no idea how persuasive his mom could be. Evelyn Jackson didn't take no for an answer.

The telephone rang. Thank the good Lord.

"Excuse me," he said as he started to get up from the table.

"You finish your breakfast," his mother insisted. "I'll get it."

When she'd scurried out of the room, Rush sat back down with a heavy breath.

"Don't feel bad," Max whispered, "I get this from my mother all the time."

Her smile broke through the tension he'd felt all morning. Or maybe it was just those big brown eyes and having her here. She wore black again today, slacks and a button-up blouse. Her hair was looped around in one of those fancy braids that looked as if she'd rushed to twist it together. And the glasses, of course, but he was getting used to those.

She was pretty.

She had a nice smile.

He liked having her here.

For all the wrong reasons.

His mother had planted this seed in his head. He just knew it. Somehow, her nagging since Anna got married had set him on edge. He just hadn't noticed until someone came along who made him sit up and pay attention.

No matter. He knew the odds of a relationship working out with someone who didn't love racing the way he did. Buck had warned him plenty about that. From what Rush had heard, Buck knew from personal experience how that felt.

Rush managed a dry laugh. "I guess all of 'em are that way."

For about half a minute they just stared at each other, enjoying this new thing they'd found in common.

"Rush."

Before he even saw her face, he knew something was wrong just by his mom's tone. Worry revved up inside him. He jumped up, knocking his chair over in his haste.

"Sorry," he muttered to Max as he straightened his chair before turning to his mom.

"It's Buck. He needs you to come into the office right away. I told him you'd be out the door as soon as I hung up."

That could only mean trouble.

"I'll get my coat."

He pecked his mom on the cheek as he passed her. "Thanks for breakfast."

"Drive carefully, Rush!"


WHATEVER WAS HAPPENING, Max didn't want to miss a second of it. She grabbed her dishes and carried them to the sink.

"Don't worry about that, Maxine. I'm sure you want to go with Rush."

Max smoothed her hands over her thighs. "Thank you. The breakfast was lovely."

"It's cold out," Evelyn warned before she could escape. "Better wear one of my coats if you didn't bring one of your own."

Max hadn't. It was ridiculous. She lived in a part of the country where a jacket of some sort was needed eighty percent of the time and still she'd managed to come up short.

Thank you, Weather Channel.

"That would be very nice."

Evelyn started to clear the table. "Check the coat closet under the stairs."

The front door slammed.

Max whirled in that direction.

"Don't worry," Evelyn assured, "he's just a little rattled. He won't leave without you."

Max wasn't so sure. She hurried to the stairs, found the closet and grabbed the first coat her hand landed on. She pulled it on as she bounded out the door and across the porch.

As Evelyn had predicted, Rush waited for her. He'd already started the truck. Moderately warm air blew from the heater making her appreciate that he'd come out ahead of her.

The ride into town was fraught with tension and

utterly silent. Max started to say something a couple of times, but she failed to work up the courage. Imagine, her, uncertain what to say. It was so unlike her usual straightforward self.

Apparently the atmosphere down here played havoc with her ability to think straight.

She really did need to wrap this up as quickly as possible. The longer she stayed, the more she felt something about her changing…something intrinsic to her well-being. Allowing the momentum to continue would be a mistake.

Several other team members arrived at the Buchanan Building as she and Rush did. Rush still hadn't said a word, but worry was lined in every angle and plane of his face.

Last night she'd watched him play the part of generous celebrity. This morning she witnessed up close the less pleasant side of what being at the top of his game meant. Stress, mixed with unyielding determination.

When the team was settled—in Buck's office rather than the den—Max felt abruptly out of her comfort zone.

"Mr. Buchanan," she spoke up, "if my presence in this meeting is problematic I'm happy to wait in the den."

He shook his head, his expression grave. "You might as well hear this from me."

Every face in the room was somber. Max wished he would speak up and get it over with. The tension was killing her.

"I got a call from a friend of mine," he said, his voice uncharacteristically weary. "The *Inquisitor* is releasing more pictures this morning. They're probably on the East Coast newsstands as we speak."

Max turned to Rush. This would be about him. The devastation that claimed his face made her feel ill.

"How bad is it?"

"Bad enough to have our sponsor calling me at the crack of dawn."

Somewhere in the room a fax machine started to whir. Max wanted to turn and look but she resisted.

"That'll be copies of what they're publishing."

Lori Houser went to the fax machine and picked up the pages received. She walked straight back to Buck's desk and handed them to the boss. Her face was pale.

Max's throat parched. This had to be very bad. The sponsor wouldn't have bothered getting involved otherwise. A certain amount of negative publicity was expected when dealing with celebrities.

After a thorough perusal, Buck handed the pages across his desk for Rush to see next.

Rush heaved a disgusted breath. "God Almighty."

Max was startled when he passed them to her. She blinked, moistened her lips and took a look.

Her heart stumbled.

Rush, his arm around a big-breasted blonde. Okay, she remembered that Kodak moment in last night's picture-taking session. It was completely innocent.

But the other picture…that was the one that made her pulse rate do strange things. The same woman with a man who looked like Rush. Only this time the two were in a bathroom stall—making out.

"This is a hoax." She hadn't meant to say the words out loud.

Someone behind her reached for the pages.

Max looked from Rush to Buck. "That didn't happen."

"But can you prove it?" McElroy's voice sounded from his position propped against a file cabinet.

"Well…" Max almost said no, but then she realized she could. "Yes, I can actually."

McElroy looked mildly surprised.

"What do you mean, Dr. Gray?"

Max turned back to Buck who'd asked the question. "I watched Rush all night. I never took my eyes off him, except once."

"Unfortunately," Buck countered, "once is all it takes." He slanted a look at Rush. "Figuratively speaking, of course."

Max shook her head. She was on her feet before she realized she'd moved. "No. No. The only time I wasn't watching him was when I went to the ladies' room." She grabbed the pages back from Farley, who was now glaring at them. She tapped the disparaging photo. "This is the ladies' room. If this wasn't happening while I was in there, and it most assuredly was not, then this isn't Rush, because he never left the party any other time."

The silence that thickened in the air after her monologue had her face heating with embarrassment.

"Sorry." She handed the pages back to Farley.

What the hell had she been thinking? This wasn't her business. She was an outsider. But then, she was right.

"And what about that blonde?" she went on, uncaring if she sounded foolish. "Won't she be able to tell who was really in that stall with her?"

Farley stepped forward and dropped the pictures back on Buck's desk. "She might, but there are a few out there who prefer to let the world think they had their moment with him. It's their claim to fame."

"But it's a lie," she urged. There had to be something they could do.

The silence settled heavily over the room.

"If Dr. Gray says it didn't happen," Buck said, shattering the tension, "then the sponsor will just have to accept that. Dr. Gray has absolutely no reason to confirm Rush's innocence unless he is innocent. That's good enough for me."

Max felt a smile push across her lips.

"Thank God," Rush breathed the words. "I swear we've got to find whoever the hell is doing this."

"Don't worry," Buck said, "I'm on top of that. I'm closer than you think."

The last he said with a long look around the room.

Max felt a sense of dread well in her stomach. Did he suspect one of their own? As she glanced around she didn't miss the way Lori Houser looked—as if she suspected Max of some wrongdoing.

Max looked away, determined not to feel any guilt. She'd just saved Rush's backside. As his PR rep, Houser should be thrilled. Max had made her job a lot easier considering the complications those pictures had raised.

Maybe she'd imagined the woman's strange look. Tensions were high right now. Max wasn't immune. She hated deceit. Anyone who altered the truth to create their own facts was despicable in her book.

Her entire adult life had been about the facts.

*Until now*, she realized with a brutal jolt. There was at least one fact in all this that she was working hard to pretend didn't exist.

Unfortunately she wasn't sure she could or should own that one. Not at the moment anyway. This might be one of those times her mother had always warned her she would someday face. Her mother had harped on the irony that Max's surname was Gray when she saw absolutely nothing but black and white. Some things, her mother cautioned, weren't so clear-cut. One of these days, she'd insisted, Max would know.

Max was reasonably sure that day had come, only seeing beyond the black and white of the situation wasn't the problem.

It was the motivation behind her epiphany that presented the challenge.

RUSH WANTED to kick something, but that wouldn't do any good. The office had cleared…except for Buck and Max.

Maybe he shouldn't say what he was about to in front of her but after the way she'd stood up for him, he figured he couldn't exclude her from any part of this.

"There has to be something I can do, Buck." Rush stood in front of the boss's desk, fighting the urge to pace like a caged animal.

"I could ignore this," Rush went on, "just let it blow over, if I didn't feel it was someone I know twisting the knife."

"You believe it's someone on your own team?" Max asked.

Rush checked Buck's expression, hoping he hadn't overstepped his bounds by letting that cat out of the bag.

"We're afraid it might be," Buck confessed,

letting Rush off the hook. "Some of the photos used have been taken in situations where that's about the only theory we can come up with."

A frown marred her smooth brow. "Why would a member deliberately sabotage his or her own team?"

The answer to her question appeared to dawn on her no sooner than the words were out of her mouth.

"Oh." Jealousy, or personal gain. The bottom line was greed, pure and simple. Make Rush look bad and maybe a new driver would take his place. Or a competitor could be providing financial incentive.

"Looks like we have ourselves a traitor, all right," Rush echoed what she was no doubt thinking.

"I did some watching of my own last night," Buck said. "I think I know where our problem lies."

Anticipation roared through Rush. "Who?" His heart thundered hard in his chest. He trusted each and every one of these people. It was hard to believe that any of them could have done this.

Buck held up his hands. "I need you to let me handle this part, Rush. I promise you it'll get done today."

Rush shook his head. "You know I trust your judgment, Buck, but you don't have to do this alone."

Buck dropped his hands to his side and drew in a heavy breath. "Yes, I do. I think this might have more to do with hurting me than you, son. This is my mess, I'll clean it up."

"What do you want me to do?" Rush needed to help...somehow.

"You take Dr. Gray and the team to Tony's driving school and give her something to remember." Buck smiled at Max. "It's the only way to understand the experience." He turned back to Rush then. "Afterward, make sure the shop's ready to shut down for the holidays. We all need a break. I'll bring everyone up to speed as soon as this is done."

"Tony's driving school" was really Tony's Racing Experience, a mini theme park all about the racing experience, including a near-regulation-size track and cars designed for two, a trained driver and a paying passenger. It was the closest experience to the real thing a civilian could get. A number of places that provided the rush of racing had popped up around the country.

Rush exchanged a look with Max. He couldn't decide if what he saw in her eyes was fear or anticipation. Either way...he always followed orders. This just happened to be one of the times that he was going to thoroughly enjoy the task.

He'd wanted to take her for a spin all night last night. This would have to do.

The sound was incredible.

Max stood on the halfway point of a mock pit road and watched Rush fly by in a blur of blue and gray. The ground seemed to shake beneath her feet, but she wasn't sure that was actually possible. Maybe she was the one shaking.

The roar of the engine had her heart pounding so hard she could scarcely catch her breath.

The cold air and the ugly, doctored photos were forgotten.

With a burst of speed that made her breath hitch, he approached turn one, hugging the apron of the track. Farley explained everything via the Bluetooth-type earpiece she wore.

Rush let out a gleeful yell as he flew down the back stretch. Hearing the excitement in his voice sent shivers tumbling one over the other on her skin.

He took the next turn and swung around on the banking. He was absolutely soaring. It was incredible…nothing like watching it on television. The very air crackled with excitement.

The power of the machine…the precision handling of the driver…made her pulse react accordingly. She'd never observed anything quite so exhilarating.

"Oh, my God."

A few chuckles echoed over the communications link, letting her know she'd said the words out loud.

He roared around the track for three more laps before coasting back onto pit road.

When the growl of the engine died, he hefted

himself out through the window and jogged over to where she stood. Seeing him in his official fire suit and helmet made her feel vulnerable somehow.

"Your turn now," he said as he dragged off his helmet.

Rush jerked his head toward the car. "She's rigged for accommodating a passenger." He grabbed her by the arm. "Come on and I'll take you for a ride."

She was shaking her head, but she couldn't form the word *no*. It was absolutely nuts. *N. O.* Simple. But she couldn't say it.

Farley tucked a helmet onto her head.

Somehow her fingers found the strap and snapped it into place under her chin. She had to be out of her mind. This wasn't part of her assignment.

"Once you're settled inside," Rush said as he came up beside her, "I'll secure your harness." He dragged the coat off her shoulders. "You won't need this right now."

Before she could argue, his hands were around her waist and he'd lifted her off the ground. She passed her legs through the passenger-side window and eased herself into the seat. He dropped behind the wheel next to her before she'd even realized he'd moved, much less had time to hustle around to the driver's side.

*Okay, Max, snap out of it.*

He buckled the safety harness around her. "You ready?"

The mischief glinting in his eyes took her breath away all over again.

"Don't worry," he said when she couldn't find her voice. "I'll keep it under one-eighty."

There was something she should say...she just didn't know what it was at the moment. The synapses just wouldn't fire with any accuracy.

"Here we go."

*Stop. This isn't a good idea.* Several reasons she shouldn't do this swirled in her head, but none made it across her lips.

He fired the engine and the car abruptly rocketed forward.

Max pressed back into the seat and did something she rarely did—she prayed.

She was certain she would fly out the window somehow as he took the second turn. She stared straight ahead. She didn't want to know how fast they were going...the world out the side windows was a blur. Staring straight ahead was the only way to stay calm. The endless circle of the track was somehow comforting...unending...hypnotic.

She could feel her heart surging mercilessly against her sternum. Way faster than normal. Her BP had to be at stroke level. The pressure from the g-force was far more intimidating than that of any roller coaster she'd ever ridden.

Max didn't know whether Rush had a set number of laps in mind to take her on when he started or if something about her expression had warned him that stopping now was a good thing, but whatever the case, he cut the engine and rolled along pit road.

When the car stopped and their surroundings came into focus once more, she still felt as if she were moving.

"You okay?"

She told herself to turn her head and answer him but she couldn't quite make the muscles work.

He tugged off her helmet as well as her own. "Max, you okay?" he repeated.

Farley was suddenly at her window. "Come on, Dr. Gray, I'll help you out of there."

Hands pulling at her, she climbed out of the car somehow. But when her feet hit the ground her knees buckled.

"Whoa there, little lady."

The next thing she knew she was in Rush Jackson's arms. "Don't worry, Doc," he murmured, "I'll take care of you till you get your land legs back."

He smiled and right then, right there, staring into those unusual blue eyes she surrendered to the inevitable.

She was hooked…swept away…bedazzled. And the only thing that kept her from kissing him square on the lips that were so very close to her face just then was the fact that the world that had finally stopped spinning went suddenly black.

## CHAPTER EIGHT

MAX WAS MORTIFIED.

The whole team had watched her faint in Rush's arms.

But no one had said a word that didn't come across as concerned or sympathetic.

Thank God, the business of dropping by the shop and ensuring that all was secure had kept everyone so busy there hadn't been time to dwell on her ridiculous display.

The only tense moments had come when Rush had driven her back to his house. Thankfully his mother had called his cell phone, keeping him occupied. Her call had been to let him know that the entire Jackson family had gathered for decorating the tree, and waited for his and Max's arrival.

She now knew every single member of the Jackson clan, family pets included. She'd been pawed by the four-legged creatures and climbed on by the wee ones and gushed over by the adults. Every time someone walked by she braced for a hug.

This never happened with her family. She had never in her entire life met people this openly affectionate.

"Shelby gets to do the star this year," Evelyn announced as she ushered her youngest grandchild to the front of the crowd around the tree.

"Well, come here, Miss Shelby." Rush lifted the little girl into his arms and gave her a big kiss.

Max's heart thumped hard just watching the man interact with the child.

He lifted her high enough for those little fingers to place the star on top of the tree. The crowd broke into applause as if the child had accomplished world peace.

With the tree decorated, the family wandered back into the kitchen for coffee and pound cake. Max didn't follow despite the urging of at least three of the four sisters.

She just needed five minutes alone.

The lights of the tree twinkled against the dark night outside the window. None of the decorations were fancy and most were old, but she couldn't remember ever seeing a tree more generously or gorgeously decorated.

Absolutely lovely.

"I guess this has all been a little overwhelming."

She turned to face *him*. The race-car driver who'd made her heart beat too fast...who'd stolen her ability to think straight.

Oh, she could explain away the fact that she'd fainted with all sorts of physiological explanations, but she knew the one fact that had made the difference.

*Him.*

She hadn't just crossed the line here, she'd pole-vaulted over it.

"A little," she admitted.

"We take a little getting used to."

The smile that tilted his lips took her breath all over again, had her taking a hopeful lean toward him.

Okay, she couldn't do this. She'd let her reason drift far enough into uncharted waters. "I really need some—" God, how did she say this? "—some space. Could you take me to a hotel?" Her request was completely unreasonable and totally thoughtless, but she had to go.

That he looked hurt or disappointed or maybe both twisted inside her with a rawness she'd never before experienced.

"Sure. I can do that."

"I'll…" What would his mother think? She couldn't worry about that. "I'll get my bag."

She hurried upstairs and got only what she would need for the night. She had to get out of this house before anyone else noticed.

RUSH COULDN'T DECIDE what to say as he headed back into town. He'd obviously overstepped his bounds with her.

But he'd thought there was something happening between them. She'd stood up for him in front of the whole team today. She'd seemed to like his family.

Maybe he'd misread her.

Should he apologize?

Just sit here and say nothing?

"Do you think we could stop by the Buchanan Building and get the tapes of some of your previous races?"

Well, at least she was talking to him. He cleared his throat. "Sure. Was there one in particular you wanted to take a look at?"

More of that silence.

"How about I just pick four or five at random?" she offered. "You don't think Mr. Buchanan will mind?"

"He won't mind."

"Excellent."

Rush drove to the office. It was past eight, the buildings all around the Buchanan Building were dark, but he was surprised to see the light in Buck's office was on. Maybe Buck was there working on the problem. *His* problem.

At this hour, parking at the curb wouldn't get him a ticket. Rush and Max took the stairs to Buck's office. Rush didn't knock, he just went on in.

"Rush, what're you doing here at this time of night?"

Tom McElroy sat behind Buck's desk.

Tension rippled through Rush. "Dr. Gray needs a couple of videos from past races." He didn't ask what Tom was doing there. He was Buck's right-hand man. Buck probably had him finishing up some paperwork that needed to be done before the holidays.

Then why the momentary awkwardness? Maybe Rush was overreacting, considering his churning emotions where Max was concerned.

"You need me to help you find them?" Tom asked as he pushed out of Buck's chair.

"That's okay. You finish up whatever you're doing. We'll be out of your hair in a sec."

Tom picked up a couple of folders. "Take your time. I'm finished here. You can lock up." He pushed in Buck's chair and rounded the desk. "Don't work too late, kids," he said with a wink as he strolled out of the office.

Rush relaxed fractionally. He was definitely overreacting. Tom and Buck went back…forever.

"The…ah…tapes are over here." Rush led Max to a bookcase on the other side of the room. "Just pick out whatever you need." He stepped back and let her make her own selections from behind the glass doors.

He glanced out the window just in time to watch Tom cross the street to where he'd left his car parked. Like Buck, Tom had never married. He imagined holidays were tough on guys like that…guys who were alone.

Like him, he realized. Sure, he had lots of family, but he didn't *have* anyone.

His career came first, he reminded himself. The rest would come later…no matter how badly he suddenly wanted it now.

MAX HAD DONE her research ahead of time. She knew some of the pitfalls and dangers of racing. For example, she was well aware that a driver and his team had to be capable of handling a car at upwards of 200 miles per hour, not to mention cornering forces that exceeded the launch force of the space shuttle. During a hot summer's race, cockpit temperatures could reach a hundred degrees or more. Drivers had been known to lose ten or more pounds during a single race.

No question, the physical rigors of the sport were tremendous.

So, the question had been simple: did Rush Jackson and his crew meet those challenges with the heart and determination of true athletes in the heat of the moment?

There was no way to answer that question without watching the real thing.

It was hours ago that Max had loaded the first tape into the VCR slot and settled back on the floor at the foot of the bed to watch. She'd wanted to be close to the television so she wouldn't miss a single detail.

It was past midnight now. She'd watched miles of footage, listened to endless audio, all the while making notes for her final report. The teamwork, from the crew chief to the spotter who kept the driver informed to the team members who changed the tires, was absolutely amazing. The timing and choreography were nothing short of fascinating.

Whatever she had thought she knew about NASCAR, she had been wrong. Totally wrong.

The physical preparations before a race, the physical rigors during a race were nothing compared to the exacting communications and mental prowess. Teamwork at its most basic, essential form.

If one member of the team made a mistake, a single mistake, there could be devastating consequences to Rush, to anyone close to him on the track.

Max ejected the tape she'd just viewed, last season's final race, then she picked up the only one out of those she'd selected that she hadn't watched. The one where Rush had crashed. She'd saved that one for last.

She slid the tape into the slot and sat back as it began to play.

The race started out like any of the others, the

stands full of enthusiastic fans, the engines grumbling with restrained power. And then they were off.

Rush moved past one car after another. By lap twenty he'd moved into first place. It would be his first win. That much was crystal clear. But she knew what was coming and that made watching all the more difficult.

Car number fifteen attempted to move into the lead—but something went wrong.

Max held her breath as number fifteen banked off the wall and spun off the track.

That was when Rush's trouble began.

The sound of Farley's voice urging him to cut left in order to sway the vehicle's rear end had her heart pounding. The spotter's voice came in next, providing quick decisive directions Rush couldn't seem to comprehend.

And then the crash.

Max's hands went over her face. She watched between her fingers, her breath stalled in her lungs and that pounding heart suddenly stumbled.

Even though she knew he'd walked away from the accident with scarcely a scratch, she couldn't drag in a breath until she saw him climb out of that car.

She pressed a hand to her throat and struggled to even out her respiration. That had been a close one. Both Rush and the other driver were exceedingly fortunate that they'd been able to walk away.

A knock on the door made her jump. Her breath caught all over again.

What time was it?

She twisted around to look at the clock on her bedside table. Almost one-thirty in the morning.

Who would show up at her door at this hour?

Another knock followed by, "Max, it's me."

*Rush.*

She pressed Pause and struggled to her feet. Her muscles were stiff from sitting on the floor so long. Three empty water bottles lay on the floor, along with the remnants of the fruit bowl room service had delivered.

At the door, she smoothed her hair away from her face, only then realizing she wasn't wearing her glasses. That made her feel naked…especially knowing he was on the other side of that door. That was the purpose of her glasses anyway. She wore them more to hide behind than to enhance her vision. What a coward she was.

"Max?" Another knock. "You okay in there?"

She took a breath and did what she had to do. She opened the door. "Hey." What was he doing here? The question instantly prompted an image of him in bed.

He held a large plate covered in aluminum foil in one hand, and two colas in the other.

Her stomach rumbled the instant the glorious scent hit her nostrils. Pizza.

"It's pepperoni. I hope that's okay. It was the only kind we had in the freezer."

The weary smile on his face was as charming as ever.

"Come in." She stepped back and let him pass. She told herself it was more about the pizza than about him but that was a lie.

He placed the pizza and colas on the table, his gaze riveted to the television.

"That was a day I won't soon forget," he said more to himself than to her.

She folded her arms over her chest, mostly to protect her heart from going out to him, but it didn't work. "I was terrified just watching," she admitted.

He looked away from the still scene on the screen. "We should eat before the pizza gets cold."

She was famished so she didn't argue, though she would have liked to ask him a few questions.

After the third or fourth slice had been devoured in silence, he finally came out with what was on his mind. "The traitor was Tom McElroy."

Max lowered her cola without taking a drink. "You can't be serious? Wasn't he Mr. Buchanan's closest confidant?" But he had been in Buck's office just a few hours ago. His comment at the cocktail party followed hot on its heels. Some part of her had recognized something was off with him...but she'd dismissed the idea.

Rush nodded. "No one can believe it. I found out just a couple hours ago. Apparently he was in Buck's office tonight trying to get rid of the evidence Buck had collected. Buck fired him. He might as well be banned from NASCAR for his betrayal of the team and dishonoring the sport, because the folks who learn about his dirty business sure won't be forgiving him in this lifetime."

She couldn't imagine how Buchanan must feel. And, good grief, they'd practically caught him in the act. "Why did he do this?" According to what she'd read about Buchanan's team, he and McElroy had been together from the beginning. This was the worst kind of betrayal.

"Buck said Tom had gotten tired of living in his shadow, always taking orders," Rush explained. "Apparently he thought he should have gotten more credit or more of Buck's attention. I don't know." He shrugged. "He thought Buck was getting too close to me or something crazy like that."

Max couldn't help herself. She had to put her hand on his. "This isn't your fault. People make their own choices. You had nothing to do with McElroy's efforts to damage the team. He clearly has issues."

They gazes held for several seconds and the urge to lean closer to him, to touch more than his hand, was palpable.

"That day was my fault," Rush said, his attention

shifting to the television screen though that final tape had been stopped and ejected. But she knew what he meant. The race where he'd crashed.

This was important, Max realized. He was about to share something very personal with her. A part of her wanted to make him hush. She shouldn't want to feel any closer to him. But the part of her that needed to know everything about him wouldn't let her say a word.

She could only listen.

"No matter how great the team, those moments on the track boil down to one crucial element."

Max allowed those intense blue eyes to mesh fully with hers even if maintaining the contact was the hardest thing she'd done in a very long time.

"Unbreakable mental focus. You see," he said, his voice low and somber, "if it's your time up to bat and you get distracted on the field, worst-case scenario you strike out. But when a driver in a race going one-eighty or more gets distracted, even for a split second, the worst-case scenario could very well mean the ultimate disaster."

And that was the way her report would read. Not only were NASCAR drivers and their crews physically fit, the specialized mental skill set and extreme, unbreakable mental focus required went well beyond ordinary definitions of athleticism.

"I let the other car wiping out distract me," Rush

went on, unaware of her revelation. "It was a mistake I won't ever make again."

She touched his hand again, unable to hold back that small comfort. "You learned a lesson and you haven't repeated the same mistake. That shows what kind of athlete you are, Rush. What kind of man."

He shrugged. "I was lucky."

She lifted her shoulders and let them fall in echo of his. "Perhaps."

For several seconds they didn't speak, just sat there and stared into each other's eyes.

This was the moment, she knew, where she could make the logical choice or the one her heart wanted desperately. If she made the *wrong* choice…she might never have this chance again.

"I should go. We're both tired."

He stood and suddenly there was no more time to decide.

She pushed out of her chair and reached for his hand, this time entwining her fingers with his. "Don't go."

Getting lost in those eyes was too easy. And yet he held back.

"Are you inviting me to stay, Max?"

*A gentleman to the very end.* She smiled.

"Yes, Rush. I'm inviting you to stay."

He pulled her into his arms and held her that way for another moment, content to continue staring deeply into her eyes—or maybe giving her the chance to change her mind.

"As long," he chuckled as his lips lowered to meet hers, "as you still respect me in the morning."

"Shut up and kiss me." Her arms closed around his neck and pulled his mouth fully to hers.

He kissed her long and deep and yet so sweetly she felt tears burn in her eyes. It had been so very long since she'd been kissed...since she'd been held like this. She was really glad it was this man. He was special.

For a guy who made a lot of left turns he'd certainly made the right one tonight.

## CHAPTER NINE

MAX EXPERIENCED TWO shocking realizations the next morning.

She, Dr. Maxine Gray, a woman and doctor with a reputation for conscientious objectivity—who operated on facts and facts alone—had slept with the subject of her study.

And, if that wasn't astounding enough, it was snowing outside. In Alabama. On Christmas Eve. Not only was it snowing, it had *snowed*, several inches.

Back home in Boston the seven or eight inches of white stuff that had fallen would be nothing. People would scarcely notice. But here the city was practically paralyzed.

Flights were delayed and canceled. Similar problems in Atlanta had caused tremendous delays there as well. No way would she be getting any farther than Atlanta in the next thirty-six hours.

"You can spend Christmas with me and my folks," Rush urged, coming up behind her and pulling her into his lean, hard body. "Your folks are off on separate vacations, right? You'd be all alone back in Boston." He pressed a kiss to her neck, she shivered. "You should stay."

She didn't mention that she always spent the holidays alone. It was safer. You didn't miss anything you didn't get used to in the first place.

She had to be firm. Last night had been great, but she knew where this was going. A one-way trip to emotional upheaval. It would never work out. They were too different.

What happened between them last night would be tough enough to put behind her. Her mother would never believe she had allowed this to happen. If Max were really smart, she wouldn't tell her. But Vivian would know. She had apparently learned mind reading in some strange little country only her mother would visit.

"I have to get back." Max turned in his arms, couldn't help herself. She was only human and he was so amazing. "This report has to be completed and filed."

He smiled, those incredibly pale blue eyes glittering with sensual invitation. "I'll bet you could do that report on that handy little computer of yours and file it through cyberspace."

She drew in a deep breath and sighed, something else she couldn't resist. He smelled wonderful, like subtle tangy lime and warm male skin. She'd never smelled anything so magnificent. Lots of that beautiful skin was exposed with him only half dressed, and he was holding her so very close.

"Is that a maybe?" He kissed the tip of her nose. "My family loves you already."

That was the truly scary part. "They probably think I'm awful for skipping out on them last night. Besides, I'd be intruding."

"You won't be intruding," he guaranteed. "One Christmas with us and you'll want to stay forever."

No, she had been wrong. *That* was the scariest part of his proposition. Because some part of her knew that what he'd just said was no untested hypothesis. It was an absolute fact.

THAT EVENING Max had a second chance to bond with Rush's family. Every single one of them. His sisters, his brother and their spouses and kids and the family dogs that she'd already learned couldn't possibly be left out of something this important. But she took it in stride. Somehow she'd even managed to get her report done and filed, via cyberspace just as Rush had suggested, before the deluge of kin hit.

Rush stole her away from the kitchen where his sisters and sisters-in-law were cleaning up. "Come on," he urged. "Let's play in the snow."

"This may be a novelty for you," Max argued, "but

I deal with this stuff all the time. Playing in the snow would not rank high on my list of fun things to do."

"Ah, but you don't know what I have in mind," he argued, leaving her to wonder exactly what he did have in mind.

Reluctant at first, she finally bundled up in one of his mother's coats while he tugged on his own coat and gloves.

He took her out back to a giant oak where an ancient wooden swing hung. "Climb aboard." He dusted the snow from the seat. "My dad made this swing for my sisters."

Hands on hips, Max surveyed the old seat and the ancient ropes holding it about three feet off the ground. "I don't know about that. I'm not so sure that thing is reliable. Perhaps at some point in the past it was, but certainly not now."

Just to show her she had nothing to worry about, he settled between the ropes and pushed off for a couple of swoops. "See, it's plenty reliable."

She still wasn't convinced. "All right, but if this thing breaks…" She left the warning unfinished as she perched on the seat.

Rush grabbed hold of the ropes at her sides and pulled her back as far as he could. "Hold on," he cautioned, then he pushed her forward. She squealed, the sound a mixture of delight and apprehension and total silliness. He laughed.

"You're not afraid, are you?" he teased, knowing that would get a reaction.

"Of course not." She sent the words over her shoulder along with a daring glance as she charged back toward where he waited to give her another boost. "Push me higher, if you have the strength."

"Oh, it's that way, is it?" He pushed with all his might.

She gasped.

He pushed harder the next time.

"Feel that?"

"What?" she demanded, pretending confusion as she swung back toward him.

He pushed her harder still. "*That.*"

She gasped before she could catch herself.

"That pull way down deep in your stomach," he explained as if she still didn't get it.

She flew back at him and he pushed her forward yet again.

"I feel it!" She surrendered the words, releasing them as she hurled forward once more.

"Doesn't that make you want to go faster and faster, just like we did in the car?"

When she swung back this time he hung on to the ropes, stopping her momentum with a soft jerk. She was breathing fast as he slid one arm around her waist and snuggled her close against him.

"It's the same thing I feel whenever I hold you close. It makes me not want to let go."

She turned her face up to his. "Then don't."

A snowflake lit on her cheek and he brushed it away. "Good idea. I guess we can work out the logistics later."

"Agreed," she whispered against his lips.

Then he kissed her and that bond the had formed between them last night sealed tight, grew stronger. This was going to be the best Christmas ever. For both of them.

And just maybe this was the real checkered flag she and Rush been charging toward all along.

She definitely wanted to find out.

# CHAPTER TEN

*Two weeks later...*

BUCK SPREAD THE NEWSPAPERS across his desk and smiled. *Go for the Gold* was a hit. Even *USA Today* had run with it, thanks in large part to yesterday's release of the New England Institute for Independent Experts' final report.

He smiled as he thought of Dr. Gray. She'd sure done a number on his driver. If she didn't marry that boy, Buck would have a hell of a time keeping him focused this season. But he had a feeling he had nothing to worry about on that score. The doc was pretty much smitten herself. Evelyn Jackson would see that there was a wedding.

Buck didn't have a problem with that. He wanted the boy to be happy.

So far he'd been able to keep McElroy's dirty business out of the media. Buck hoped he could keep it that way. He preferred salvaging NASCAR's honor over pushing criminal charges.

It had been a long time since anyone had injured him the way McElroy had.

But Buck was tough. He wouldn't let this get him down any more than he had any of the troubles he'd faced in the past.

He had a team to manage after all. And he had every intention of staying on top no matter what fate threw his way.

Too many people were counting on him to allow any wallowing in pity. All he had to do was stay focused on that goal just like back in his driving days.

Life went on.

There were races to win.

\* \* \* \* \*

*Watch for an edge-of-your-seat
romantic suspense and more
NASCAR thrills with
Debra Webb's DANGER ZONE
coming in February 2007.
Read on for a sneak peek.*

JENNA WILLIAMS WAS exhausted when she got off work at the hospital that evening. It was bitterly cold outside and she'd forgotten her scarf. The wind whipped through her hair, nipping her ears and slapping her cheeks with its harsh sting.

A few minutes later Jenna wouldn't remember how cold it was or even that she'd worked a double shift. She would only know that her daughter wasn't at the school soccer field where she was supposed to be. She hadn't gone home with a friend when her mother was late picking her up for the third time in a row.

Jenna's daughter was gone…vanished.

A million-dollar ransom was the demand if Jenna ever wanted to see her daughter alive again. She had no one to turn to…except one man. A man Jenna hadn't seen in more than a decade. Still, she had no choice. She needed Buck Buchanan…and she needed him *now*.